Some kids are just dying to be perfect little angels . . .

"Daddy? Mommy?"

She listened again. There was a creak in the floorboards, and a shadow moved in the far right corner. Whoever was standing there, stepped forward. She turned slowly toward him. The weak, yellow light peeled away the darkness slowly and revealed the corpselike face, it's teeth as white as bone. She couldn't scream; she couldn't move. For a few moments, she felt as if she had already died. None of her limbs obeyed her brain's commands. A chill gripped her heart, making her wonder if it had already stopped beating.

Then something glimmered in the light, and she saw the machete. . . .

Perfect Little Angels

The Shocking New Novel by Andrew Neiderman

Berkley Books by Andrew Neiderman

PLAYMATES
SURROGATE CHILD
PERFECT LITTLE ANGELS

ANDREW NEIDERMAN

PERFECT LITTLE ANGELS

BERKLEY BOOKS, NEW YORK

PERFECT LITTLE ANGELS

A Berkley Book/published by arrangement with
the author

PRINTING HISTORY
Berkley edition/September 1989

ISBN: 0-425-11775-8

A BERKLEY BOOK ® TM 757,375
Berkley Books are published by The Berkley Publishing Group,
200 Madison Avenue, New York, NY 10016.
The name "BERKLEY" and the "B" logo
are trademarks belonging to Berkley Publishing Corporation.

PRINTED IN THE UNITED STATES OF AMERiCA

10 9 8 7 6 5 4 3 2 1

*For all my former students
who became my present fans*

PERFECT LITTLE ANGELS

Prologue

HE PRESSED THE palm of his hand against the glass and pushed out, but the thick storm window was as hard as cement. He studied the way the tips of his fingers whitened with the effort. Where did the blood go? he wondered. My blood. He's taking my blood in little drips and drabs, studying it under his microscope, and leaving it on slides until it dries into a dark amber blotch and no longer looks like a part of me. As well as a part of him, for I am a part of him.

Or, at least, I was.

Vaguely now, he understood that his doctor father no longer treated him as a person. He saw him as a creature.

But doesn't that make me still a part of him? he thought. He created me again, didn't he?

It struck him as funny, so he laughed. And yet, the sound of his laughter seemed to come from somewhere else—not from inside him. Where was he? Gradually, he was losing contact with his own body. Yesterday, he had awakened to find a strange leg in his bed.

Another one of my father's sick experiments, he'd first thought. He'd touched the leg and made it bend at the knee, surprised at how flexible and warm it was. He's keeping a human leg alive, keeping the blood beating through it, keeping the muscles limber, keeping the skin hairs growing, even keeping the toenails growing. And then, as part of his treatment for me, he put the leg in my bed, he concluded. The indignity of it all.

"I want my own bed!" he'd screamed.

Naturally, she'd come running in, Mrs. What's-her-face. He couldn't recall her name; he didn't want to.

"If you can't remember my name, just call me 'Nurse,'" she had said. But he even forgot that.

"What is it? What's wrong?" She was still slipping her faded light blue robe over her sheer gray nightgown as she came rushing into his room. Her big breasts shook so hard, he thought they might come falling down over him.

"Unstrap me. Quickly," he demanded. *"Quickly!"*

"Not until you tell me what's wrong," she said. She had gotten hold of herself; she was a professional. His father usually left her in charge. She reached forward and put the palm of her hand against his forehead, just the way he was pressing his hand against the window now. She had pushed, too, pushed his head back to the pillow and forced the thoughts that had spilled out over his forehead back into his brain. He feared his head would crack like an eggshell, and what was left of his brains would come pouring out, yolk and all.

"I've got to get out of this bed," he said. He tried to tug at the strap, but his hands were bound, too. He could feel the veins in his neck straining like rubber bands pulled a little too far. Soon they would snap, and little drops of blood would appear all over him. He would look as if he had the measles.

"You have to calm down. If you don't control your-self, you can't get up today," she said. He saw by the way her eyes narrowed that she meant it. He had learned to read her gestures well—as well as he'd once read books. But he hadn't read a book since . . . since the accident.

"All right," he said, forcing himself to calm down. "I will." He swallowed emphatically to show her he was gaining control of himself. "It's morning and I want to get up. Isn't it morning?" he asked to be sure. Light filtered through the dark brown curtains on his windows.

"It's morning, but it's early. I haven't even washed or dressed."

"But I can still get up, can't I? If I control myself?"

She studied him a moment. "There's something mak-ing you want to get up earlier than usual this morning. What is it?"

"Unstrap me and I'll tell you. I promise," he added quickly. He made an attempt to raise his hand as if taking an oath, forgetting for the moment that his arms were restrained. He was always strapped down at night. The doctor ordered it that way.

He could see she was thinking about it, considering his promise. He watched her eyes. The pupils darkened and deepened, moving in and out like tiny microscopes. Most of the time, he thought she was fat and ugly. Sometimes, he could see the very pores in her skin, and her face resembled perforated cardboard. When that happened, everything around him was magnified; she was only the ugliest thing. Fortunately, right now, she didn't look any bigger than usual, he thought. He couldn't take that, too.

She reached down and unfastened the strap around his

waist. He closed his eyes. Only a few more moments, he thought, and he would be away from it. He felt her undo the bands around his arms, and a rush of freedom washed over his chest. He didn't get up too quickly, however. He knew that might incite her to strap him in again. It wouldn't be the first time he was kept in bed or made to wear a straitjacket. In fact, the straitjacket hung on the wall above his bed as a reminder that it would be used any time it became necessary. And he knew the jacket was eager to be used, eager to embrace him and suck out his energy.

"Now, what is it?" she demanded.

"This," he said, pointing to the leg. "It's disgusting. How could he do such a thing? No matter what I did, how could he do that?"

"I don't understand."

"The leg, the leg. Christ, the leg!" He reached down and grasped it around the calf muscle. When he looked up at her, she was staring at him with new interest.

"What about the leg?" she asked.

"It's in my bed. That's disgusting. I won't share my bed with someone's leg," he added, pushing the leg off the bed. He tumbled off with it, following it to the floor.

That was when he realized it was attached to him. The realization drove him to tears, and the tears made his body limp and weak.

She had to help him back onto the bed. She pushed his head onto the pillow again, and tucked the gray wool blanket under his chin.

"It's too early to get up," she barked. "I told you. Sleep some more, and I'll come in and wake you when it's time."

He didn't say anything, but merely stared at the ceiling.

Right now, he continued to study his fingers. The whiteness around his nails was spreading, moving down to his knuckles. His blood was retreating rapidly. It would all join together in a ball in his stomach, and his stomach would explode. It was getting late. Soon he would have no chance, no chance at all.

He looked back to see if she were watching him, and he was glad to see she had gone out of the room. Her magazine still lay open on the chair where she had been sitting, doing some kind of needlepoint.

He moved slowly across the room and took the needle out of the cloth. He crossed the room, still studying the needle, its blue and green threads trailing behind him on the dark brown carpet. When he reached the window again, he took the needle and drove it into the tip of his right forefinger. He didn't even feel the pain, and for a moment, he had to consider whether or not he was driving it into his hand or into someone else's hand. He concluded that it was his hand, but he was losing it, just the way he had lost his leg in the bed. He worked faster, turning the needle harder and wider, until the hole in his finger permitted a nice size glob of blood to emerge.

Then he took his finger and began to write on the windowpane. Every once in a while, he had to squeeze the finger to draw more blood. Finally, he had to drive the needle into his left forefinger to take over the printing, though it didn't work as well because he was right-handed.

After he wrote the word, he stepped back to appreciate it. It looked good; it looked promising. He stepped forward again and pressed his face against the windowpane to look down at the houses and people in the development below. Surely someone down there would glance up soon and notice the word on the window.

He waited. It was as quiet below, as usual. His father kept it that way, but his father wasn't here right now, so maybe someone would come out of his house and look up. He wanted to shout, but he remembered that shouting did no good. No one could hear him because of the thickness of the windows and walls. In fact, his father, smirking at him one day, had said, "Shout your damn lungs out, if you want."

He would have screamed, too, only his father had stopped him—the way he always stopped him from taking action.

It was so frustrating. There was another him trapped inside this body.

That's why I don't know this body, anymore. The thought excited him. That's it. It's not my body. My body is inside. This is a shell my father made. I know his secret.

He laughed, only this time the laughter remained within because it was his real laugh. He was still laughing when she returned to his room and interrupted him.

"What are you doing? What have you done?" she screamed, rushing across the room. "You fool." She ripped the needle out of his fingers. "Get away from that window. Get away now," she demanded.

He stepped back obediently.

"Don't move from that spot," she ordered, stomping out of the room.

He didn't move.

She returned with a wet rag and quickly washed away

his word. But even after it was gone from the window, he still saw it. It had sunk into the glass and embedded itself within the pane. He smiled.

"What are you grinning at?" she demanded.

"It's still there," he said. "You can't wash it away."

"*It's still there,*" she mimicked and shook her head. "Follow me. I want to clean and bandage those fingers."

He followed her, but he looked back once before leaving the room just to be sure the word was still there.

It was. He could see it as clearly as he had seen it after he had written it in his own blood. The sunlight even lit it up and made it stand out more.

Soon, someone below would notice. They would look up and see HELP written on his window.

And then, they would come and take him out of here.

1

JUSTINE FREEMAN PRESSED her face against the rear window of the metallic blue Mercedes and looked out at the rich green lawns and the bright flower beds. Despite the beautiful landscape, the view seemed grim, as though she were looking through gray-tinted glass. The moment they had driven through the security gate, she felt her depression deepen. As if losing her friends wasn't bad enough, she'd also been torn from city life just to move out to the suburbs. She couldn't feel happy about being here, even though her parents were so pleased. Her father went so far as to describe the development as hypnotic. How could a place be hypnotic? Eyes could be hypnotic, like the eyes of Tom Cruise, for example, but a place?

They turned up Long Street and passed the Dukes' residence, a large, milk-white colonial-style house, not unlike the one they had bought. Her mother said both houses had fronts like Tara in *Gone With the Wind*, and she always wanted to live in a house like that. Justine had never seen the movie and couldn't imagine giving your house a name.

Michael Duke and his wife Christy stood in front of their house and waved enthusiastically as they drove by. When Justine's father pulled into their cobblestone driveway, the Dukes hurried toward them.

Right now, Justine disliked Michael Duke. He was one of her father's law associates, but from what she understood, he was chiefly responsible for talking her father into selling their co-op on Seventy-first and York and buying a home in this housing development called Elysian Fields. She didn't even know what "Elysian" meant, but she'd never asked because she didn't want to show her father she was interested.

"Welcome, Elaine, Kevin," Michael said even before any of them stepped out of the car. "Hi, Justine."

Michael Duke's eyebrows went up as though they were on little springs. His hair was midway between brown and red, but his eyebrows were even a shade lighter. Justine imagined he could go without shaving for days.

He took her mother's hand to help her out of the vehicle. Justine thought her mother looked like one of her teenage friends beside him; not that he was that big a man. Michael Duke was probably six feet tall, but her mother was only five feet four. Her father was five feet ten, but only weighed about one hundred and sixty-five pounds, so her parents didn't look awkward together. Her father wasn't physically impressive, but he was a confident, bright man who usually commanded the respect of those who met him. Justine was proud of her father most of the time; she was just upset that he and her mother had been persuaded to make this move.

"Hi," Christy said, coming around to meet them.

Justine knew her mother liked Christy Duke. They had

so many common interests: Both women were trying to
be artists, and both had a relaxed, youthful appearance.
Although Christy was nearly six inches taller, they could
be mistaken for sisters. Both women wore their light
brown hair long and straight. Christy had soft, symmet-
rical facial features, highlighted by cerulean blue eyes
and a dimple in her left cheek. Elaine Freeman's features
were diminutive, but she, too, had sky blue soft eyes.

"Let us help you with some of those things," Michael
said, reaching in to take a carton from the back seat.
"Brad and Steven should be home any moment, Justine."

Justine faked a smile. Brad and Steven, she thought.
She had met them only twice before, and although Brad,
a senior in high school, was quite good-looking, she
found him rather dull. Steven was her age, fifteen, but
quite immature, in her opinion. Life for teenagers was
different out here, she concluded sadly. She wouldn't
expect them to be as sophisticated as her friends back in
New York.

"Hey, thanks," Kevin said. Justine saw his hazel eyes
sparkle with excitement. He'd told her that nothing he
had done during his seventeen years of marriage was as
exciting as this. What was so exciting about moving into
a housing development? she wondered. Will I get this
way when I'm their age? It was a frightening thought.

She could see why her mother was impressed with the
place. The house was enormous compared to their co-op,
and the development had its own tennis courts and
Olympic-sized swimming pool, and clubhouse. There
was also a private golf course adjacent to the development.

Her father had talked her mother into it, however, by

emphasizing that like Christy Duke, she would have the space for a studio in the house. "And plenty of land-scapes to paint."

What could Justine offer in opposition to all this? That she would miss her friends? Her father didn't like many of them, anyway. That there wasn't much to do? Her father was always complaining about her hanging out in the streets, and New York was less than an hour's drive. They could still go to the theater, and her mother could still go to museums.

The big kicker was the security here. The entire development was fenced in, with a beautiful stone wall in the front, and a booth at the entrance manned by a security guard twenty-four hours a day.

The whole thing was designed by some famous doctor who'd bought all the land, then decided to build a special housing development. At least, that's how Justine understood it. He lived here, too. Michael Duke had mentioned him frequently, and now Justine's father was always talking about him. Dr. Lawrence. She never understood what he was doctor of, anyway. Doctor of developments?

"I'll help you organize your kitchen things," Christy told Justine's mother.

Justine contemplated her new home. The two other times she had come out here, she had been so stubborn about it, she really hadn't looked. Now she studied it more seriously. No matter how she felt, it was going to be her home, and she took a certain pride in it, even though she wanted to resist that feeling. She hoped she wouldn't become a snob, as her city friends had predicted.

Her eyes skimmed over the house. To the right of the

portico were privet hedges shaped in an S. The blue
flagstone walkway to the portico was edged with blood-
red impatiens. The driveway was lined with stained
railroad ties, and low-growing vines were woven over
them to create a smooth linkage with the lawn itself.
There was a small rock garden in the center of the lawn,
and an egg-shaped fountain at the center of that.

The front entrance had double doors built out of rich,
dark oak. The pillars and the siding of the house were
only a shade darker than the Dukes' white. There were
light blue shutters on the windows and a triangular
stained-glass window just above the front entrance. Her
mother particularly liked the backyard patio and the fruit
trees behind it.

Her mother turned around and saw that she was
lingering by the car. "Come on, honey," she said.
"We've got a lot to do. Grab something and follow us."

"She's a little frightened by the move, huh?" Christy
asked, looking back at Justine.

"Justine's been a city girl all her life, and she had to
leave all her friends," her mother replied.

"So? You were a city girl all your life," Kevin
Freeman said. "And you left friends behind."

"I'm not a teenager, Kevin." Elaine shook her head
and frowned at Christy. "Men. Such sensitive types!"
Both women laughed.

"Nevertheless, you'll be amazed at how quickly
Justine adjusts and forgets her past," Christy said. For a
moment, Justine felt as though she weren't there, or as if
they were observing her through thick glass walls and
didn't think she could hear what they said. "Like Dr.
Lawrence always says, Elysian Fields has a way of

winning you over," Christy added, turning to her husband. "Right, honey?"

"That's what he says," Michael confirmed. "The man himself. He says Elysian Fields has a way of protecting its inhabitants." He took a deep breath and looked around. "It embraces u: . He spoke about the development as if it were a livin₅ thing.

"That's his house on the hill, right?" Elaine asked just before they all started for the front door. "The one with the fence around it?"

"Uh-huh," Michael said, smiling. He looked up at it with admiration. "We've become good friends, rather good friends. For me, it's like having the brother I never had. An older and wiser brother. He's helped Christy and me in a number of ways," he said, glancing back at Justine. "And he will be able to help you, should you need him."

"I meant to ask you last time, Michael. Why does he have a fence around his land?" Elaine asked. Curious, Justine moved a little closer to hear the response.

"His was the first house constructed in the area. Back then, Sandburg Creek was so rural, the fence was a necessity. When Elysian Fields was built, he never removed it. He likes his privacy. But don't let that fool you," he added quickly. "He's a very sociable man. And creative in many ways. You know, he designed this place, even down to the shape and quality of the street-lights."

"Really?" Justine's mother turned to look at the street-lights.

"When those lights are on at night, it's like daytime out here," Michael said with great pride. Justine noticed he was gazing up at the streetlights the way people look up at a statue of Jesus in a church.

"They do have a strange design," Elaine said.

Justine studied them, too. The blue-tinted, incandescent bulbs were housed in a rust brown, wood-faced container that seemed to be a natural extension of the pole. But the container was an unusual shape—wide in the center and narrow at the top, which pointed directly at their house like a finger of accusation.

"Anyway," Michael said. "I'm sure you'll be impressed with Dr. Lawrence when you meet him. You'll be surprised at his interest and concern for the development and all its inhabitants. He happens to be the president of the Elysian Fields Development Organization. We've elected him unanimously for the last ten years."

"Ten years? I thought you were here only five," Kevin said, a quizzical smile on his face. Michael and Christy looked at one another as though to confirm.

"Well, it seems like ten," Michael said and laughed. "Right, honey?"

"I've lost track," Christy said. "Days and months just merge into one another and become a single line of time," she said.

Elaine Freeman nodded thoughtfully, but Justine thought the whole thing sounded weird.

Probably only something a couple of artists would appreciate, she thought. She turned to look up at the house on the hill again, as though her eyes were drawn to it magnetically.

"What kind of doctor is he?" Justine asked. The question just slipped out like a burp. She was embarrassed about it, but Michael Duke smiled.

"He's a psychologist. Started his career by working in schools, matter of fact. But he's also well known as a nutritionist these days. We're all proud to have him in our development."

"What's his wife like?" Elaine asked.

"That's a tragedy," Christy said. "She was killed in a car accident." Her face took on what Justine thought was an exaggerated look of sorrow. It reminded her of an elementary school teacher reading a story to first graders.

"Oh, that is terrible. And his children?" her mother asked.

"His seventeen-year-old son was driving. They had only the one boy. The terrible thing was, his son was on marijuana," Michael said. His face assumed a somber expression.

Justine looked from him to Christy, then back to him. Because of their dramatic facial expressions, the couple seemed comical, even though they were discussing a tragic event.

"My God. He lost his wife and son?" her mother said, moving closer to her father instinctively.

"No, his son lived, but he had some problems. Guilt . . . whatever," Michael Duke said, his expression changing to utter disgust.

"How terrible," Elaine said. "Institutionalized?"

"No, he lives in the house. The doc has a nurse there full time."

"He's in that kind of shape?" Kevin asked.

"Well, he suffered a rather traumatic experience. But Dr. Lawrence is devoted to helping him, and is willing to go to any expense.

"Anyway," Michael said, his voice taking on a

happier tone, "I'm sure Dr. Lawrence will make it a point to stop by and see you before long. He likes to greet newcomers personally, and he always brings a valuable gift along."

"What kind of gift?" Elaine asked, picking up the upbeat tone. "Something for the house?"

"Better. Something for the inhabitants. As I said, he's a nationally known expert in nutrition, and he has designed his own vitamin. You're going to get more than a year's supply for the entire family, and believe me, they make a difference. You know that Christy, my kids, and I have not had a single cold since we began taking them. Right, honey?"

"Mike's right," she said. "I don't even have headaches, anymore. I used to get horrible sinus headaches from time to time." She turned to Justine. "And the vitamins make the boys so energetic. It even helps their brain power," she said, pointing her forefinger at her temple.

"Really?" Justine said dryly. She couldn't see how anyone could get so excited about vitamins, even in today's health-crazed world.

Sensing Justine's skepticism, Christy stepped back to her. *"Really,"* Christy said, putting her arm around Justine. "I'm so glad you're here, honey. You'll love it; you'll see."

Justine smiled at her. Maybe there was something to the vitamins. Christy had such vibrancy. She was like a woman who would never age.

"I can't wait until he gives those vitamins to us," Elaine said.

"Neither can I," Kevin added. "Justine can use some brain power." He laughed.

"Very funny, Daddy."

"I'm sure you won't have to wait long," Michael Duke said, smiling. "Dr. Lawrence knows you're here." As he turned to look up at the house again, Justine sensed that odd, religious air about him. And this time, though she couldn't explain why, it gave her the creeps.

She stared up at the house, too, and thought about Dr. Lawrence's son. That aspect of Elysian Fields was interesting—the most interesting thing in the whole development, she thought.

He stood in the bathroom with both hands held high, each of his forefingers bandaged tightly. They are still bleeding, he thought. Underneath the bandages, they are still bleeding, only she can't see so she doesn't know. If he didn't hold his hands up like this, all of his blood would drip out on the tile floor. And then, he would collapse in a fold of skin and bones. His father would take his remains and hang them out on a clothesline in the back. After he shriveled and dried sufficiently, his father would put him in one of his albums, paste him to a page, and label him, "Homosapien Failure."

He would invite his puppet friends up here for a drink of carrot juice, and when they were all sitting around in the living room, he would say, "Oh, by the way, does anyone want to see what became of my fucked-up son?"

Of course, they would all want to see, and he would bring out the album and open it to the page. He would look up at them with disc eyes because, amazingly, he would still be alive even though pasted to the page. He would scream with this miniaturized voice, like the man who had become a fly in the first version of that horror film . . . "Help me, help me, help . . ." But no one would hear. Or even if they did, they would only look up and smile at his father. Who would smile back and say, "That's his favorite word."

"You can put your hands down," she said, snapping him out of his dream. He didn't do it. "Put your hands down," she commanded, and he did so immediately.

All right, he thought. She'll be sorry; she'll have to clean it up.

"What's going on in here?"

He turned to see his father, dressed for work, distinguished looking, as perfect as a mannequin. Where were his blemishes? Where were his cold sores? Where was his dandruff? Didn't he miss a single hair when shaving? His skin was like alabaster. Maybe his super vitamin did work.

"He went a little wild this morning," she told him. She was putting the bandage wrappers into the wastebasket, being aseptic, neat, the immaculate nurse. No germs would ever touch those hands.

"Wild? How?" he scowled.

He hates to look at me, he thought. It puts him into pain. He could almost see the line of pain just under the skin of his father's forehead, shooting back and forth like submerged lightning. He wondered if the electricity in his own head was as visible.

"He punctured each forefinger and started writing on the window in his room." She stopped working, put her hands on her wide hips, and considered him alongside the doctor.

He stared back at them both. They were beginning to look like twins. She was growing his face. Something from his face contaminated her face, burrowed in her fat cheeks, and was now taking it over. Already she had his eyes and his mouth. The nose was coming. Soon the nose, then the forehead.

"How did he puncture his finger?"

"He got a hold of my needlepoint needle," she said in the tone of a confession. The doctor's eyebrows lifted. "I realize it was careless of me to leave the room without taking it," she said quickly. "It won't happen again."

"See that it doesn't," he said. He turned away, and then stopped. "What did he write on the window?"

"He wrote 'Help,'" she said and shrugged.

The doctor smiled. "Interesting. Very interesting. Later on today, give him a note pad and a pen, but be sure he doesn't puncture his skin with the pen, and let him write whatever he wants."

"Very well." She nodded, then watched as the doctor left the room. "You see how you got me in trouble?" she snapped. "Take off your pajamas and step into the shower. Move it!"

He did so, and she turned on the water, keeping it ice cold. As always, he stood under the spigot, screaming while the water ran over his body.

"Scrub yourself," she said, handing him the soap. "Then rinse off."

After he did that, she handed him a towel.

"Wipe yourself dry and go to your chair."

"No food?" This morning, he remembered what his mouth and his teeth and his tongue were for, and the memory encouraged him.

"Afterward," she said. "You'll be hungry. We'll both be hungry." When he was dry, she took his towel and nudged him down the hallway to the room with the chair. The door was opened, so he walked in and sat down.

He faced the windows that opened to the rear of the

house. From this room, he could see only the wooded area his father had not permitted to be developed. In fact, no land above their house had been touched. Images of himself playing in the forest flashed across his eyes, but all of them were disjointed. It was like turning the channels rapidly on a television set.

He saw himself camping out, running, chopping wood, and hiking through the forest. Someone was walking alongside him in a few of these images, someone he liked a great deal. Who was it? She held his hand, but when he turned to look into her face, she had no head. He struggled with that visual memory, but struggling did no good.

Suddenly there was a humming in his ears, and then he heard the nurse enter behind him. Without saying a word, she walked past him. She was totally naked. Her stomach ballooned like the belly of a pregnant woman, and her skin was almost as white as her uniform. Rolls of fat under her breasts jiggled as though they were small, rubber tubes filled with water.

She didn't look at him, but merely walked across the room to open the other door. The familiar hum emerged from the connecting room. Like Pavlov's dog, he anticipated what was next, and shifted in his seat, spreading his legs to make himself more comfortable. He heard that high-pitch ringing, and suddenly his penis became erect, rising like a mole that had been sleeping between his legs. He looked down at it with surprise.

A moment later, she reappeared, a smile on her face. She came to him and put her right palm on his chest. He looked up at her and saw that she was miraculously changed. She was beautiful. She looked like Rhonda Thomas, that girl he'd had such a crush on when he was

a senior. Her eyes were just as blue; her nose was just as
cute and small; her long, flowing red hair gleamed as
richly.

She had Rhonda's body, too: well-shaped, firm breasts
that peaked at the nipples, a slim torso, and a narrow
waist. Her peaches and cream skin looked so inviting.
He wanted to press his lips everywhere on her body.

"Come on," she said, taking his hand. "You're
cooked." He heard her laugh, but it was a distant sound,
as if it came from the television set in the other room. He
rose from the seat and followed her to the bed.

She lay back, then pulled him to her, working him
between her legs as though he were made of clay and she
had to mold him. She fit him to her, then placed her
stubby hand on his buttocks and pulled him forward
roughly, her hands like cold claws.

"My fringe benefits," she said, and she laughed again
until her laughter ended with a series of moans.

Oh, Rhonda, he thought, I love you so. I mean it; it's
not a line. I'm not just saying this to get you to be with
me. You are the most beautiful girl in Sandburg Creek.

He kept his eyes closed. Somehow, it was all right. He
was really making love to Rhonda again. The hum from
the next room grew louder and louder until he climaxed,
and then it turned back into a high-pitched ringing.

She pushed him away from her and dismounted the
bed. Then, she went back into the next room. A moment
later, she reappeared, a smile on her face.

Why was she smiling? he wondered, and didn't she
look disgusting without clothing?

"Breakfast is on its way," she said, "and then we'll go
into the laboratory and finish the work your father set out
for us to do."

He watched her leave the room; then stared at the chair. Wasn't he just sitting on it? How did he get to this bed?

Why did he have these bandages on his fingers?

And who was that woman holding his hand in the forest, the woman with no head?

He brought his hands to his ears and pressed as hard as he could. If only he could crack his head open and spill the answers out on the floor. He had to find a way to do that; he had to.

Justine stood by her father's Mercedes in the driveway and gazed forlornly at the moving men as they carried one piece of furniture after another from the van to the house. With each piece of furniture lugged from the van to the house, the reality was driven home. She was here, separated from her friends, ripped out of the world she had known and loved. It all seemed so unfair.

Saying good-bye to her friends had been painful, even though everyone had promised to visit. She thought Mindy Boston would probably be the only one to actually make the trip, and that was only if Justine's parents permitted Mindy to visit. She knew her father didn't like Mindy, but she couldn't help feeling sorry for the girl for exactly the reasons her father disapproved of her.

In Justine's mind, she was Mindy's best friend. Although Mindy had other friends, none of them helped keep her out of trouble as much as Justine did. Whenever she was with the others, she was apt to smoke pot or shoplift or get a little too wild.

Of course, Justine's parents were afraid it would work the other way around. Instead of her influencing Mindy for the better, Mindy would influence her for the worse. She could understand their fears; she just felt she was stronger than they thought she was. And, anyway, there were other things about Mindy that she liked. Justine liked the wild way her friend dressed, sometimes looking like Madonna, sometimes looking like Vanity; Mindy had once "jazzed her hair," streaking it green! No one else she knew had the nerve to do things like that. Mindy was special. Justine liked her offbeat view of other kids, and her cynical view of school. Mindy was a renegade, but she could also be a lot of fun.

Justine turned and looked at herself in the window of the car, straightening a few strands of hair. She knew she looked much older than fifteen, and it wasn't only because she had a full bosom and a firm, mature body. She had developed a look of sophistication, an awareness that suggested experience beyond her years. It had come naturally to her. She was very bright and very perceptive, even though she was the first to admit she rarely applied her intelligence fully to schoolwork.

Physically, she resembled her father. She had his rusty brown hair and his hazel green eyes, and often took on some of his facial expressions, like pressing her teeth down on her lower lips and nearly closing her eyes when she was angry or frustrated. She was two inches taller than Elaine, but she had Elaine's graceful hands and shoulders. Although she had Kevin's smile, she had Elaine's diminutive features.

She was about to go back into the house to help her parents unpack when she noticed the half dozen teenagers coming up the hill toward her house, walking so closely together they looked attached. They were led by Brad Duke.

"Hi," Brad said as they came up the driveway. Justine thought he had rich looking, light brown hair, even though he kept it too short and wet looking. Brad's big, vividly blue eyes were unforgettable. She couldn't remember being so taken by a boy's eyes. There was a hunger in them, a curiosity. Her mother had told her Brad inherited his father's intense look, but Justine found more innocence in the way his eyes fixed on her. It was as if she held as much interest for him as would a teenage girl from another country.

"Hi." She looked at the six boys and two girls. Four of the boys wore slacks and short-sleeved shirts. Brad and Steven wore jeans and white T-shirts. One of the girls wore a red hair clip on top of her head, a bright blue and pink oversized shirt, and dark blue dungarees. It was hard to tell because of the shirt, but she seemed to have a nice figure.

The other girl had her hair pinned back in a bun. She wore an ankle-length, dark blue skirt, and a frilly white blouse buttoned to the neck. She had a long neck, a small bosom, and rather large hips.

"I can't even remember when we first moved in," Brad said, smiling as they all drew up in front of Justine.

"Can't remember? Why?" she asked, remembering his parents' confusion about that same date. How could people be confused about such important facts and events in their lives?

Brad shrugged, as if the answer weren't important. "Dr. Lawrence says, life began for us at Elysian Fields," he said, smiling. "Everyone, this is Justine Freeman. Justine, this is Mark Bronstein, Scott Halsey, Paul Kotein, Benjamin Billups, Lois Wilson, and Janet Bernie."

"Hi," they said, almost in unison.

"Hi."

"Lois is a sophomore, too," Brad said. "Janet's a junior. The rest of us are seniors this year."

"Really." She couldn't help but be curious, especially because of the way they stared at her. They all seemed friendly, but it was as if they were wearing masks with permanent, identical smiles. These boys certainly didn't look as mature as the senior boys she had known in New York, she thought, reinforcing her original fears.

"Uh-huh." Brad, his hands on his hips, surveyed the scene before him. "We all walk to school together in the morning," he said. "It's only three-quarters of a mile from the front entrance of Elysian Fields. Janet and Lois will show you around the first day, right, girls?"

"Oh, sure," Lois said. Her smile warmed and became more sincere. Justine decided she might like her.

"Of course we will," Janet said. Justine thought she had a rather deep voice for a girl. She pressed her hand against the side of her head and stroked her hair back, as though to be sure there wasn't a strand out of place.

"Thanks," Justine said.

"You're not interested in being on the school paper by any chance, are you?" Paul Kotein asked. "I'm the editor, and we need some good writers." His mouth turned up in the corner when he finished his sentence. His hair, cut even shorter than Brad's, exaggerated the size of his ears. He wore light yellow framed glasses, the lenses of which magnified his eyes.

Justine thought he looked like a frog. "I don't know," she said.

"Give her a chance to get orientated," Scott Halsey snapped. Justine was surprised at his sudden burst of anger. It was as though these kids turned emotions on and off like a faucet. Scott's face was so narrow, his nose so long, and his eyes so beady that Justine was reminded of a rodent. He was the tallest boy there, but he had an awkward-looking, gangly body, with arms that brought his fingers down just above his knees. His dull, dark brown hair looked as though it had been cut under a bowl. "Maybe she wants to be on the debate team."

"I don't know whether I want to belong to any clubs yet," she said. "I didn't belong to any at my old school."

"Nothing?" Janet asked. When Janet smirked, Justine thought she looked like a disapproving schoolmarm.

"I didn't, either, before I came to Sandburg Creek," Lois confessed softly. Almost immediately after she said it, she looked as though she regretted it. "I was kind of lazy and unproductive," she added quickly. Her sudden excuse sounded automatic, memorized.

"What changed you?" Justine asked. She wondered if her father was right with his predictions of change for her. Lois looked at the others again before replying.

"I started taking better care of myself physically, vitamins, exercise, and my parents had me see Dr. Lawrence. He gave me a pep talk I'll never forget."

"Dr. Lawrence? What's he, the development's private shrink or something?" Justine laughed at her own joke, but the others, except for Lois, seemed angry, as if she'd just insulted them personally. "I gotta go in and help my parents," she said. Something about those kids made her uncomfortable. "See you all later." She headed for the house.

When she turned back, they were all still watching her. Lois looked like she wanted to follow, but the others stood so still, their posture so erect, they seemed to be planted in the ground.

Justine opened the door quickly and stepped into the house. Her mother was supervising the delivery of the cartons, directing the movers here and there. Her father was upstairs, organizing the placement of furniture in the bedrooms. When Elaine saw her, she paused. Justine thought her mother looked kind of cute, dressed in an old sweat shirt, jeans, and sneakers. Her hair was disheveled, with strands falling over her forehead, and her face was flushed from the activity.

Justine searched the long, wide entryway for the boxes that contained her clothing and possessions. Her room in this house was considerably bigger than her bedroom in New York. She was anxious to hook up her stereo and see what kind of sounds she would get when she set up the speakers farther apart then they had been in the apartment.

"Where are my things?" she asked.

"Everything's been brought up to your room. You can start unpacking the cartons."

"Okay, I—"

"Hi, Mrs. Freeman," a voice called from behind her. Justine turned around to see all the teenagers enter the house. "We thought we'd drop by and see if we could be of any help."

"Why, that's nice of you, Brad."

Justine stepped back as Brad introduced everyone to her mother. The placid gloom that had come over their faces when she left them outside was gone. All of them were friendly and bright. They began to help carry cartons upstairs, and moments later, she heard Brad introduce the other teenagers to her father. Soon afterward, the boys were helping him assemble furniture. Lois and Janet followed her to her room.

Her new bedroom, a good twenty-by-fifteen feet with two windows facing the front, was open and airy. A thick, mauve-colored, tightly woven nylon carpet covered the floor. The walls were papered in a darker pink, floral pattern. Her mother had already hung matching curtains. There was a full-size walk-in closet to the left on entrance, and another, smaller closet to the right. Justine had decided to store her tapes, some books, albums, and other personal articles in the smaller closet. Her queen-size, cherry-vanilla tinted canopy bed was already set up against the far wall. Matching nightstands stood on both sides of it.

A large, matching dresser had been placed to the left of the bed, and a small vanity table with a square, white wood framed mirror stood beside it. She and her mother had planned the arrangement of the room the last time they were here, and Elaine had marked where each piece of furniture would go.

"I love organizing clothing," Janet said, digging into a carton on the floor. "I love organizing anything. I just love it when things are neat."

"I'm afraid I'm a slob," Justine said.

"Sometimes I am, too," Lois admitted.

"No you're not," Janet snapped at Lois. "Why are you saying that?"

"Well, I used to be," Lois corrected quickly. "Janet's right. I'm not anymore." The smile fell from her face, peeling down slowly. First her eyes faded from a bright, eager look to a dull glaze, and then her lips became a thin, knifelike slice.

Justine realized that neither of the girls wore makeup,

not even a touch of lipstick. Janet had harder, sharper features. Justine thought her mouth was too long and her nose had an ugly bump just at the bridge. Her dark brown hair looked dull, and it was brushed and pinned back so tightly, it made her forehead look even wider than it was. She couldn't understand why the girl didn't shape her eyebrows.

Lois, smaller and more attractive, had a smoother complexion and softer facial features. Her tiny, delicate hands reminded Justine of a doll she'd once had. Her almond brown hair, brushed down around her shoulders, seemed shiny and natural. The red hair clip seemed out of place, as if it had been added hastily, just for effect.

"You want your top drawer for socks and the second for lingerie?" Janet asked.

"Lingerie?" Justine said. Janet held up a pair of panties, but she looked pained, as if her fingers were burning and she had to get rid of the garment quickly. "Oh. Yeah, sure, put it in there."

She watched them fold her things carefully and shook her head. She found her tapes, records, and magazines far more interesting than the prospect of getting organized. She began to set up her stereo.

"You're going to like it here, Justine. Wait until school starts," Janet said with sudden enthusiasm.

"Oh, I just can't wait for that." Justine expected a familiar grimace, but Janet missed the sarcasm and only smiled. On the other hand, a twinkle of understanding glimmered in Lois's eyes.

Justine turned back to her stereo, and the girls continued to unpack her clothing. As she watched them work, she smiled to herself. Actually, this wasn't too bad, she

thought. They were doing a hell of a job, and they were
saving her a lot of work. She hated looking after her
things, except for her albums and tapes.

The moment she got her stereo set up and placed the
speakers where she thought they would be most effec-
tive, she inserted a tape of The Cult, one of her favorite
rock groups. Then she closed her eyes and absorbed the
blast of music, much like someone who had been a
prisoner of war for years and finally was biting into a
hamburger.

"Do you really like that?" Janet asked. "It's so loud,"
she said, pursing her lips together. "Isn't that being
inconsiderate?"

Before Justine could respond, Kevin was at the door.

"Hey, sweetheart, tone that down, will you. It's hard
enough shouting orders up and down the stairs and
across rooms."

Justine grimaced and turned off the stereo. The girls
stood there looking at her. Janet had a self-satisfied
expression on her face, but Lois looked sympathetic.

"We're going down to see if we can help your mother
with the kitchen things. Want to come?" Janet asked.

"In a few minutes," she said and turned away from
them, still sulking about having to turn down her music.
When she glanced back, Janet was gone but Lois
hesitated in the doorway.

"That was The Cult, wasn't it?" she asked.

"Yes," Justine said, encouraged. "You have any of
their tapes?"

"No," she said.

"Aren't you coming?" Janet called from the hallway.

"Oh, yes." She looked at Justine longingly for a
moment, and then disappeared.

Weird kids, Justine thought, shaking her head.

The teenagers of Elysian Fields spent the rest of the day in the Freemans' new home. Both Elaine and Kevin kept thanking them for their help. Before they left, the girls were dusting furniture, organizing cabinets, and washing down windows. The boys were a great help to Kevin. They seemed to have interminable patience, moving couches and chairs from spot to spot while Elaine decided on the best arrangement.

Justine noticed the way Elaine took to Janet and Lois, how they were at her side, wiping down dishes and silverware and jabbering about detergents and sprays. She couldn't help feeling jealous, but she couldn't believe the conversation these girls were having with her mother. Justine didn't know the differences between one detergent and the next, much less when it was better to use powders instead of liquids. How could girls this young be interested in such things?

Late in the afternoon, Christy Duke arrived to help Justine's mother set up her studio in the rear of the house. The large room boasted an enormous picture window facing the west, which permitted a great deal of sunlight.

At suppertime, Christy returned home to fetch Michael and covered dishes of food. Right behind them came Sid and Sylvia Bronstein, who lived in the house beside the Dukes. The Bronsteins brought breads and cake and a bottle of wine. They were eager to help, but the kids had done so much, there was very little left to do. Kevin and Elaine couldn't stop raving about the helpful teenagers.

Justine was glad when everyone finally left. Her parents flopped on the couch and looked about the large living room. Justine sat in the blue cushioned easy chair. At least having the same furniture made her feel at home, she thought. She liked curling up in this deep, soft blue chair. When she was little, her father told her it was a magic chair because she could only wish for things when she was sitting in it. As she had received some things she'd wished for, she had a child's faith in the magic.

"Do you believe how friendly people are here?" Kevin asked. "I mean, we're really moved in for the most part."

"Down to the dishcloths hanging on the pole above the sink," Elaine agreed. "Those kids are fantastic. You're going to make some wonderful new friends here, Justine."

"Sure, Mom." She glanced at the mute television set. "Can we get MTV out here?"

"We'll see. The cable will be hooked up tomorrow."

"No television tonight?"

"You won't wilt, will you?" Kevin laughed. "I have a unique new idea for you," Kevin said, jumping up dramatically. "What about a book? You know, like reading?"

"Very funny, Daddy."

He laughed and gave her a playful pat on the head.

"Well," Elaine said, standing. "Let's enjoy the food they brought. Everything looked delicious."

Justine had to admit the food was good. After dinner, she went up to her room. Her father had promised her her own phone if she started school well and brought home some good marks, and she was confident that she would be able to wrangle a phone out of him before long.

She went back to her stereo immediately. Now that the commotion had died down, she could close her door and play her music, just as she always did. Actually, with so much more living space, her parents would have less to complain about, she decided.

But when she reached for a tape, the box was gone. Her first reaction was confusion. In the middle of all that turmoil, she must have forgotten what she had done with them. She smiled to herself as she looked around the room. Everything was so neatly organized; it wouldn't be hard to find the tapes here.

But a perusal of the furniture, the chairs, the bed, and the closet floor turned up nothing. Where had she put all those tapes? She started to open drawers and pull out articles of clothing. She practically crawled over the closet floor. She looked under the bed and rifled through the drawers in her desk twice, but found no tapes.

Frustrated and angry, she bit down on her lower lip and thought. All she could picture was Janet's expression of disgust and Lois admitting she didn't have The Cult. Now she realized they were just pretending not to like her music so she wouldn't suspect them of snatching her tapes. The nerdy bastards, she thought, charging out of her room. Something made her hesitate, beside the empty cartons in the hallway. Slowly, she peered down into the first large box, and then she screamed.

Her mother and father came running up the stairs.

Justine stood by the carton, embracing herself, trying to staunch the tears of anger.

"Justine, what is it?" Elaine asked.

"What's wrong, sweetheart?" Kevin was at her side.

"My . . . tapes . . . look," she said, pointing to a carton.

Kevin looked down into the carton. Her cassette tapes

were there, but they were a jumble of smashed plastic and unraveled tape.

Elaine took his arm. "Kevin . . ."

"Must have gotten smashed in the moving," he said.

"They weren't in that carton," Justine said. "They were in my room."

"Why would anyone want to smash your tapes, Justine? Huh?" Kevin said. He looked at his wife, but she only shook her head. "Tomorrow we'll go downtown and buy some new ones."

"They probably don't sell these recordings here," Justine said. "They probably never even heard of Twisted Sister."

"Maybe they're lucky," Kevin said. It was a weak attempt at humor, but Justine didn't appreciate it. She ran into her room and slammed the door.

"Oh, Kevin." Elaine scowled at him.

"I was just trying to cheer her up. Hey, Princess," he said going to Justine's door. "Make a list, and I'll pick them up when I go into the city Monday."

Justine didn't respond. After a few moments she heard her parents go back downstairs, their voices low, their words indistinguishable.

And suddenly, even in this beautiful, new house, she felt a terrible foreboding.

2

GAZING OUT THE front window, Justine saw the black Cadillac pull up in front of her house and Dr. Felix Lawrence step out, carrying a small carton in his hands. The fifty-four-year-old man was a trim, one-hundred-and-eighty-pound six-footer. His salt and pepper hair was swept back neatly with a slight wave in the front. As he walked toward the front door of the Freemans' house, his deep blue eyes focused intently before him, giving him the air of a man with a determined purpose.

Even before he reached the door, it was opened. Kevin and Elaine had been expecting him, and had called Justine down from her room to meet him. Still depressed about her tapes, she had left her room reluctantly and come down to wait in the living room. Dr. Lawrence's secretary had called only a half hour earlier to ask if he could stop by on his way home.

"First time anyone ever made a formal appointment to pay a social call," Elaine said, but she was impressed and anxious to meet the famous man.

"Hello there, Kevin, Elaine," he said, "and welcome to Elysian Fields. I'm Dr. Felix Lawrence."

"Come in. Please," Kevin responded. He and Elaine stepped back, and Dr. Lawrence entered the house quickly.

Despite her mood, Justine couldn't help but be curious about the founder of Elysian Fields. His house, the story about his son, his glorious reputation all made him a very intriguing man. As soon as he appeared at the entrance to the living room, she stood up.

"And this is Justine," he said, as if he had met her before or had seen her picture somewhere. He made her feel as if she were greeting a long lost uncle.

"Yes, it is," Elaine said.

As Dr. Lawrence approached her, Justine noted how he held his shoulders back in a stern, almost military posture. He wore a dark jacket, a tightly knotted light brown tie, and a cream-colored shirt. Although he was cleanly shaven, his complexion was so dark, it suggested a Middle Eastern background. There was a handsome quality to his finely chiseled features and firm mouth. His jawbone was a trifle sharp, but it added to his intense look.

He reminded Justine of Mr. Donnely, a teacher back at her old school. She'd had such a crush on Mr. Donnely that she'd found excuses to stay after class.

"Hi, Justine," Dr. Lawrence said.

"Hi."

He shifted the carton to his left hand and held out his right. She shook it, expecting a quick, almost instantaneous squeeze and release. But he held onto her hand, forcing her to look into his eyes.

His smile was warm and his eyes full of interest, but she couldn't help being self-conscious. His gaze was so intense, he made her feel naked. She felt a soft flush stain her neck and cheeks.

Finally, he turned to her parents. "Sorry I wasn't here to greet you as you were moving in, but I had to be out of town. I hope you were warmly welcomed."

"We couldn't have had a better reception," Kevin said.

"Oh, yes," Elaine agreed. "Everyone's been so helpful and friendly."

"That's my development," Dr. Lawrence said, as if he not only had owned the land, but owned the inhabitants, as well.

"Please, come into our living room," Elaine invited. "Things aren't totally organized yet, but I'm sure you'll forgive us."

"Don't fuss over me. I just came by to officially welcome you to one of America's finest communities, and present you with this." He handed Kevin the small carton. "When you open it, you'll find enough of my vitamin formula to last your family more than a year. And when that's all used, there'll be more."

"Thank you so much," Kevin said. "We have heard a great deal about it. Please, have a seat."

"Can I get you something to drink?" Elaine asked.

"No, thank you, nothing for me. So," he said, following her farther into the living room, "I hope you find our little community comfortable." He nodded approvingly at the furniture and the handful of wall ornaments Elaine had put up. She had hung one of her early landscapes above the couch and he smiled at it appreciatively.

"We love it," Kevin said. "Every bit of it."

"Of course, I've got to get used to the wide open,

quiet space," Elaine said, indicating that Dr. Lawrence should take a seat. The doctor settled in Justine's favorite big blue cushioned chair, just across from her, smiling at her all the time. "I've been a city girl all my life," Elaine added.

"So I hear. It won't take you long to shake the noise and turmoil out of your ears, believe me. After a month here, you'll think you lived here all your life," Dr. Lawrence responded. His smile evaporated quickly, and his face took on an intensely serious look.

"That's what people tell us—in almost exactly those words." Kevin sat on the couch beside Elaine and Justine.

"Well, it's true. A number of years ago, I sat in my house on the hill and looked out over these beautiful grounds and said to myself, Felix, what a location for a picturesque community. What a waste, what selfishness it was to keep it all to myself. And so I began the development."

"You've certainly created a paradise," Elaine said.

"And designed it all yourself, we understand," Kevin said.

"Well, I dabble in things. I understand you're something of an artist, Elaine," he said, nodding at the painting.

Elaine blanched and looked at Kevin. "No, I'm just . . ."

"Oh, never say I'm just anything, Elaine," the doctor said, shaking his head. "You're never *just* anything." His face tightened with intensity. "If you have an inclination toward art, that's something significant. I hope being out here will stimulate the creative juices.

Perhaps one of these days I'll come by to purchase an
Elaine Freeman original," he added, smiling.

"Oh, I don't know." Elaine blushed and looked at
Justine, who was fascinated with the way the doctor
spoke. There was something about him that held her
attention. When he did speak to her parents, he was
constantly aware of her presence, too, and directed his
attention more at her than at them, she thought. Usually
adults made her feel like another piece of furniture when
they sat and talked with her parents; but not this man. He
was different.

"I do know. It's part of my business to build people's
confidence. And when they have a real talent to begin
with, that task becomes easier. So, Kevin," he said,
turning his attention to Justine's father, "you work with
Michael and handle tax cases, I understand."

"Yes, but one of these days I'll get to do some of the
more dramatic law Michael handles."

"You mean the malpractice cases?" Dr. Lawrence
winked. "I know what you lawyers are all about." He
laughed. "You don't have to worry about me, though. I
recognize the need sometimes to protect the victims. I've
testified on behalf of patients myself, you know."

"No, I didn't."

"Emotional problems, procedural things . . ." He
waved the air as though he wanted to chase away the
topic as one would shoo away a fly. "But even you will
find that living here is stimulating career-wise. It will
make you a better attorney. You'll be more relaxed." He
looked directly at Justine and smiled. "You'll worry less
about Justine—not that you worry about her much, I
imagine. How about it, Justine? Do they bug you like
most parents bug their children these days?" he asked.

"I don't know," she said, glancing back at her parents. "Yeah, I guess they do."

"What's that?" Elaine said, feigning indignation. Everyone laughed.

"Michael tells us you've counseled just about every teenager in this development," Kevin said.

"A little exaggeration. I have seen many, off and on. I'm nearby, easily available, and inexpensive," he added. He turned to Justine again, apparently impatient with anything that pulled his attention from her. "You've got a pretty daughter who takes after her mother," he added, nodding at Kevin.

Justine couldn't help but blush.

"Agreed," Kevin said.

"Thank you," Elaine said.

"Justine, you're going to like it here. I know you miss your friends back in the city, and you probably think these kids are different or snobby or boring, but after a short while, you'll be one of Sandburg Creek's and Elysian Fields' biggest cheerleaders," Dr. Lawrence predicted.

Justine shrugged.

"She's a little nervous about it all," Elaine said.

"Of course. That's understandable. Even expected. Well, any time you have trouble adjusting or even if you just feel like talking, feel free to call on me, okay? No charge for pretty girls," he added. Justine smiled. "And when you smile, you're even prettier."

"Thank you," Justine said. She didn't know what to make of an adult who was so direct and flattering.

"Well, I won't hold you people up any longer. I know you've got plenty to do," he said quickly.

"Oh, that's all right," Elaine said. "We were just relaxing, anyway. Right, Kev?"

Kevin nodded as he studied the doctor's gift. "These vitamins are supposedly quite the thing."

"Been out for five years with remarkable results," Dr. Lawrence said, sitting back proudly.

"What do you call them?" Elaine asked.

"Simple name for a complex thing," Dr. Lawrence said. "I call them 'The Good Pill.'"

"I've never seen them in the health stores," Elaine said. "Or I'd remember that."

"I haven't put them on the open market just yet. I'm not really in the vitamin business, but I can tell you they are being used by America's astronauts even as we speak." He turned to Justine. "Do you take vitamins, Justine?"

"Not really."

"Well, you're never too young for vitamins, and you never get enough of the right amounts in today's processed foods. I have what some might call a holistic approach to mental well-being. I think emotional health is dependent upon good nutrition, as well as other things."

"If Michael Duke and his family are examples of people on your vitamin, that's enough for us," Kevin said. "Justine will be taking them, too."

"Good. If you don't mind, I'd like to hear about it. I don't mean to sound as though I'm checking up on Justine," he added quickly. "What I mean is, I'd like to hear how you all feel after you've been on them a while."

"Sure," Kevin said.

"Not that we need any more proof of its success; it just

makes me feel good. Sort of like the father of the child, proud, if you know what I mean."

"Sure do," Kevin said.

"Well, fine. I'm on my way." He stood up quickly, and so did Justine and her parents. "Once again," he said, taking Kevin's hand, "welcome and best of luck to you and your family."

Justine watched as the doctor gripped her father's hand and stared directly into his eyes, as would a hypnotist.

"Thanks again," Kevin said.

"Elaine, I meant that about one of your pictures," he said, looking up at the landscape. "I sense a certain sensitivity to things natural. You're going to flourish as an artist here," Dr. Lawrence said, then headed for the door.

"I'll be happy just to do work good enough for my own home," she said.

"Uh, uh, uh." Dr. Lawrence paused at the door. "There you go again, underestimating yourself. Be confident, and you will be good," he said, his eyes catching hers and holding them for a long moment. She brought her hand to her throat and smiled.

"So long, Justine." He winked. "The moment you have trouble with your parents, pick up the phone."

"Thank you," she said in a voice just above a whisper.

Elaine and Kevin followed the doctor to the door and watched him walk down the flagstone path to his car. He waved before getting in.

"What a charming man," she said as he pulled away.

"Really is. You can feel his enthusiasm. When he took my hand, I felt energized," Kevin said.

"And wasn't it nice of him to learn so much about

us before coming? He knew Justine's name, that I paint . . ."

"I didn't like him," Justine said, still standing behind them.

"What? Why, honey?" Elaine asked.

"He was too . . . too nice," she said. "I don't trust people who are too nice."

"That's ridiculous," Kevin said. "You trust some of those city freaks you go around with, but you don't trust a nationally known doctor?"

"I don't go around with freaks," Justine protested.

"Kevin." Elaine grimaced.

"Well, why would she say she didn't like him, for god's sake?" He raised both his arms in frustration. "What did he do that would turn anyone off? As far as I can see, he's everything Michael said he was. You couldn't tell from talking with him that he was such an important man. He's not arrogant; he's almost like the guy-next-door. Why doesn't she see that?" he demanded.

"She's only a teenager, Kevin. She's not going to have the same reactions to people."

Justine's father shook his head.

"I'm just being honest," Justine said. "And I'm not going to take his stupid vitamins."

"Oh, yes you are, young lady," Kevin said. "I've been meaning to get you onto vitamins, anyway. Maybe that's why you've been so lethargic lately."

"Vitamins can't hurt you, Justine," Elaine said. "And you heard the Dukes talk about them."

"We'll all take them, once a day," Kevin said. "We need them." He went over to the carton and tore open the cover. "He wasn't kidding," he said, reading the label on a bottle. "They're called 'The Good Pill.' How's that?"

"Stupid," Justine said.

He opened the bottle and poured three pills out into his palm. "Come on. Let's toast our first meeting with the famous Dr. Lawrence and the beginning of a healthy, happy life in Elysian Fields."

"I can't take a vitamin without water," Justine protested.

"So, let's get some water." He headed toward the kitchen. "Justine."

"Do I have to?"

"It's a good idea, honey," her mother said, "a good habit to get into."

Reluctantly, Justine followed her parents into the kitchen and took the cup of water.

"Open," her father instructed. He placed a vitamin pill in Justine's mouth, the way a priest would place a communion wafer there. Then he lifted his cup.

"To us," he said. Elaine put a vitamin pill into her mouth, and they each swallowed a pill. "There. Now we'll be just as healthy as the rest of the people who live here," Kevin Freeman said.

He stood staring out of his bedroom window, looking down at the development. For a long time now, he thought of it the way he used to think of toy houses and toy people. There was something unreal about it all, and, in his father's eyes, Elysian Fields was indeed a toy world.

Sometimes, when he looked down at the houses and people, they seemed so tiny. He imagined how his father must feel—gigantic and powerful, able to reach down at

any time and move them at will. He could make them
almost anything he wanted to make them—happy or sad,
angry or docile. He knew that his father had been doing
it to him. The nurse had shown him proof. Confronting
him with it was part of the treatment.

There were pictures of things he loved, pictures he had
torn to shreds.

"Why did you do this?" he asked her.

"You did it," she said.

He didn't believe her, so she made him watch the
videotape that showed him attacking the pictures. He
couldn't believe the hateful expression on his face, the
intensity with which he'd sliced the pictures or ripped
them apart. And his self-loathing had been so great, he'd
even destroyed pictures of himself.

In the beginning, he hadn't cared what was done to
him. Right at this moment, he couldn't remember why
he'd felt that way, but he remembered that he had.
Sometimes isolated words returned to his memory,
words like "embarrassment," "freak," and "killer," and
those words made him feel so bad that he didn't mind the
physical and emotional torture.

But now he was starting to resent it. He couldn't put
it into words yet, not words that made any sense to him.
It was just a new feeling. Something bothered him. But
when he tried to focus on it, his mind went blank. No
matter how he struggled, he was unable to recall. He
imagined that this memory lapse was also his father's
doing.

His father was like God. His father gave and took
away. His father made pronouncements and dictated
commandments. His father created miracles, or at least
some miracles. He couldn't or he wouldn't change the

past. Actually, he was no longer sure what his father could and could not do. That was all blurred. He would have to wait to see.

He saw his father's car weaving through the development, the black vehicle moving like some large insect, prowling the quiet streets, looking for a new opportunity to pounce. Sure enough, he found one, for he stopped at one of the houses, the house that was actually the closest to his. It had been empty for so long, he hadn't thought much about it; but from what he could see now, there were new toy people inside.

He caught a glimpse of his father getting out of his car with one of his cartons tucked in the crook of his arm. The carton contained a mousetrap to be set in the house. Soon it would snap over the inhabitants and squeeze them silly. They would only get relief when his father deemed it necessary.

It was the same for him.

He stood there, staring down until his father emerged from the toy house and slipped into his large black insect. The vehicle crawled up the rest of the hill and turned into the driveway to disappear in its cocoon. Soon afterward, he heard the sound of doors opening and closing, and then he heard voices.

First his father was on the phone, and then he was conferring with the nurse. Moments later, his father was at his door. He felt him come in.

That was something his father didn't know he could do. He had spent so much time in this room, it had become a part of him. There were invisible threads, no bigger than the threads spun by a spider, connecting him to the walls, the ceiling, and the floor. His blood traveled through those threads and into the walls that actually had begun to pulsate with his life. He could feel it every time he placed the palm of his hand against it or pressed his cheek against its cool surface.

The walls had become walls of his flesh; the windows were his new eyes and ears. He wouldn't have to get up out of his bed to see out of the room or hear what was going on outside. It would all be brought to him via the invisible, thin threads.

The door was now an eyelid. When it was opened, he could see into the rest of the house; but when it was closed, he was blind to what went on out there. So, he thought, when his father came through the door, he passed through his eye ball and entered his brain.

But he had been doing that all along, anyway. His father had found all sorts of paths into his brain. He came in through his ears and mouth and, sometimes, through the strands of his hair, traveling down into the roots. He bounced around in there, scraping and pulling, twisting and turning, molding his brain cells the way a child might mold clay.

The funny thing was, it didn't hurt; none of it hurt. He was beyond pain. Pain had been cut off, disconnected, like a severed wire. Instead of pain, he felt a dull, continuous nudge, as if a finger were probing, pressing.

He felt his father's footsteps on his brain and closed his eyes. When he closed them, however, he saw his father standing there clearer than if he had turned and looked at him with open eyes. There was no escape from his father, because his father was inside him.

"Sit down," he commanded.

Aren't I already sitting down? he wondered. He looked down at his legs and saw that he was standing, so he went to the chair and sat. His father was beside him.

Suddenly his father had nine heads. He was the Hydra from Greek mythology. If one head was cut off, two would grow in its place.

More than a dozen eyes were staring down at him. There were hands all over him. Every part of his body was being prodded and examined at the same time. He began to panic, pushing the hands off his head, off his neck, off his legs; but as fast as he brushed them away, they returned.

"Relax," his father said. He had to say it only once. "How many fingers am I holding up?" he asked.

"Forty," he replied.

"Put your right forefinger on the tip of your nose."

He started to lift his leg, but found that impossible; so he thought about it and remembered what was attached to his shoulder. He brought that appendage up and peered at his hand. He must have just had it pressed against the wall of his room, for it was blood red. He didn't want to touch his nose with it.

"I'll get it all over me," he said.

"What are you talking about? Get what all over you?"

"The blood."

"There's no blood," his father said. "She bandaged your fingers this morning. You can't touch your nose?" he asked.

"Sure I can." He brought his fingers to his face until he found his forehead. Then, remembering the route, he traced down until he came to the space between his eyes and worked his way to the tip of his nose.

His father stood back and folded all six of his arms across his torso. He felt the nurse standing in his eye, so he turned to the doorway. She was there, waiting.

"Cut the dosage," he told her. "No radio stimulation

this week, either. I want to test his recall, and I want him to become more useful," he added.

Recall? What did he mean by "useful"? These were like foreign words. His father continued to look at him through thick lenses.

What happened? Had he shrunken until he was tiny enough to be put on a slide and shoved under a microscope?

"What do you want?" his father asked him.

"I want you to get out of my head," he said. "It itches inside, and I can't scratch."

"Does it?" his father asked without emotion. "What about your mother's itch?" he asked.

Mother? he thought.

His father left the room quickly. Then, they closed the door, and he was blind to the rest of the house.

Mother?

He stood up and went back to the window.

She was coming up that hill a hundred years ago, and he had been waiting for the sight of her car, standing right by this window, waiting. He was still waiting, but now that his father reminded him, his waiting paid off.

She was coming back. He wanted to run out to greet her. He snuck out the door quickly and ran to the front entrance. They didn't hear him; they were in the kitchen, talking. He opened the front door.

Her car was pulling into the driveway. He rushed out to greet her. She turned off the engine and opened her car door and stepped out.

Only . . .

She had no head.

He screamed and ran back into the house.

They were there to meet him.

"My fault," his father said. "I left his door unlocked. Help him back," he said.

And the nurse led him gently back to his room, where he curled up in the corner to be comforted and warmed by the walls of his own flesh.

Late the next morning, Justine stepped out of the house and looked down Long Street, past the Dukes' house. Then she turned and looked in the opposite direction. Everything was so quiet, it reminded her of a film she had seen that took place after a nuclear war. Even the birds seemed lethargic. They looked reluctant to move from one tree to another. It was almost as though they had to break their claws free of the sticky branches. And when they landed, they didn't strut about nervously as birds did on the branches of trees in Central Park. Instead, they were more like stuffed birds, staring out at the world through glass eyes.

She turned and looked up at the house on the hill, Dr. Lawrence's home, and thought about the man. Why had she told her parents she didn't like him? What had made her jump to that conclusion so quickly? There was something fascinating about him, and he was kind to her, actually seemed interested in her. Perhaps she just couldn't believe that an adult could be that understanding when it came to teenagers. Especially not a psychologist. Mindy had told her that all psychologists were phonies.

But the other teenagers in Elysian Fields liked Dr. Lawrence so much. Everyone couldn't be wrong, she thought. Maybe he was really an exceptional man. Her father didn't stop raving about him all night, and from what he said and what Michael Duke and some of the other adults in the development said, Dr. Lawrence was an important man. He was the first real celebrity she had ever met.

Suddenly she felt guilty about being so negative and causing her father to get so angry. The only excuse she could think of was she didn't like being uprooted like this. It wasn't her fault; they had to expect her to be a little testy.

She was walking toward Blueberry Street, which she had learned would lead her down to the tennis courts and the game room. According to rumor, wild blueberry bushes grew along that street. She'd heard Mrs. Bernie and Mrs. Wilson, who had come to visit, tell her mother that after their daughters, Janet and Lois, picked the berries, they would make pies.

Justine was intrigued with the idea of picking blueberries for a homemade pie. Of course, it wasn't the kind of thing a friend like Mindy would appreciate, but she was still curious about it.

Reluctantly, she decided she had to give this place a chance. She studied the map of Elysian Fields, trying to memorize where everything was located in relation to her house. Of course, she still hadn't gotten over the destruction of her tapes. One or all of those kids was responsible. And she would find the culprit, if it was the last thing she did. They weren't going to make a fool out of her.

She wished Mindy were here already, so she could get her opinion on some of these nerds. Mindy was usually pretty perceptive when it came to other kids.

If all went well, Mindy would be here later this week. Before Justine had left New York City, they had made tentative plans. They would have lunch together and listen to music. Mindy would fill her in on all that had

happened since Justine had left the city. She wondered if
Marty Stewart was sorry she had left. Their relationship
had just sparked to life before she left town. And though
he wasn't the kind of boy her father would approve of,
he was so sexy looking in a disarming way, like Andrew
McCarthy in *St. Elmo's Fire*. She smiled, remembering
the way she and Mindy had pursued him.

Only the memory didn't last as long as she would have
liked. It seemed to slip out of her mind, the images, the
words, and the vents all sliding into darkness, pushed out
by the events of the present. She lifted her right hand as
if to reach out and pull the memories back, and then
stopped, conscious of how she might appear to anyone
observing her.

She brushed some strands of her hair off her forehead.
A stiff, but warm breeze cut across the development as
Justine moved down the hill toward the pool and the
courts. She had to admit that from her new home, the
view was beautiful. But all the homes in the development, except for Dr. Lawrence's, were laid out like doll
houses. Everything was green and plush. The lawns
were like carpets, and flowers, still in full bloom,
painted streaks of red and yellow, purple, and orange
across the entire vista. Her mother was going to love to
paint this.

She could see that all six tennis courts were in use.
The players made her think of toy figures moved by
magnets hidden under the hard clay. Women and children were clustered around the pool. Despite the distance, sounds of laughter carried up to her. Some
maintenance men were working around the administra-
tive building, pruning hedges and weeding around

flowers. It looked like the center of a beehive, bustling with activity.

As she walked on, she found herself growing more and more relaxed, despite the inner turmoil and frustration she felt. Her nervous system was used to being bombarded by traffic noises, loud conversations, laughter, and the grinding of machinery on city streets. She was having trouble adjusting to the slow pace and stillness around her. She felt like someone going into withdrawal. It was hard to fall asleep only to the sound of crickets.

When she'd told her mother about it during their conversation this morning, her mother had admitted to having the same problem.

"Maybe we should have recorded some street noises," Elaine had said, "and played them all night long."

They'd both laughed, but now Justine thought that maybe it wasn't such a funny idea. At least she wouldn't toss and turn in expectation of something more. If things continued at this rate, she could have a nervous breakdown.

But almost as suddenly as it had begun this morning, the uneasiness had ended. She'd heard a soft ringing in her ears, and then she'd felt herself relax. When she went up to her room after breakfast, she'd gazed out of her bedroom window and noticed the recreational complex. The pool had looked inviting.

Now, somewhat closer to it, she regretted not having put on her bathing suit. She considered returning to her home to do so. When she turned around, she saw a car approaching.

It was Brad Duke.

"Hi," he said, pulling up beside her. He was wearing

a T-shirt and jeans and, for the first time, she realized that he was a very well-built boy. The musculature in his chest and shoulders was outlined clearly under the thin cotton material of his shirt.

"Hi," she said petulantly.

"Finally came out of your house, huh?" Brad asked. Justine just shrugged. "I heard about what happened to your tapes," he said. "Your mother told my mother."

"Yeah? Well, one of your wonderful friends did it."

"I don't know," he said. "The willful destruction of someone else's property is a criminal act."

"You sound like a lawyer's son, all right."

He laughed.

"People act out for different reasons," he added. "When I was with Dr. Lawrence once, he told me he used to punch holes in the eggs in his mother's refrigerator just to get her to pay more attention to him."

"You saw Dr. Lawrence, too? What's everybody have a problem here?" she asked.

He smiled wryly. She understood he hadn't always been the angel he seemed to be now, and that suddenly made him more interesting.

"I was headed for the pool. Want to come along?"

She hesitated. That feeling was coming over her again. There was even a return of that faint, but enticing ringing in her ears. Almost against her will, she was softening. Something made her turn toward the pool and gaze at the sparkling blue water. She couldn't remember a pool ever looking so inviting. She longed to glide through the soft, cool liquid, moving in pursuit of endless pleasure. Her skin tingled in anticipation.

"I don't have my suit on," she said, surprised at how disappointed she sounded.

"No problem. I'll drive you back to your house and wait."

For some reason, all of Justine's senses were heightened. She turned when she heard the flutter of bird's wings and saw a robin cruise, almost in slow-motion, to a nearby branch.

"Get in," Brad said.

Justine climbed into the car. As soon as she closed the door, Brad backed the vehicle into a driveway and turned around to take her home.

Her mother was sitting in the living room, talking on the phone when Justine reentered. She put her hand over the receiver and looked up, an expression of disappointment on her face.

"What's wrong, honey? I thought you were going for a walk."

"Just getting my bathing suit," she said. "I'm going to the pool."

"Oh, good." Elaine smiled.

Justine ran up the stairs and opened her bottom dresser drawer. For a long moment, she stared down at her three suits. She had a one piece, a turquoise two piece, and a black bikini so abbreviated, her father had told her to throw it out. She'd pulled a tantrum, and he'd relented after they had one of their father-daughter discussions.

She quickly stripped down and put on the bikini. Then she looked at herself in the mirror. She was a lot paler than someone like Christy Duke, but she was happy with her figure. She should have spent more time at the beach this summer, she thought. Even so, she was anxious to see the reaction on Brad's face when she came out of the house.

Her mother was off the phone by the time Justine came

down the stairs. She was at the front door looking through the four-panel window.

"Is that Brad out there waiting for you?"

"Uh-huh."

"That's very nice. He's a wonderful boy."

"It's just a ride to the pool, Mom. Hold off on the wedding arrangements," she sang and left the house, her mother's laughter chiming behind her. She wrapped her towel over her shoulders and started down the walkway to the driveway, anticipating Brad's smile of pleasure at the sight of her.

Instead, he grimaced as if in pain. She slowed down, sensing a radical change in him.

"What's wrong?" she asked.

"I . . . just remembered something terribly important that I have to do," he said. "I'm sorry."

She didn't respond for a moment.

"You don't want to go to the pool?"

"I can't," he said. "I gotta go. Sorry." He started the car and backed out of the driveway so quickly, she felt as though she had just had a terrible fight with him. She stood there, watching him drive down to his house, pull into his driveway, get out of his car, and rush into his house.

"I don't believe this," she muttered, turning back to her house. When she slammed the door behind her, her mother came out from her studio in the rear of the house.

"What happened? Why are you back so soon?" she asked, wiping her fingers with a rag.

"Don't ask me. Brad suddenly remembered something important that he had to do."

"Oh. Do you want me to go to the pool with you?"

"No. I don't care now."

"I wonder what could be so important," her mother mused aloud. She was wearing one of her father's old gray sweat shirts and a pair of worn jeans, her "artist's outfit."

"He's weird. They're all weird here. I hate it here. I hate it," Justine repeated and ran upstairs quickly. She slammed the door of her room, then flopped over her bed in disgust.

After a few moments, she got up and went to her window again. The pool still looked so inviting, which only made matters worse. What was Brad's problem?

He didn't have something important to do, she thought. Something changed when he looked at me. What?

She got up and studied herself in the mirror again. So she was a little pale; she was still attractive, and the bikini was quite revealing.

Maybe that was it, she thought.

But why would a boy that age be upset about this?

She wondered if it had anything to do with the reason his parents had sent him to see Dr. Lawrence. Maybe he had committed some sort of sex crime. All sorts of possibilities passed through her mind.

What kind of a place was this? she thought. Maybe the people here weren't as wonderful as her parents first thought. Maybe they all had terrible pasts and came here because they needed the doctor's psychological guidance. But then, why did her parents move here? They didn't have a terrible past. It was all so confusing and so . . . annoying, like an itch you couldn't get to, an itch under your scalp.

She decided to go out onto the back patio and get some sun, after all. Why waste the day? she thought. So she went out and set up a lounge chair. She rubbed in some suntan oil and sat back, hoping to relax and forget the scene she had just experienced.

From this vantage point, Dr. Lawrence's house stood directly above her. She paused for a moment before lying back. Someone was peering out of a window. Was that the doctor's crazy son? she wondered.

She closed her eyes, shook her head, and lay back. But a few moments later, she opened her eyes again and sat up to look up at the house. She thought she'd heard someone scream. Whoever had been there was gone, but the scream had frightened Justine. Even though the sun was bright and the air was warm, she was left with a cold chill.

Something wasn't right; something was just not right.

But moments later, she couldn't recall thinking about it. She even had trouble remembering why she was mad about what Brad Duke had done. In fact, when her father came home and asked her about the incident, after her mother had mentioned it, she drew a blank.

"I don't remember," she said.

He thought she didn't want to talk about it.

But the cold truth was, she didn't remember, and that was the most frightening thing of all.

3

HE COULD SEE the toy girl down there, stretched out on a lounge chair. His eyesight was still very good. It wasn't a matter of seeing objects; it was a matter of identifying them. He was interested in the girl because she was wearing one of those skimpy bathing suits, the kind his father did not approve.

How did he know his father did not approve of it? he wondered. How did he remember that?

Things were coming back. Whatever it was that had blocked the past was moving aside to permit it to be heard and seen and remembered again.

The sound of his father's voice made him spin around, but his father wasn't in the room. From where was his voice coming?

He looked around. Was that his father on the television set? He remembered now. When he was very young, perhaps no more than three or four, his father used to place him before the television set and then play the video cassette recorder. His father played tapes he had made of himself speaking to him, teaching him things, telling him things. He was forced to sit there for hours, watching his father on the screen, listening to his words.

He grew up with this. Through the years, when he returned from school, there were messages and lessons waiting for him on the video cassette recorder. He would get a glass of milk and a box of cookies, and turn on the machine to look at his father and listen.

The toy girl below had evoked one of those video memories. It was a memory that took him back to when he was a teenager. and his father was complaining about the breakdown of values. His head took up the whole screen, and he was glaring out at him with those magnetic eyes so that he couldn't turn away from the set.

"Look at the clothes young girls are wearing. Think about it. They are just discovering themselves, and they are pushing too hard and too fast toward maturity. Parents who permit their daughters to wear suggestive, skimpy clothing like bikinis are only contributing toward the degeneration of our moral values.

"Don't have anything to do with such girls. Don't even talk to them. And never, ever bring one home to meet your mother or me."

That wasn't fair, he thought. He liked those girls; he wanted to bring them home. Other boys weren't forbidden to spend time with them. Why was he?

Other boys didn't have a father in the television set, a father who packaged himself and his ideas to be sold to desperate parents looking for easy ways to raise their children. Other boys didn't have a father who was in the very walls of their homes, shaking his head in disapproval or nodding in approval, judging, watching, studying their every thought and action.

He erased the tape. He rewound it and pressed record

and left it running, so that when his father came home that day, he discovered that the tape had been ruined.

He pretended it had happened by accident.

"You have to be more careful with my things, Eugene," his father said. He was very understanding about it. One thing about his father, he was very understanding because being understanding was his profession.

He looked down at the girl again. Didn't she know his father didn't approve? Hadn't her parents played the tape? He knew everyone in the development was given copies of the tapes. In houses throughout Elysian Fields, at a specific time in the early evening, families sat in front of their television sets, and fathers turned on the videotape.

"Here is a gift from Dr. Lawrence," they announced, and the tapes were begun. They watched, a captive audience in every sense of the word.

His father was everywhere; his voice echoed throughout the development, and his image haunted everyone's mind. So why was this girl sitting out there like that?

Hey, hey, girl! he thought—or did he call out? She sat up again and looked up at him. Had she heard him? He pulled back from the window, back into the shadows of the room. And suddenly, he was shivering. The sun was beating down outside, and he was shivering.

Why should I be shivering? he wondered, staring down at his feet.

The floor of his room had become a pool of icy water gradually turning into a sheet of ice. His feet, in fact, were becoming frozen within it. He moved quickly and rushed to the door. Hard, snowy chunks of ice were running down his walls. He could see little puffs of his breath. His room had been turned into a freezer. He pounded on the door. Someone had to hear him; someone better hear him, or he would die in here, he thought. He had had a dream like this many times before. Remember Bobby Bienstock who did get shut up in his father's butcher shop freezer? They said he died standing up. He pounded the door again.

She opened it abruptly and glared in at him. He thought she had a meat cleaver in her right hand. Was he to be butchered now? Was that the plan? That was why his room had been turned into a freezer.

"No, please, don't . . . don't cut me up and cook me."

"What the hell is it now?" she demanded. Then she put her right hand on her heavy hip and smirked. "Your father doesn't realize the residual effects of the pills. It will be days before you become anything like you were, considering the dosages you were taking."

What was all this gibberish? Was she speaking another language? Those foreign words again?

"No hablas en Espanol," he said, shaking his head.

"Here," she said, thrusting the meat cleaver at him. "He wants you to take this pad and write your thoughts on it. I'm giving you a ball-point pen, but if you stick it in any part of your body, I'm warning you . . ." she said, waving a finger at him. Only it wasn't a finger, it was a long, thick worm. In fact, it was a leech. He cowered. "Take the pad, damn it," she repeated.

He reached out and took the meat cleaver carefully so he wouldn't cut his hand. Then she put the pen in his other hand. He looked down at it.

I remember this, he thought. He smiled. I remember this. Words came out of it. He would point it down and words would leak out all over the paper.

"What do you want me to do?" he asked her.

"Write me a story," she said. "And don't forget to start with 'Once upon a time,'" she added and laughed. "Don't close this door," she commanded and turned away. He watched her walk down the hall and turn the corner. Then he went to the desk and put the pad down.

It had become a pad in his hands. He stared at it a moment, then sat down.

I remember doing this, he told himself. I remember sitting down with . . . what is it . . . in my hand and getting the words to leak out on the paper.

Words that were called poems when they were all together.

She liked his poems. He would go to her as soon as he had completed one, and she would say, "Wait. Don't read it until I close my eyes. I want to envision what you say." He would wait, and after she closed her eyes, he would begin.

A moth fell asleep on an unlit light bulb.
When someone flipped the switch and the bulb lit up,
The moth thought it had fallen into the sun.

"I can see that," she said. "I can see it." She opened her eyes. "I like it. It's simple, but it's beautiful. And it says something."

He smiled. She made him want to write another.

"Leave it, and I'll show it to your father later," she said.

He shook his head.

"Oh, don't be that way. He likes your poetry. Some of it, anyway. He'll like that one. Leave it, Eugene. Please."

He'd left it, but his father had never said anything about it. Some time later, he'd asked him.

"What moth?" he'd said, looking up from his "official" mail.

"The one on the light bulb."

"What the hell are you talking about now? Listen to me," his father had said sternly. "I heard today that you have been hanging around with the Fenton boy. That boy's trouble, the personification of trouble. His parents are both alcoholics. I've had sessions with the whole rotten family. Stay away from him, understand?"

"He likes some of the music I like," he'd replied.

"I don't care. You stay away from him, and never, never bring him to this house." His father had scowled at him a moment. "Moth . . . On a light bulb? Go do your homework and forget about moths. And take that pen out of your ear. You look like a stock boy, not a student."

A pen. That's what this was, a pen. And the words didn't come from it; they came from him, from his mind, down his neck, through his arm, and through his hand and fingers into the pen. Then the pen dropped them on the paper.

He remembered, and he felt encouraged.

He started to write.

"The toy girl like a sponge soaked up the sun."

He liked that. She would like that, too, he thought. He jumped up from his seat and rushed to the door. Nurse had left it open, so he crept out into the hall and turned left.

She heard him and came after him. "Where are you going?" she demanded.

"To show her my new poem," he said. He rushed into

his mother's room, only she wasn't there. The bed was stripped. All of her things were gone. The dressers were bare. He looked around stupidly. "What . . . where is she?" He turned around to face the nurse, who was right behind him. "Huh?"

"She's in the ground," she said. "Where you put her."

And suddenly, he wondered why he had a meat cleaver in his hand.

Justine sat quietly at the dinner table, chewing her food slowly and looking ahead as though she were in deep thought. And yet, she wasn't in deep thought. Her mind was literally blank. Both her parents ate the same way, staring ahead, chewing slowly. It wasn't until the phone rang that they all came out of their daze.

For a moment, no one got up. Then Kevin went to the wall phone. After he said hello, he just listened, cradling the receiver in his hand. Then, he hung up.

"Who was that?" Elaine asked, smiling when Kevin returned to his seat at the table.

"Oh, it was Dr. Lawrence inviting us to tonight's Elysian Field Development Organization meeting at the clubhouse. Seven thirty," he said.

"How come you didn't say anything to him?" Justine asked. "You just listened and hung up."

"What do you mean? I thanked him, didn't I?" He looked to Elaine to confirm it, but she didn't hear what he said.

"Wasn't that nice of him to give us a personal invitation," Elaine said. Kevin didn't reply. He continued to eat, lost in his own thoughts. "What should I wear, I wonder."

"Wear something blue," Kevin said, suddenly remembering.

"Blue? Why blue, honey?" she asked, a slight, inquisitive smile on her face. Kevin paused as if he had forgotten the reason. Then he smiled. Justine thought it was a weird smile, like a little boy.

"Because Dr. Lawrence said . . . wear something blue. I'm sure he said that."

"Something old, something new, something borrowed, something blue," Elaine said and laughed.

"What's that?" Justine asked. Her parents were acting very strange tonight.

"What you're supposed to wear on your wedding day."

"Well, you're not getting married to Elysian Fields tonight, are you?" Justine asked. Elaine shook her head.

"Dear Justine," she said, reaching across the table and patting her daughter on the top of her hand. "How can a person marry a development?" She looked at Kevin, and they both laughed.

Confused, Justine tilted her head, then giggled, but she wasn't really sure why she was laughing. It was as if everything her parents did and felt was contagious. Everyone was just in a silly mood.

After dinner she helped her mother with the dishes, then went into the den to call Mindy. But when she lifted the receiver and started to dial, she had to stop. She couldn't remember her best friend's number. It put her into a panic. She must have called Mindy a thousand times during the last year. How could she forget the number? Struggling to recall, she finally succumbed to defeat and ran upstairs to her room to look it up in her pink leather address book. She found it in her desk drawer. But a strange thing happened when she located Mindy's number. There was still nothing familiar about it. It was like a brand new sequence of numerals, one she had never used before. How could that be? she wondered.

Deciding not to think about it anymore, she ran back downstairs to the den, sat behind her father's dark pine desk in his smooth, black leather swivel chair, and called Mindy.

"You sound different already," Mindy said. Justine's friend had a thin, high-pitched voice, but it had never seemed so annoying as it did at this moment.

"Why? What's different?" Justine demanded. She'd never liked criticism, but suddenly she was a great deal more sensitive to it.

"You sound . . . stuck up," Mindy said.

"That's ridiculous," Justine replied. She grimaced as if Mindy were there in the room with her. "I'm just bored, that's all," she added, slouching back in the chair.

"No good-looking boys?" Mindy inquired hopefully.

"Yes, there are a lot of good-looking boys here," she snapped, then thought, why did I say that?

"Good. But you better not be lying to me."

"I'm not lying. It's nice here, very nice. The pool's beautiful, and the grounds are very pretty."

"Is it nicer than the city?" Mindy asked sadly. It was as though Justine were betraying her.

"Yes, in many ways."

"You're stuck up," Mindy concluded.

"I am not. Don't be silly. Have you seen Marty?" she asked, happy she had remembered to ask about him.

"Yes, I saw him," Mindy replied quickly. This gave

her opportunity to strike back. "And he keeps asking about you. He wants to see you very much."

"Maybe he'll come out here with you," Justine said.

"I don't know. I don't even know if I want to visit you there," Mindy said petulantly. "I hate stuck-up kids, and that's probably what they all are."

"No, honest. Please come out," Justine cried, leaning forward on the desk. "You said you would. My parents aren't going to let me go into the city. Please," she pleaded.

"I'll see," Mindy said, deliberately still sounding reluctant. "But Marty probably won't want to come along. He's already looking at Dede with desire," Mindy added, exaggerating her pronunciation of "desire."

"But he would like it here," she said, her voice filled with unexpected enthusiasm. "It's really beautiful."

"You told me that. Jesus."

"Well, it is. I can't help it. I can't help saying it," Justine added, as if just realizing it herself.

"You're right," Mindy said. "You must be bored. Look, I gotta go. I'm meeting Colleen and Nancy at Donnie's house."

"Oh."

"We're goin' to have a good time."

"You'll have a good time here," Justine said. "It's very . . ."

"I know. It's very beautiful. Good-bye, Justine. Jesus," Mindy said and hung up before Justine could reply.

"But it is very beautiful," she repeated into the dead receiver. Then she cradled the phone and sat back in her father's desk chair, staring ahead blankly until her mother appeared in the doorway.

"How do I look?" Elaine asked. She was wearing a light blue sleeveless cotton dress with a white belt. She had her hair brushed back neatly and pinned. She wore only a touch of lipstick, and no eye shadow or any other makeup.

"Very nice."

"Your father's wearing a pair of dark blue slacks, a light blue shirt, and his sea blue sports jacket, with his blue Pierre Cardin shoes," she said, sounding like someone describing a fashion show. "And here he is," Elaine announced, turning around. Justine's father appeared at her side. "Doesn't he look dapper?"

"Yes, he does," Justine said. "Mom, do you think I might be able to go into the city to see my friends this weekend? Please?" she said quickly.

"We'll talk about it when we return from the meeting," Elaine said.

"I'll take the bus in the morning and come back before supper," Justine said. "Please?"

"Kevin?"

"Well, we might arrange something," he said. "Let's talk about it when we come back. Okay, princess?"

"Okay," Justine said, recognizing the familiar signals of agreement in her father's voice. If he didn't reject something outright, he was susceptible to her pleas. It never failed. "Have a good time."

"How can the two best-looking people fail to have a good time?" Kevin said, and Elaine laughed.

Justine watched her parents leave the house. She stood in the doorway until their car disappeared around the corner of Long Street.

It was easy to see clearly up and down the street, because the powerfully bright streetlights held the darkness at bay. The network of streetlamps created walls of light and, for a moment, she had the sense of being within the walls of a castle or fortress.

She embraced herself and tried to see beyond the streets, deeper into the heart of the development, but the brightness of the lights made it difficult to see beyond them. She held her hand over her eyes and peered to the right, and then to the left.

The darkness turned into an oozing black liquid trying to penetrate the shield of light. As the wind moved tree limbs, their shadows slid over the ground toward the wall of light, only to be driven back by the illumination. She waited a moment and listened for some sound of other people, other voices, but there was only the monotonous hum coming from those bright streetlights.

Bored, she closed the front door and wandered aimlessly through the house. They still hadn't gotten their television hooked up, so that was out. She thought about going up to listen to her music, but the usual enthusiasm just wasn't there. She thought about her conversation with Mindy and put all her hope into the possibility of her parents permitting her to go to the city. She was confident now that if they returned from their meeting in a good mood, she could continue to pursue the idea and get them to agree.

She went to the rear of the house, to her mother's art studio. The canvas on the easel held the beginnings of a painting. She stared at it a moment, then went to the window and looked out. Her mother was painting a landscape of the grounds behind the house, but she had also included the house on the hill. In her drawing, it loomed much larger than it really was. Justine was surprised at the minute details her mother had included, especially details of the house. The painting looked more like a photograph.

She moved on, passing through the kitchen to go back to the living room. She flopped in her blue, cushioned chair and stared out the picture window until she saw the figure of a girl approaching the house. Happy for some company, she got up quickly and went to the door before the girl even had a chance to press the buzzer. It was Lois Wilson.

"Hi," she said. Justine just stared out at her. "Don't you remember me? I'm Lois."

"Oh, yeah, sure. Come in," Justine said, backing away.

Lois entered tentatively and looked about the house. She was dressed in an oversized black sweat shirt with SANDBURG FOOTBALL SQUAD printed in gold on the back. Her jeans were dark blue and tight at the calf muscles. She wore a pair of light pink sneakers, and white tube socks.

"Your parents went to the meeting too, huh?"

"Yes. Yours did?"

"Never missed one in two years. That's how long we've been here," she said. "You see, unlike Brad, I can remember," she added. She peered through the entrance-way as though she didn't trust Justine and thought her parents might still be there.

"Where are you from?" Justine asked.

"Bridgeport, Connecticut," Lois replied. She continued to look about the foyer, reminding Justine of a curious dog, sniffing and studying its environment.

"So, how do you like it here?" Lois asked cautiously.

Justine shrugged. "It's all right, I guess." She glanced toward the doorway as an image of the pool and the beautiful grounds flashed before her. "It's very beautiful," she added.

"Uh-huh," Lois said and nodded, as if confirming a diagnosis. She stared at Justine, then looked away quickly. "You've got a nice house, too. And I love your room," she added, her voice a little louder. It was as if she were saying things so someone would hear them. Did she still think her parents were hiding behind a door?

"Thank you," Justine said, then thought a moment. "You were in my room?"

"When you first moved in. I was with the other kids who helped. Don't you remember?" Lois grimaced. "You don't, do you?"

"Yeah, I do," Justine said defensively, but she really didn't.

"But you remember Dr. Lawrence visiting you, don't you?" Lois said accusingly. For a moment, Justine just stared at her. The girl seemed so angry about it. She nodded, though she felt guilty, as if she were confessing to a crime.

"Yes. He was here. We all sat in the living room and talked."

"And he brought you a present . . . his vitamins," Lois said. "And you've been taking them," Lois added as if finishing a story. She shook her head and turned back to the door. "I've got to go."

"Wait. Why do you have to go so soon? Can't you stay awhile and talk? School starts tomorrow, right?" she asked quickly to keep the girl there.

"Now you can't wait, huh?" Lois asked, smirking. "When we first talked about it, you weren't very interested."

"Well, it's boring just doing nothing, and starting at a

new school can be exciting," Justine said. "Come on in. Nobody else is here," she added, taking Lois's arm gently to lead her. Lois reluctantly followed her in and sat on the couch. She looked around blankly. Justine sat on her blue chair and stared at her expectantly. "Are the boys nice?"

"Just like any place else," Lois said. "There are nice ones, and there are ones that aren't so nice. The townies are different."

"Townies?"

"Kids from Sandburg Creek who don't live in Elysian Fields. You'll see. They think we're stuck up," she said. And then she muttered, "And they're right."

"What?"

"Nothing. Look, I've got to get back and see what my little brother's doing. I'm responsible when my parents go out."

"How old is he?"

"Ten, and he's a brat."

Justine nodded as if she knew. Lois got up abruptly. She was determined to leave.

"Why did you come here if you had to go so quickly?" Justine asked. She wasn't angry; she was just curious.

"You wouldn't understand. Not now. Maybe later," she added, speaking rapidly. She started for the entry-way. Justine rose quickly and followed her out to the door.

"Why wouldn't I understand?" she asked.

Lois looked around. "You can't when you're in here—or anywhere on the grounds of Elysian Fields," she said.

"Huh?"

"Forget it."

"This isn't very nice, leaving me like this," Justine said. "It makes me feel peculiar, like I did something to hurt your feelings."

"And that bothers you," Lois said in a dry monotone, as if reciting something she had been hearing for years and years.

"Yes. And that's not fair," Justine added quickly.

Lois contemplated her a moment. "I came to tell you something, but I don't know if it matters now."

"What?" Justine's eyes widened with interest.

Lois peered into her face, as if looking for a blemish. "Your tapes," she said.

"Tapes?" A smile froze on Justine's face.

"Janet smashed them. I saw her do it."

"Smashed them?" Justine tilted her head, then looked up toward her room. "Smashed them?"

"Didn't you find your cassette tapes smashed?" Lois asked.

Justine didn't respond.

Lois shook her head. "I told you, it doesn't matter now." She opened the front door. "I'll see you in the morning, since we all usually walk to school together. We meet at the bottom of the hill, by the security gate."

"Okay," Justine said, realizing the girl was determined to leave. "Thanks for stopping by."

"Yeah," Lois said, smirking again.

Justine watched her go down the walkway to the road. Then she closed the door and started back to the living room, thinking about the things Lois had said. Something lingered in her mind. She looked at the stairway, and then started up to her room.

When she got to her room, she went to her cassette container and peered inside. Her father had bought her a number of new tapes. They were still unwrapped. She had put them there herself.

Why did he bring her the new tapes?

What did Lois mean when she'd said that Janet had smashed them? Why was it so hard to remember unpleasant things about this place? And why had she forgotten her old friends—her old life—so quickly? She shrugged, and then went downstairs to wait for her parents. She fell asleep in her favorite chair, waiting, and woke up when she heard them come in.

"What are you doing?" her mother asked her. Her parents stood side by side in the doorway looking in at her. They had strange expressions on their faces, scowls that suggested they had caught her doing something illicit. Justine rubbed her eyes, trying to remember what she'd been doing.

"I just fell asleep in the chair, I guess." She shrugged, unable to think of anything she had done to upset them.

"You just sat there in a chair all this time?" her father said. "You didn't pick up a book, or do something worthwhile with your time?"

"I wanted to watch television," she remembered, "but—"

"Forget television. You can live without television for a couple of nights," he snapped.

Justine felt her face crumble.

"How about we all have a nice hot chocolate?" Elaine said suddenly, "and relax," she added, but she made it sound like some kind of psychological technique. "Come on, Justine. Help me in the kitchen."

Justine followed her mother out of the living room, walking past her father, who glared at her with a look of annoyance. She was frightened by the fire in his eyes, something she rarely saw there.

"We had a wonderful meeting," her mother began in the kitchen. "We met a lot of nice people, and had a great discussion. You're going to love it here. We all will. And Dr. Lawrence . . . he is such a charming and resourceful man. We told him we were thinking about getting another car, you know, since I'll be driving again, and he introduced us to a car dealer who practically made your father a rock bottom offer on the spot. Such cooperation . . . such eagerness to help one another." She paused. Justine was standing in the kitchen doorway, listening. Elaine smiled.

"Look at me, going on and on like a chatterbox. Can you ever remember me a chatterbox? You know how I hate sitting around and gossiping. I hate clubs and I hate organizations with weekly meetings and organized activities and . . . what's the matter? Why are you staring at me like that?" She brought her small hands to the bottom of her throat.

"Nothing. I don't know," Justine said quickly. "I was so bored. Mom," she said, grateful for the idea that was returning. "You said I might be able to go to the city to visit my friends. You said we would talk about it."

"Absolutely out of the question," her father said, coming up behind her. "Forget it."

"But Daddy, you said—"

"I never said anything about it. It's a bad idea."

"Yes, you did," she continued. "Right before you two left for the meeting. I had just called Mindy and—"

"And that's another thing. I don't want you to have anything to do with the likes of Mindy Boston. She's a bad influence. Now that you're out here—"

"That's not fair. You're lying. You did say we could talk about it. You're lying!" Justine exclaimed, her face reddening.

"Justine!" Her mother stepped forward.

"You're both lying. And I hate you for it. I hate you!" she screamed and ran from the kitchen.

She rushed upstairs to her room and closed her door. Then she went to the front window and stared down at the street. She wanted desperately to cry, but the tears wouldn't come. It was as though they were being blocked, and the frustration was so great, it made her heart pound.

She turned from the window in disgust and started for her cassette recorder, but almost as soon as she had inserted the tape, she stopped. There was a gentle ringing in her ears. She listened to it for a moment, then returned to the window.

The streetlights of Elysian Fields made it look as though the sun shone only on the development, even at night. She could see the pool and the tennis courts and the pretty houses, all neatly arranged.

"It is beautiful here," she muttered in a monotone reminiscent of a recording.

There was a soft knock on her door.

"Justine?" her mother called softly.

"Yes?"

"We're going to sleep now, honey."

She went to the door and opened it. Her father and mother stood there, both staring at her expectantly. Neither parent looked angry now.

"Night, Mom. Night, Dad," she said. Her mother kissed her.

"Night, princess," her father said. She kissed him. "Don't you think it's wonderful here?" he said.

"Uh-huh."

"I can't wait for the morning," her mother said. "I want to get right to my new painting. I can't remember ever having such enthusiasm for my work. Dr. Lawrence was right—being in a beautiful, serene environment does stimulate the creativity. Aren't you happy Daddy brought us here?"

"Yes," Justine said. "I'm happy."

"Great," Kevin said, raising his arms in an overly dramatic gesture.

Were her parents drunk? Had booze been served at their meeting? The possibility brought a smile to her face, but her father misinterpreted her amusement and his smile widened.

"Sleep tight," he said. "And don't let the bed bugs bite."

"Oh, Kevin," her mother said, "there are no bed bugs here." They started toward their bedroom.

"I know that. I'm just joking," he said.

Then she turned away from the door, and feeling very contented, got ready for bed.

It was only moments after she'd pulled the soft cotton blanket around her that she fell asleep, unable and unwilling to think of anything at all.

4

THERE WAS SOMETHING different about this morning,
he thought as soon as he opened his eyes. He felt lighter,
stronger, more alert. And the sunlight coming through
the window didn't have that usual yellowish tint that
reminded him of banana skins. It was cleaner, softer, and
brighter than ever. Most importantly, it filled him with
an energy he couldn't recall having for some time. He
didn't have this usual indifference to waking up, either.
Now he was impatient with the nurse. She should have
already come to unfasten the straps.

He called out and waited, called out and waited. Soon
he heard her ponderous footsteps in the hall, and the door
opened. She stood there in her diaphanous nightgown,
her large breasts pointed accusingly at him, the nipples
like slices of carrot. She put her hands on her hips, and
pressed her large, worm-colored lips together until she
looked like a fish. Her dull black hair was unpinned, and
it draped around her head unevenly, some of the strands
curling up, some hanging limply.

"I want to get up," he said. "I have to go to the bathroom, and I want to get dressed and have breakfast and
take a walk through the woods."

"I want, I want," she said. "As soon as he reduces the dosages, you remember to want. I'm not a baby-sitter."

"You'll have to change my diaper if you don't let me up," he said, and she laughed.

"I forgot you have a sense of humor," she said, coming over to him. She began to unfasten the straps, deliberately leaning across him so her breasts would graze his chest. They felt like two water-filled balloons.

As soon as he was free, he sat up. He washed his face with his dry palms, excited by the feel of his own skin, by the realization that he was touching his mouth, his nose, and running his fingers over his closed eyes.

"It's me," he said. "I've been sleeping with myself, for a change."

"Congratulations. You remember how to go to the bathroom, don't you? You remember you've got to point your pecker at the toilet and not at the sink, right?"

"Sure. No worries."

"Easy for you to say. You don't have to clean it up. Go on," she commanded, and he slipped off the bed and hurried to the bathroom. There was a moment when he had to actually consider the two porcelain objects and make a conclusion as to which was the toilet, but that moment passed quickly.

When he was finished, he came out and dressed himself before she returned to tell him his breakfast was on the table. He put on his dark blue cotton, short-sleeved shirt, and a pair of light blue slacks that had been hanging in the rear of his closet for ages. They were still sharply pressed. For a moment, he recalled a scene in school—his friends kidding him about the creases in his pants always being so sharp, so perfect.

As a result, one afternoon he had come home after school and had taken all his pants out of his closet. He'd put them on a chair and sat on them, ruining their sharp creases. His father had been upset, but his friends had loved it. He could still see them—dozens of kids standing up in the cafeteria when he entered, everyone applauding.

"Eugene lost his crease; Eugene lost his crease," they cheered.

He smiled like an impish cherub who had deserted God and joined forces with Lucifer. In Hell, none of the sinners have a sharp crease in their pants.

The memory faded almost as quickly as the images and words had appeared, and he looked around guiltily. His father might find out what he had been thinking about.

He hurried out to the kitchen, looking at everything as though for the first time: the plaques on the walls; the family pictures; the grandfather clock, its face looking stern and austere; the place whose molding he'd nicked when he'd brought his bike in the house. His father had refused to have it repaired. It was to remain as a reminder.

There were dozens of reminders all over the house— every tear in the furniture, every muddy fingerprint on the walls—symbols of the times he'd misbehaved as a child. The house was a museum, tracing his behavioral development. There would be no escape, no forgetting. "We must be haunted by our deeds; it's the only way to grow," his father proclaimed in his Ten Commandment style. In his dreams, his father stood bedecked in a long, flowing robe, looking out over Elysian Fields.

"Behold what I have made," he said, raising his arms with a flourish.

As soon as he got to the kitchen, he sat down and began to eat his breakfast. He gulped down the orange juice like one who was afraid all his food would be seized, and attacked the bowl of cereal, enjoying the taste and the crunchy sensation between his teeth.

She was drinking a cup of coffee and standing against the far wall, peering at him over her cup. Then he heard his father's footsteps and paused.

"Eugene looks rather together this morning," his father said, coming into the kitchen. He took a glass out of the cabinet and poured himself some orange juice.

He couldn't take his eyes off his father.

"He didn't need me to do anything for him this morning," she said.

"Oh?" His father turned around and studied him with clinical eyes, scrutinizing, peering down through an invisible microscope. "Yes, I see. So, Eugene," he said. "What are you thinking about this morning?"

"I wanted to go for a walk through the woods. Maybe just run between the trees, hop over stumps, plow through bushes, listen to the birds scream."

"You think the birds scream?"

"When someone invades their place, yes."

He looked at the nurse as if to say, "See?" Then he poured himself some coffee, and came to the table.

"You know you're a sick boy, don't you? You know I'm treating you myself, trying to make you better than you were before. You remember all that, right?"

"Some of it," he said. He didn't remember anything like that, but he knew enough to agree. His father, still staring at him closely, nodded. Then he thought of a question. At first he was afraid to ask it, but his father sensed his hesitation. He was beginning to think his father could really see into his head. When he was younger, he had that fear because other kids his age, kids whom his father treated, told him they felt he could see into theirs.

"What is it? Something's troubling you, right? What do you want to know?"

"What . . . what was wrong with me?" he asked. His cereal spoon remained poised between his mouth and the bowl. He looked quickly at the nurse to see if she would laugh at his question, but she seemed just as interested in the answer.

"Good question, Eugene. You're coming back." His father sat back and sipped his coffee. Then he leaned forward, tilting his head and taking on his teaching face, a face characterized by eyes that looked off as though he were reading cue cards. He also had that pedantic tone in his voice. "Evil is sickness, Eugene. Most people don't understand. Misbehavior, antisocial behavior, delinquent behavior, whatever you want to call it, is a sickness. Something goes wrong in here," he said, pointing to his temple.

"Psychologists, psychiatrists, have been groping for ways to cure it. They are like blind men in a maze. Some go rushing down Freudian tunnels, reading and interpreting symbols on the walls."

"If they're blind, how can they read?" he asked quickly.

His father smiled. "That's what I want to know. That's very perceptive of you, Eugene. The whole thing is ridiculous. Imagine trying to talk someone out of having cancer. It's a disease. And so is evil, understand?"

He nodded. "*I* was evil?"

"I'm afraid so, Eugene. During the next day or so, I'm going to let you find your way back so you can see what you were and what you did, and then we'll go on with your treatment—with less resistance on your part, I hope. Of course, you must understand that I am feeling my way about, too. Nothing's perfect yet. There are some flaws in the process, flaws I'm discovering out there." He gestured toward the window and the development below.

"But," he said, leaning back again, "on the whole, things are going very well, very well, indeed. Right, Mildred?"

"Whatever you say, Doctor," Mildred said.

He laughed. "That's what I like about Mildred," he said, turning back to Eugene. "She's devoid of any feelings that might influence her behavior. Mildred's indifference is her biggest asset, at least for me."

"Can I walk through the woods today?" he asked.

"No, I don't think so. Not yet, Eugene. I want you to go into my office and read things, things about yourself. I'll be back later this afternoon, and we'll talk about them. Then we'll see. Go on, finish your breakfast. I'm glad you're hungry."

He looked down at his spoon, and then brought it to his mouth. For a while, his father just watched him. Then he went back to his room to finish dressing for work. Before he left, he stopped in on him and the nurse.

"Stay close to him," he told her. "And record anything significant."

"Okay," she said.

"You should give yourself a shave, Eugene," he told him. "A breakdown in personal hygiene is a symptom of sickness, evil sickness. That's why so many people, adults, I should say, hate these filthy looking rock stars. We know inherently that they are rotting away inside, and that rot is contagious. Understand?"

He nodded.

"I think you might be making progress," he said. "And if you make enough of it, you're going to become useful again, useful to me." He smiled. "I've got to drive through my laboratory and check on the animals," he added. Mildred laughed and shook her head. "Watch him closely today," he said, then left.

"I'll go shave," he said.

"Fine," Mildred said. "Only don't do it with your toothbrush," she added as he walked out of the kitchen and went to the bathroom.

Shaving was harder than he'd anticipated. He had to look at himself in the mirror, and the sight of his own face, a face he now clearly understood as his own, was terrifying. It was like standing face to face, inches apart, from a known killer who at any time might make him the next victim. He worked quickly, never taking his eyes off himself, set to flee if the image in that mirror came at him.

When he was finished, he put the electric razor down quickly and fled from the bathroom as though it had caught fire.

She was waiting for him in the hallway. "Calm down," she said. "And follow me."

She took him to his father's office.

"Sit here," she commanded, and he took a seat in the leather chair by the standing lamp. Then she retrieved a folder from the file cabinet and brought it to him. He looked up at her as she thrust it into his hands. "It's your file; he refers to you as patient 001."

"How many patients does he have now?" he asked.

"Quite a few. Just look out the window and you'll see the waiting room," she added with a chilling smile. "Your father has a sense of humor, too, you know. I bet you didn't know that."

He shrugged. He didn't know that. At least, he'd never thought of his father as a funny man.

"Sure," she said. "Sometimes he does things, or, I should say, has things done, for humorous reasons. Of course, he's proving something to himself, demonstrating something. The other day . . . the other day," she said, holding her stomach as if her laughter pained her, "everyone here was wearing something blue." She laughed as though she'd just delivered the punch line to a terrific joke. Only he didn't understand why it was so funny. "What's wrong with blue?" he asked.

She laughed harder and pointed at him. "What's wrong with blue! I like that. What's wrong with blue?" She laughed on. "Go on," she said, catching her breath. "Read. I'll be back in a few moments. What's wrong with blue?"

Her laughter filled the hallway. He listened until she was gone.

Then, he took a deep breath and opened the folder.

They were all waiting for her at the bottom of the hill, right before the main entrance—a cluster of about a dozen teenagers. All the boys were dressed in slacks, short-sleeved shirts, and ties. The girls were wearing blouses and skirts, and their hair was neatly brushed or

pinned. Everyone carried a notebook. Some of the boys
had briefcases.

As soon as she appeared at the top of the knoll, they
turned toward her in one motion, as though the move
were choreographed. She stopped and stared down at
them. Unsmiling, they gaped at her. She wore a long
sweat shirt that reached below her knees, with tights and
sneakers. She had put mousse in her hair and had blow-
dried it, giving it a fuller look. Her mother had wanted
her to wipe off the eye shadow and blush. They had
compromised when she'd agreed to wear a bra.

"Good morning," Brad said, stepping out of the
bunch.

From the first day Justine had met teenagers from
Elysian Fields, she'd been amused and intrigued by the
manner in which they huddled so closely together. They
reminded her of pigeons crowding together in the park
when people cast peanuts at them. Sometimes, the girls
held hands when they walked.

"Hi," she said.

"We were waiting for you," Janet Bernie said. "You
have to get here about five minutes earlier. It's important
that we get to school on time—especially the first day."

Justine stared at her. Usually teenage girls did not
intimidate her. She had met tough types in New York
City, but this girl was different, harder in another sense.
She looked young, but acted old. It was almost as if an
adult had been placed in a teenager's body. Justine felt as
though she had just been reprimanded by a teacher.

"You don't have to wait for *me*," she said, lifting her
voice dramatically.

"Oh, but we want to," Janet Bernie said, stepping
forward. Her eyes widened with such odd sincerity that

Justine could only stare. The girl sounded frantic about it. "We always have so much to talk about on the way to school, right, Lois?" Janet turned to Lois Wilson, who had been standing quietly to the side, observing Justine.

"Yes," she said with a sudden enthusiasm to match Janet's. "That's right."

"Let's get started," Steven Duke said. Justine saw how excited Brad's younger brother was. He moved in place like an impatient race horse, frustrated with the wait in the starting gate.

When Justine joined the pack, Brad introduced three other boys she had not yet met, and Janet introduced two other girls, Stacy Weinberger and Martha Lowe. They were both sophomores, although she couldn't imagine that they were her age. They seemed so much younger. Also, both girls seemed shy, as they stared away whenever she glanced at them.

She checked out the boys. None of them were really unattractive, but Justine wasn't impressed with any of them, any more than she had been initially impressed with Brad. The only thing that kept her interested in him now was his apparent leadership role. They were all waiting for his signal to move on. When he said, "Okay," they started for the gate.

"I feel like I'm in a wagon train," she said with a laugh. She looked to the girls, expecting one of them to smile with understanding, but they all gaped at her as though she spoke a different language. Justine was struck by the notion that all the kids wore the same, masklike expression. No one was willing to risk a reaction or comment without first confirming it with the group.

Except for Lois. She scrutinized Justine differently

and seemed more alert. Justine wanted to fall back to
walk with her, but Brad had taken a position at her side.

Justine noticed that all of the teenagers carried themselves in the same way. Their posture was nearly perfect;
their gait was in sync. They all held their books the same
way, too. It was as if they had all attended the same class
to learn the proper way to stand, walk, and talk.

The day guard at the security booth stepped out to
greet them. Justine noticed that he looked at her with
special interest as if he had been given the assignment of
monitoring her behavior. His intense glare made her
uncomfortable, but she didn't show it. When the others
said good morning to him, practically singing it, she
remained silent and simply glared back at him as they
passed the booth. She didn't have to turn around to know
that he was still watching her walk away.

Brad was the only one who spoke to her during the
walk to school, telling her how she would get a locker,
what was expected of her in homeroom, why some of her
teachers were nicer than others.

After they had walked a few dozen yards from the
front gate, Justine began to relax. It was as though a
heavy weight had been lifted from her shoulders. She
had a feeling of freedom and looseness in her body. The
tightness in her arms and torso eased. She swung her
arms and turned her shoulders with more abandon,
feeling more like her old self.

She took a deep breath and looked about. Colors,
sounds, even scents had an old familiarity. The world
around her didn't seem as new and as different as it had
since she and her parents had moved to Elysian Fields.
She imagined all this was happening because she was

excited about going to a new school and because she was regaining her self-confidence.

Looking at Brad in his sharply coordinated outfit, Justine had to admit he was a very good-looking boy. Even though she wasn't completely impressed with him, she decided he was worth some effort. Maybe she could loosen him up a bit.

"You going with anyone?" she asked him.

"Going?" He looked confused, as if the word was never used in that sense. Was he dense? she wondered.

"Have a girl friend?"

"Oh." He looked back at Janet Bernie, and then shook his head. "No, not really." He seemed to anticipate her line of questioning, so he deliberately walked faster to move ahead of the bunch.

"Don't tell me you don't like girls," she teased.

"I didn't say that." He looked serious. "We're just too young to get seriously involved with anyone."

"Who says you have to be serious about it?" The look on his face made her laugh. He was cute, she decided. "Why don't you drive to school? That way, you could pick me up in the morning, and we wouldn't have to leave so early."

"It's not that far."

"That's not the point. It's nice to be able to talk privately sometimes." She moved closer to him, but he didn't respond. "Can't you get your father to loan you the car?"

"Oh, yes. Whenever I need it, I ask."

"So?"

"I don't need it to go to school."

"Jesus."

"You shouldn't say that," he said quickly. He looked

at the teenagers behind him again. "Some people get offended when you take the Lord's name in vain," he added softly.

"Are you and your parents very religious?" she asked, keeping her voice a few decibels above a whisper.

"No, it's not that." He looked troubled by the need to explain. The struggle was revealed in his face, in the way he squeezed his eyes and frowned.

"So what do you say when you're pissed off?"

He slowed down, and she saw that he was recalling something.

"Whenever I'm angry at someone or something, I use a number from one to ten to correspond to how important I think it is," he replied in a singsong manner.

"What?" She smiled quizzically. "I didn't understand."

"If it's very important, I'll say, 'ten.' If I say 'three' or 'four,' I know I'm getting myself excited over a relatively minor thing. Then I'll try to step back and evaluate it intelligently."

"What if it's a high number?"

"Then I'll start to think of ways to correct or solve the situation," he said, as though the solution was obvious.

"Who taught you that?" she asked, still holding a half smile on her face. She didn't know whether he was kidding or not.

"Dr. Lawrence," he said.

"Oh, during your sessions with him?" He nodded quickly. "What do you do, just sit and tell him everything that's bothering you?" she asked, recalling Mindy's descriptions of her sessions with the school psychologist.

"I suppose," he said.

"Suppose? Why, don't you remember what you do when you're with him?"

He shrugged.

"I guess he's not so impressive after all, if you can't even remember what you and he do."

"Dr. Lawrence is very impressive," he said quickly.

"What about his son? You ever meet his son?"

Before responding, Brad looked back to check on how close the others were. "No, never."

"How impressive can he be, if he can't even help his own son?" Justine asked and smirked.

Brad stopped walking. "I said he was very impressive."

He looked like a spoiled little boy, stubbornly refusing to accept his parents' denial of his request. She started to laugh at him and stopped. The others were all gaping at her angrily, all except Lois, who looked more curious than angry.

"Big deal," she said, and then added, "Jesus." She laughed nervously.

His grimace faded. Then, suddenly, he said, "ten," and her laughter ended abruptly. The look in his face and the faces of the others were sobering. Sensing the underlying anger in expressions, she took a deep breath.

They started to form a circle around her. As they moved, they kept so closely to one another that their arms and hips touched. Their eyes intense, the pupils darkening and losing color. Mouths writhed, lips twisting like worms trapped on dry concrete.

"Forget it," she said quickly to Brad. "Let's get to this wonderful school."

She started away. When she looked back, she saw that

the others hesitated until Brad moved to catch up with her.

"I'll teach you the technique," he said, his voice much softer, "so you won't ever get angry again."

She looked at him and realized he was indeed doing what he said he would—he was looking for a solution to the problem that had caused his "ten."

Part of her wanted to laugh, but part of her was intrigued. Brad was smiling, and he did have such a nice smile when he wanted to.

"Great," she said. "Why is everyone so damn serious about Dr. Lawrence?" she asked. When he didn't respond, she became sarcastic. "I can't wait to hear all the techniques he's taught you. Tell me more," she said.

He turned and saw she wasn't serious. "Maybe he'll have to teach them to you himself," he said. But instead of a promising possibility, his words sounded more like a threat.

Justine couldn't help being impressed with the school. Although the building was ten years old, it looked brand new. The classrooms were bright and clean; the halls were spotless. Her teachers didn't seem as burdened and pressured as the staff at her other school. She didn't sense the familiar tensions in the air, tensions she had come to expect between students and members of the faculty. Of course, some were more relaxed than others.

Mr. Spiegel, her homeroom teacher and her English teacher, was erudite. Simply listening to him take attendance and discuss the rules and procedures was a vocabulary lesson. He made homeroom seem like a fascinating interlude. In fact, when she looked around the classroom, she couldn't believe that the teenagers from Elysian Fields were actually taking notes. What did they expect? she wondered, a test on how to behave in homeroom every morning?

She was happy to see that most of the other students from Sandburg Creek and its surroundings were not like the teenagers of Elysian Fields. These kids dressed more like she dressed and acted as carefree as her friends in New York—despite the sanitized atmosphere in the school. She was more comfortable talking with them.

However, they all grew suspicious once they learned she lived in Elysian Fields. She understood that in their minds she was "one of them." She assumed that meant another rich kid, so she did her best to play down her home and background. Instead, she talked about her life in the city.

She did her best to avoid the Elysian Field teenagers, but she found that almost impossible to do, mainly because of the subtle way they surrounded her. They reminded her of mother hens protecting their chicks. As soon as she would enter a classroom and take a seat, the teenagers from Elysian Fields who were in that class sat behind, in front, and next to her. After every class, they waited for her or walked beside her. When she deliberately avoided them and started to talk to other students, they still hovered about, making the other students conscious of their presence. Usually, the other kids fled from her because of them.

All the while she sensed that Lois Wilson was trying to get a private word with her. Finally, just before the lunch period ended and they were all headed back to class, Lois came up beside her.

"After the last class, go to the bathroom in the forties

corridor, and then go out the west-end exit," she whispered.

"Why?"

"I'll be waiting out there, and we can talk without the rest of them listening in. I've got to talk to you before you go back to Elysian Fields," she said, her eyes small and her gaze intense. "You remember me coming to see you yesterday, right?"

"Of course."

"Good," she said. "Good," she repeated, as if Justine had performed a significant feat. "The west-end exit. Stay in the bathroom for a good five minutes, so the others will go outside and wait on the east end," she added, then quickly moved off to walk beside Janet, who had just started to look their way with jealous eyes. A moment later, she was surrounded by the other teenagers from Elysian Fields again.

By the time the last period of the day began, Justine felt haunted. All day long she had been trying to make friends with Bonny Joseph, a girl who reminded her of Mindy, and Tad Donald, a boy who reminded her of Marty Stewart.

Nearly every sentence Bonny uttered was peppered with words like "screw" and "bitch." She had come to school dressed in a gray sweat shirt with a man's undershirt sticking out from beneath it. Her jeans were faded and tight, and her sneakers were covered with slogans and sayings she had written over them. There were even some profanities.

She wore her light brown hair teased and sprayed with sparkle. Justine thought she had a cute, pudgy face. There were little patches of freckles at the peaks of her soft, slightly ballooned cheeks, but the freckles stopped at the bridge of her small nose. Her bright red, wet lipstick highlighted her full lips.

Justine made a number of attempts to have conversations with her, but it took most of the day for her to learn that Bonny lived in Flora, a village about ten miles north of Sandburg Creek, that she was supposed to be a senior but had failed math and English, and that she lived with her mother and stepfather. Her real father was in a drug rehabilitation center.

Justine could see that the teenagers of Elysian Fields thought it was practically a capital offense to have a conversation with Bonny. Whenever she did, they were standing off to the side, grimacing with disgust. On two occasions, she was tempted to go over to them and tell them to mind their own business.

Before the last period began, Brad came up to her in the hall and pulled her aside.

"I should have warned you about some of the kids here," he said, "but I didn't want to overwhelm you with too much the first day."

"What kids?"

"Bonny Joseph is a very bad influence. She's gotten into a lot of trouble. The teachers dislike her. She's this close to being expelled," he said, holding his thumb and forefinger close together.

"I don't care. She's the only one I've spoken to who knows what the hell's going on. Anyway, who I hang out with and who I don't is none of your business," she said, working up her indignation. The crimson tint in her cheeks brightened into a tomato red. Her parents were always trying to influence her when it came to friendships. She wouldn't tolerate any other teenager doing the same thing.

"Just trying to be helpful," he said. He did look concerned, so she softened a little. "Dr. Lawrence says we are often judged by the friends we keep."

"Well, I'm old enough to make up my own mind about people. You don't have to worry about me."

"Going to sign up for anything after school?"

"I don't know. Probably not."

"Well, what are you going to do with your spare time? You can't just go home and listen to music every day."

"What are you so worried about?" She shook her head. "You act like my father, for Christ sakes."

He blanched. "I just . . . idle hands get into mischief," he recited.

"Jesus. What's that, another one of Dr. Lawrence's messages?" She shook her head and started away.

"Hey," he called after her, "Janet and the other girls will wait for you after school."

Without another word, she marched down the hall toward her last class, social studies, where she was able to sit away from Martha Lowe and Stacy Weinberger. She took the desk right behind Tad Donald.

The teacher, Mrs. Kaufman, had a very distinct nasality in her voice. Not ten minutes into the class, Tad was making fun of her, imitating everything she said. Justine couldn't keep her laughter contained. Mrs. Kaufman stopped her instruction to reprimand her.

"What is it you find so funny, Miss Freeman?"

"Nothing," Justine said quickly.

But Tad muttered, "Your face," and she began to laugh again. Everyone in the class turned her way. When she looked at Martha Lowe and Stacy Weinberger, she saw that same look of anger that had frightened her earlier. They're probably going to go home and tell their parents, who will tell mine, she thought. "Sorry," she said. It was enough to get Mrs. Kaufman off her case.

After the class ended, she poked Tad in the back.

"That was your fault," she said.

"Big deal."

She stood with him in the hallway, just outside the classroom. The students were rushing about, digging into their lockers and hurrying out to catch school buses. Although there was a great deal of conversation and noise, Justine didn't sense the same wild excitement the end of school brought back in the city. Everyone moved through the halls in a more orderly manner.

As they walked down the corridor, Tad exchanged playful punches and greetings with other boys and waved to some girls, but he didn't move away from her, and she lingered beside him.

Justine liked the way his licorice black hair fell in long, thin strands down over his ears. The front was swept to the right in a soft wave. He wore jeans and a faded charcoal T-shirt, with rolled sleeves. He was only an inch or so taller than she was, but he had a hardness about him that suggested tough, menial labor rather than a program of physical training.

She liked the way he studied her body, his dark eyes lingering over her bosom and hips. His cheek dimpled in an appreciative smirk. He had a narrow face with an emphatic jawbone, but she didn't think he was attractive as much as he was dangerous. She sensed his hunger, his undisguised lust for excitement, as well as for sexual pleasure.

"You live in Elysian Fields?"

"Uh-huh."

He looked at her again, this time with an expression of amusement.

"Where do you live?" she asked.

"Out there," he said and gestured toward the exit.

"What, do you sleep in the streets?"

He laughed and looked her over again. "I don't know about you," he said.

"What's that supposed to mean?" she asked quickly.

He shrugged. "Come on. You're puttin' me on, ain't-cha?"

"Putting you on?"

"You live in that big development?"

"Uh-huh."

He smiled suggestively and shook his head. "You better stop laughing at Mrs. Kaufman," he said and walked away. She watched him go around the corner of the hall, and then she turned to see Martha Lowe and Janet Bernie standing by the exit.

"Damn them," she muttered, realizing their presense had driven Tad away from her. She went to her locker and tossed in her books. When she looked back and saw they were still at the door, she remembered what Lois had asked her to do. She hurried away to the forties corridor and went into the girls room. She waited a good five minutes, and then emerged. The hallway was practically empty and there was no sign of the Elysian Fields teenagers. She went directly to the west-end exit and walked out. Lois was waiting for her, standing with her back against the building as if she wanted to hide from view.

"Quickly," Lois said. Without waiting for Justine to catch up, she headed toward Sandburg Creek proper, walking quickly and not looking back. Justine had to run to catch up with her.

"What's the big secret? Why are we going in this direction?" she asked.

"Just walk," Lois said. "I want to get as far away from Elysian Fields as I can. And then," she added turning to her with a completely new expression on her face, a face that was animated and lively, "I'll tell you everything I know."

5

AS HE READ his file that day, it occurred to him that his father had considered him an experimental subject from the day he was born. Indeed, his very conception was treated like a laboratory project. The time of his conception and the month of his birth were duly noted, as was his length and height, but not the way proud parents normally do in scrapbooks. Instead of a his name, 001 was used to denote "the subject." His weight and length were included under "statistical data."

Apparently his father had played a major role in his infant care, citing all sorts of developmental stages—when he first could see things clearly, when he exhibited familiarity with his surroundings, how often he cried for nourishment, what made him comfortable and uncomfortable, how he handled infant toys, when he began to discern shapes and colors, when he recognized words and sounds and applied them to objects. On and on, the actions were noted, the dates and, in some cases, the times cited.

He was particularly interested in the record his father had kept of antisocial or deviant behavior—when he broke a toy, or when he was disruptive and disobedient. Beside the notations, there was evidence, like a photograph of a broken toy, or a picture of a wall marred with a crayon. On one page was a picture of his father marked up with a pen, the eyes gouged.

There were little descriptions of him, paragraphs detailing his habitual gestures, his physical attributes, and even his speech patterns. There were lists of his favorite words and expressions, his color preferences, his tastes in foods, books, television shows. Some of it was in amazing detail.

Then there was a section dealing with his reaction to "treatments," activities and things that other people might refer to as education and training. Different techniques were explored and evaluated.

When he came upon the section on the television technique, using videotapes, he read with interest. His father explained his clinical reasons for taking certain actions, forbidding certain activities, and encouraging others. Once again, incidents of his behavior were cited, and then measured against his father's techniques to determine their effectiveness.

Things he had once thought were given to him spontaneously as gifts, as lovingly as other parents gave their children gifts, were justified with behavioral theory. Even the Santa Claus myth had been utilized as another device for research and evaluation.

There were long sections describing his relationship with his mother, and he gathered from the descriptions and discussions that his mother was unaware that she was being employed as a part of the research. She, too, had been manipulated, her actions and decisions evoked with a specific behavioral goal in mind.

In short, the family had been made into a laboratory experiment in which the parent and child relationship was completely controlled and designed. However, as he read about himself, he didn't grow angry. He read with the same kind of interest anyone has in evaluations of himself, whether they be palm readings done by a gypsy fortune-teller, or medical reports carried out in a clinic.

His father had couched the language and the writing technique in such a way that it was possible to remain aloof, to feel he was reading about someone else, this patient, 001.

The teenage years were the most interesting, he thought. There were long narratives describing his behavior, their discussions about that behavior, and his subsequent reactions to the discussions. Included was all sorts of analytical data from the school, typical things like IQ scores, aptitude tests, report cards, etc. As a school psychologist, his father had obviously had access to everything.

Much of it had slipped out of his memory, of course, but when he read the section entitled, "Antisocial Disease," which described his romance with marijuana, cocaine, and crack, he really felt as though he were reading about a totally different person. Apparently, his father had permitted him to go in this direction to see just how far it would take him.

Finally, he turned the page and reached the detailed description of that fatal day when, under the influence of marijuana, he'd gotten into the car accident that had resulted in his mother's death. The crash was described with the objective indifference of a news story.

The subject, his blood filled with highly toxic elements, lost his sense of depth perception. Approaching an intersection, he thought he had much more time to slow down to stop. The subsequent collision with an automobile approaching from the right resulted in the death of his passenger when the passenger's side door was sheared by the impact. It sliced off the passenger's head, dropping the head into his lap.

The subject suffered shock trauma, repressing all memory of the accident as a self-defense mechanism. Catatonic for a prolonged period, he became a prime subject for the LRT, the Lawrence Radio Technique. *See glossary, subparagraph four, section three.

He took a deep breath before attempting to go on. His heart was beating so hard and so quickly, he thought he was on the verge of passing out.

Mildred noticed. She got up from her chair quickly, putting her needlepoint down, and came to him. She took his wrist into her fingers and checked his pulse.

He swallowed, closed his eyes, and lay his head back against the top of the straight-back, leather chair.

"Take deep breaths," she said. "Slowly. I'll be right back."

She returned with a sedative and a glass of water. He gulped it down eagerly, then leaned back so his head rested on the seat again. It wasn't long before he felt calmer and more relaxed. Along with that calmness came a familiar sense of detachment from everything related to him.

"Why don't you just lie down for a while," she said. "Just go over to the couch and rest awhile."

He nodded, and she helped him to his feet and guided

him to the couch. He sprawled out and placed his hands on his stomach. When he opened his eyes again, she was standing beside him and looking down at him intently, her beady eyes again like two tiny lenses set in a naked skull, focusing and refocusing.

"I feel sorry for 001," he said. "I really do. How can he live with himself?"

"He doesn't," she said, picking up on his use of the third person point-of-view. He heard the words coming from her skull, but he didn't see her lips moving because her lips had evaporated along with her cheeks and forehead.

He nodded with understanding. "My father has his work cut out for him, doesn't he?"

"Yes, he does, but he is always full of optimism. He believes in himself, in his abilities."

"Do you think he'll be able to help him, then?" he asked hopefully.

"I'm betting on your father."

"Me, too," he said. "And I want to help him," he added. "I want to help him in any way I can. It's about time I was some help to him, huh?"

"I'd say so. Why don't you just rest for a while, and then you can start again. I'll call your father and give him a report." She started away.

"And tell him I want to help him, will you? Please."

"Sure. He'll be glad to hear that. Nothing would make him happier than your being of some assistance to him. Rest," she said.

He nodded.

Rest. He closed his eyes and saw himself sitting in the car. There was blood all over him, splattered over his neck and shirt as though someone had dipped a paint brush in a can of red paint, and then flicked the brush at him. He looked down into his lap.

She was looking up at him with opened eyes. She wasn't angry; she was . . . disappointed, and that hurt even more.

Of course, he was sorry, but being sorry was not enough. Did it help to keep saying it? No. But he couldn't stop saying it.

If he could only put it back and make her work again, fix her like a toy he had broken. He couldn't do that, could he?

No.

But his father could. That's what his father was doing right now. He was putting him back together.

What a man, what a genius, my father. He's going to put my head back on my shoulders. It wouldn't be long now. He relaxed some more. Not long. Soon, he would look in the mirror and know all of himself, and he would never wake up again with strange arms and legs.

Lois led Justine to a small luncheonette not far from the school grounds. Some of the "townies" were there. When they entered, she saw Tad Donald in a front booth with two of his buddies. He eyed her and Lois with surprise as they made their way to a booth in the rear of the store.

It was a very clean-looking luncheonette, with a beige tile fountain counter and light pine wood walls. The shop's large windows afforded it a great deal of light, giving an airy, open atmosphere. One woman in her early fifties served as a waitress, and the owner, a short, bald man wearing a white apron, worked behind the fountain making ice cream sodas, sundaes, hamburgers—whatever the high school crowd demanded. He had a cheery, perpetually sunburned face and knew most of the students by name. Justine saw that he didn't know Lois, but he smiled and nodded when they walked past the fountain.

"Why did we come here to talk?" Justine asked.

"I've only been in here twice and just recently," Lois offered in explanation. "But I like it here. It makes me feel . . . normal," she said, sliding into the booth.

Justine looked back at the townies gathered at the front of the luncheonette, then sat down across from Lois. "Well, what do you want to talk about?"

Before Lois could respond, the waitress was at their table.

"You want a Coke or an ice cream soda?" she asked.

Justine thought a moment. "Just a Coke," she said.

"I'll have a black-and-white ice cream soda," Lois told the waitress, who took their order without speaking and left. "That's a chocolate soda with vanilla ice cream," Lois explained.

Justine shrugged. It was nice here, pleasant and even fun. She had an urge to go up front and talk with Tad, but she also had another, even stronger urge to return to Elysian Fields. She couldn't help thinking about it, how pleasant and beautiful it was there. All day in school, images of the development had been playing on the back of her mind, reminding her what awaited her once she entered the front gate. She was looking forward to taking a nice walk through the development and getting some afternoon sun at the pool.

"Well, what did you want to talk about?" she asked again, not hiding her impatience.

"Elysian Fields, Dr. Lawrence, you . . . me. You're

the first new girl who has moved in since . . . since my . . . my emancipation," she said. "You remember what that word means, don't you?" Justine shook her head. "Freedom."

"Freedom? What freedom? Freedom from what?"

"From chains, only these are chains you can't see." Justine shifted in her seat. Lois Wilson's eyes grew threateningly small as her face turned angry. The patches of tiny freckles under her eyes and over her cheekbones brightened, as if some light had been turned on inside her head. Her skin was so pale, it was nearly translucent. "I wanted to speak to you alone that day you arrived and warn you then, but Janet was right at my side the whole afternoon. And then, by the time I got back to you, Dr. Lawrence had already arrived with his present."

"You mean the wonderful vitamins. I do feel better," Justine began. "I feel more energetic and . . ."

"It's an illusion. You don't feel any better than you did before you took them, believe me. I know, because . . ." Lois looked up to be sure no one was close enough to eavesdrop. "Because I've stopped taking them."

"I don't understand," Justine said, her impatience giving way to irritability. The waitress returned before she or Lois could go on.

"I don't understand it all, either," Lois said softly, after the waitress put down their drinks and left. She sipped some of her soda and took the long spoon out of the tall glass. "But something very strange and very frightening is happening in Elysian Fields. I know it, and I'll tell you exactly how I know it, but you've got to try to be a little patient, okay? I know you're sitting there on pins and needles. All you want to do is go home, right?"

"Right?" she repeated when Justine didn't reply. Justine nodded. "That's part of it, don't you see?"

"No, I don't. I'm beginning to think you're crazy." She sipped some of her Coke quickly, her nervousness becoming more intense. Her eyes darted from side to side, and she fidgeted with her napkin. When Lois pushed her soda aside and reached across the table to take Justine's hand, Justine pulled away. "What is it with you?"

"Listen, just listen. When did you ever want to rush home like this before? Did you want to do it in the city?"

"No, but it wasn't as beautiful there."

"A few days ago, you liked it better there, didn't you? Or can't you remember that?" Lois asked.

Justine shrugged. "Maybe I did, but I didn't know what it was like here yet. So what?"

"This is what. I was just like you are now. I didn't know any better. I did whatever I was told, thought whatever Dr. Lawrence wanted me to think. Just like my stupid parents. Then one day, I didn't take my vitamin. My parents didn't know it. I felt a lot different that day, even though I still loved Elysian Fields. I always loved Elysian Fields, just like you. I love it now, only I can think more clearly, and I can resist it when I'm off the grounds. That's part of it, don't you see?"

Justine shook her head.

"My parents wanted me to take the vitamin the next day, of course. I took it into my hands and put it under my tongue. When they weren't looking, I threw it out. I did that every day for a week, and suddenly I began to see things differently. I remembered my parents the way they were before we moved to Elysian Fields. They're like strangers to me now.

"I realized how weird all the other kids are, just like you thought they were the first day you arrived, right? Try to remember. You're just starting; you still have a chance to remember something, if you try. Try," she demanded. Justine winced. "Damn it, you're my only hope right now," Lois said with more aggressiveness. "My parents won't listen to anything, and I've learned that if I say one negative thing about the development or his highness, Dr. Lawrence, I reveal my emancipation. Understand?" Justine didn't respond, but chewed on the straw of her soda.

"What I've been doing," Lois said in a voice just above a whisper, "is pretending. I look at the others and do and say whatever they do. So far, they don't seem to notice, but I can tell that my parents are getting suspicious. Soon they're going to make an appointment for me to see Dr. Lawrence."

"So? Maybe he can help you," Justine said and sipped some more Coke.

"Oh, God," Lois said, shaking her head. "He won't help me. He'll realize I'm not on the vitamins, and then he'll tell my parents. I don't think I can hide things from him. He's too perceptive . . . he's like some supernatural monster.

"I need someone else who's not under his spell. Someone else to stop taking the vitamins. If you do that, you'll realize what I'm talking about; then maybe, between the two of us, we'll be able to figure out what to do."

"I don't know what you're talking about," Justine said. "And I've got to get home."

"I know." Lois thought hard. "Sometimes, don't you

hear a ringing in your ears, a slight, high-pitched ringing?"

Justine stared for a moment. Then she nodded. "So?"

"That's got something to do with it. I don't know what, but it has. I still hear it, even though I'm not taking the vitamins. But when I'm off the grounds, like now, I don't hear it, and I can think clearly and remember everything. Don't you see?" Justine stared at her. Lois saw that there was some recognition in her eyes. Encouraged, she went on. "Don't you feel different now? And when you were in school all day, wasn't there a difference?" She looked frustrated by Justine's silence. "Did you like the other kids from Elysian Fields as much?" she asked pointedly.

Justine shook her head. "They can be a pain in the ass."

"Good, good," Lois said, smiling widely. She sat back and sighed with relief. "Good," she repeated.

"What's so damn good?" Justine asked.

"The fact that you said 'pain in the ass' and 'damn' just now. You'll never say things like that when you're home. Not after you've been with Dr. Lawrence in one of his sessions. Believe me."

Justine thought about it, then nodded slowly. Things were coming back to her.

"Brad's weird, isn't he?" she asked, her eyes hazy with the memory.

"They are all weird, but it's not their fault. My parents are weird. Your parents are weird. The whole place is weird, but only you and I realize it. And you'll be weird, too, unless you stop taking the vitamins. Do you think you can stop?"

"Why not? Only . . . they're good. They're The Good Pill."

"That's what Dr. Lawrence wants you to believe."

"I like him," Justine said. "Although, I didn't want to, at first," she added, vaguely recalling her initial impression.

"I liked him, too. Sometimes, I still do. I can't help it. He's handsome and charming and understanding. See. Those words just flow from my mouth. Oh, how I wish you were clean."

"Clean?"

"Off the vitamin."

"You make it sound like a drug," Justine said, growing a little defensive.

"That's because it is. I don't understand anything about it, but believe me, there's more in that pill than just vitamins."

"I've got to go," Justine said again. She started to rise, but Lois reached across the table and caught her wrist.

"Wait. There's something else. You know about his son, don't you?"

"Son? You mean, Dr. Lawrence's son?" Justine asked, sitting again.

"Uh-huh." Lois hesitated, staring hard at her. "I've *seen* him," she said. "And there's nothing weirder than him."

"What do you mean?" Justine's curiosity was aroused. This she wanted to hear.

"If you promise not to take the vitamin tomorrow, I'll go up to his house with you and show you. We'll have to go at night and sneak up to the windows. Will you promise? Will you try—because I'll know if you took it. First of all, you won't want to sneak up to Dr. Lawrence's house."

Justine thought about it.

"I don't know."

"Just one day without the vitamin, and then the next day will be easier. It was for me. You won't believe what you'll see up there."

The image of the dark figure in the window of Dr. Lawrence's house returned. Justine felt her curiosity piqued even more.

"Just skip it one day," Lois pleaded.

"All right," Justine said. "One day."

"It's going to be hard to do it," Lois warned. "Do your parents stand over you when you take it? Mine often do."

"Yes, they do."

"Then do what I do. Take the vitamin," Lois said, demonstrating, "and put it under your tongue quickly. Swallow the water, then walk away and get rid of the vitamin. Hide it, throw it out, anything. Will you do it?"

"I said I would. But then, you've got to show me Dr. Lawrence's son."

"I will. Don't worry about that. I need you to see him. I need someone else to know." She released a breath as though she had been holding it for an hour.

"I've got to get home," Justine said. "I've got homework to do."

"Too bad Janet destroyed your tapes. I'd come over and do mine while you were listening to them."

"I have tapes. My father bought me new ones."

"Right. *Before* Dr. Lawrence arrived," Lois pointed out. "And you still want to listen to them because you haven't met with Dr. Lawrence," she concluded. "Can I come over?"

"Sure."

"But we're going to have to be very careful about it," Lois said. "We can't let the other kids know, because they'll run right to their parents or to Dr. Lawrence and tell."

"Tell? Tell what? That's ridiculous," Justine said.

"No. It's not ridiculous. It's frightening," Lois said, "only you don't know how frightening it is yet. But you will. You will," she repeated and signaled to the waitress for the bill.

As they were headed out, Tad Donald turned to Justine.

"You ain't followin' me, are you?" he asked.

The two other boys stared at her with interest. She looked at Lois, who suddenly looked very frightened.

"What if I am?" she replied.

"I might have to report ya to the principal." The boys laughed.

"If you're afraid of me, go ahead," she teased, swaggering past them to join Lois, who was paying their bill at the register.

The boys howled, and Tad caught up with her, tapping her on the arm.

"Why don'tcha hang around a little longer?" He looked back at his friends.

"I can't," she said, still seeing the look of fear on Lois's face.

"Yeah," he said. "Usually the girls from Elysian Fields got to go right home. Unless they have a sewing club meeting or something," he added. His eyes twinkled with ridicule, but she surprised him by laughing at the joke.

"Maybe tomorrow I'll stay longer," she suggested. "If I don't join the sewing club." She teased him with a wink, before turning to Lois, who was practically in flight. Tad stared after her, and Justine cast him a casual glance through the big front window.

Then she had to run to catch up with Lois. "Now who's rushing to get back?" she said. Lois slowed. "He's good-looking, isn't he?" Justine said.

"Yes," Lois said under her breath. "But if I showed any interest in him, they would know."

"I might just meet him after school tomorrow," Justine mused, not really listening to what Lois had said. "I've got a friend in the city who would die of jealousy if she saw me with a boy like that."

Lois stopped walking and spun around toward her. "If you take the vitamin tomorrow, you won't even remember talking to him today, and you'll never meet him after school. And another thing, in a few days, you're not even going to remember your city friend's name, much less invite her here," she added.

"That's ridiculous," Justine said, looking back at the luncheonette. Lois started walking away again. She was just jealous, Justine thought. Jealous that I made time with Tad, and jealous that I have a friend in the city, she concluded. I could never forget Mindy.

She started walking again and stopped. She remembered now. She had forgotten Mindy's phone number and had to look it up. Suddenly an icy finger of fear seemed to probe at her insides.

"Wait," she called, rushing to catch up with Lois, who stopped and turned to her. They stared at each other for a moment. "I'm not going to do it. I'm not going to take the vitamin, no matter what."

"Good," Lois said, her eyes filling with tears. "Because I need a friend I can trust."

"Let's go listen to some music," Justine said, and the two of them hurried back to Elysian Fields.

He awoke in a sweat. Although he had been sleeping for hours, he had no concept of time. He saw from the length of the shadows that it was late in the afternoon. One of the shadows looked like a person flattened and smeared over the floor and spread up the wall opposite him. Suddenly, it had independent movement. It shifted to the right, then came off the wall and took three-dimensional form to become his father.

He sat up slowly and looked down into his lap, but his lap wasn't there. His torso emerged directly out of the couch. Where was the rest of him now? He was already misplacing part of himself. Had he left his body, from the waist down, in his room?

"Where's the rest of me?" he asked his father.

"On ice," his father said.

"Oh, so that's why there was all that ice in my room before," he replied.

"Keeps it from drying out. Maybe you ought to just lie back again," he said, gently pressing his right palm against his forehead. The top of his head started to slide off. He reached up quickly to keep that from happening and then, his hands on his head, he lay back.

"When will I be completely whole again?" he asked.

"It takes time. These things can't be done overnight. I've been working for years and years on this project. I've got a couple of lifetimes invested in it."

"I want to help you," he said. He looked up at the shadowy figure with anticipation. When would the darkness leave his father's face?

"I heard. That's good. We're going to try some new things. You're going to go out more. Slowly at first, making small circles around the house, and gradually enlarging the circle until you can venture into the project."

"Am I ready for that?" he asked, not without some trepidation. He wanted to go out, but he was afraid he might float away. "I mean, what's to bring me back? What's to keep me from being blown away, carried off in the wind?" In his mind, he weighed less than a pound.

"You won't be able to see it," his father explained, "but there will be invisible cords, wires, chains, tying you to the house. When I feel it's time, I'll merely reel you in like a hooked fish. You used to go fishing in that pond in the woods. You remember how it worked."

"Yes. The fish had such accusing eyes, though, that I ended up throwing them back in. She would say, if you're going to do that, don't put a hook on the end of the line. Just tie a piece of bread there. So I did. It was enough just to feel them nibble and know that I would have caught them. I began to count how many pieces of bread were eaten so I knew how many fish I would have caught. It worked the same. She was just as proud of me, maybe even prouder."

"I can't take the hook off the line," he said. "You would blow away. No doubt in my mind about that."

"That's all right."

They were both quiet for a long moment as the words took shape in his mind. Letters floated in from all directions and drew closer to one another to form ideas.

The idea was the magnet, and the words were metal shavings.

"What will I do out there?" he asked. "I don't remember what I'm supposed to do."

"Hopefully, you'll do exactly what I tell you to do, so don't worry about it."

"Good. I'm getting hungry," he said. "Maybe if I keep eating, my body will grow back," he said, looking down at his aborted torso.

"That's possible. Now you're thinking constructively. See, already there has been an improvement. Mildred," he said, turning to the wall. Another shadow lifted off and stepped toward him. "Bring him something to eat."

"Why doesn't he just come to the kitchen?" she asked with her usual air of indifference.

"Because I have no legs yet," he said.

"Oh, shit," she said.

"Just bring the food here," his father commanded.

"When does it start to get different?" she asked. There wasn't any anger in her voice, just curiosity. "I thought he was making progress."

"On and off for a while. I'd say twenty-four to thirty-six hours more. You have to take into account the trauma of revelation. He read one hundred and fifty odd pages. What am I doing explaining all this to you?" his father suddenly asked. "Just bring the food."

The shadow laughed, only the laugh reverberated, growing in intensity until he had to cover his ears.

"Easy," his father said. "Just take it easy now. We really are making progress." He pulled up a chair beside him. When he sat down, some of his head began to emerge out of the shadows so that he could see his father's forehead now. He was rising from the darkness like Lazarus from the dead. "You want to be my assistant, right?"

"Yes," he said.

"I've always dreamed of my son beside me, assisting me in the project. Lawrence and son astound the world," he announced, then laughed. "Now we're going to do it." More of his father emerged. He could see his eyes and his nose and his ears.

"What will I do? I don't remember what I can do."

"I told you—you'll do what I tell you to do. Stop worrying about that."

He nodded and closed his eyes. When he opened them again, his father's entire head and neck had risen.

"Your body's coming back. What about mine?"

"It will come," his father predicted with the confidence of an Old Testament prophet. "You will rise from the dead. I will bring you back. You'll be born again, thanks to me."

"Thank you, Father."

"What's the rest of it?" his father demanded.

"Forgive me, for I have sinned," he said.

"That's it."

"She forgives me though, doesn't she?"

"Can't say. Imagine she would, remembering what she was like. She forgave everything—the birds that dropped bird shit on the patio, the rain that pounded the flowers to pulp, the wind that tore off shingles— everything. She had this habitual smile, this soft, gentle smile. You, especially, could do no wrong. She either didn't understand or didn't want to understand the things I told her."

"But I did. I did do wrong."

"That's good," his father said. "You're really coming

along." His father's entire body was now in the light. The nurse entered, and she was in the light, too. All the shadows had retreated. His father stood up. "Now you'll eat, and the rest of you will return," he said.

She put the tray on a small table and brought it to him. "He can feed himself," his father said. "Go on," he instructed. "Feed yourself."

"I will." He sat up. His lower abdomen had already returned. They both stood aside and watched him eat. "This is how you do it, right?"

"You're doing fine," his father said. "Mildred?"

"You're doing fine," she said indifferently.

"Later, after your legs are back, we're going to go outside, and I'm going to tell you some more about the project. It's about time I had someone to talk to, someone who will appreciate me," he said, turning to Mildred. She laughed. He turned back to him. "That sound all right?"

"Yes," he said quickly.

"See you later," his father said and started out of the room.

"Dad," he called. Where did that word come from? Dad? His father turned back, a curious smile on his face. "Thanks," he said. "For forgiving me."

"Oh, but I haven't done that yet, Eugene. I said she probably would, but it's going to be awhile yet for me. Understand?"

He didn't, but he nodded. Then his father left.

Mildred stood there, smirking.

"You don't think he's going to forgive me, do you?" he asked her.

"What difference does it make if he does?" she replied.

He stared at her for a moment.

He couldn't think of the answer, but knew the answer was out there, waiting for him.

Like one of those fish, eager to nibble on the bread.

Sorry, he thought; this time I have to use a hook. I've got to have the answer.

He continued to eat. His thighs were already back. Soon he would have his knees, and then the rest of him would return, and he could stand up and take a walk with his father.

6

"Wait," Lois said a block from the entrance to the Elysian Fields development. She stopped, looked around cautiously, then juggled her books to rip a sheet of paper from her notebook. "I want you to write something on here."

"What?" Justine smiled quizzically.

"Write: I hate Elysian Fields, and then sign your name. It has to be in your handwriting, something you did yourself."

"You're kidding?" Justine said, stepping back as though Lois were tempting her with drugs.

"No. Please do it. I know you can do it right now, before we go in there."

"I can do it. I just don't see the point," Justine said, eyeing the blank sheet of paper as though it were something terribly forbidden.

"Just trust me. Please," Lois pleaded. "Hurry," she added, looking down the street.

Justine shook her head. "I feel silly doing this," she said, but she took out her pen and wrote it, signing her name.

"Thanks." Lois placed it back into her notebook carefully.

"So? What are you going to do with that?"

"You'll see later," Lois replied. "Don't worry, I'm not going to show it to anyone else," she added. "Come on," she said, moving toward the entrance. Justine followed quickly.

As soon as they entered the grounds, the security guard, the name Dobson embroidered on the front of his khaki shirt, stepped out of the booth to greet them. A man in his early fifties, he wore his dark brown hair very short, in military style. Although he nodded and smiled at them, he had a stern, no nonsense look in his eyes. He looked more like a correctional officer than the security guard at a housing development.

Both girls smiled at him, then sighed as they started up the small knoll. The security guard watched them closely until they disappeared over the top.

"I'll just run in and tell my mother where I'm going," Lois said when they reached her home.

Mrs. Wilson, a tall, slim woman with birdlike features, was hovering at the door already. She wore a light blue cotton skirt and a loosely fitting matching blouse. Her thin arms looked lost in the wide sleeves. She had a very fair complexion with the same tiny freckles on her forehead that Lois had on her cheeks. As Justine and Lois approached, Justine could see the tiny blue veins in Mrs. Wilson's temples. They looked like the legs of small aqua spiders pressed under the skin. Her amber-tinted hair was brushed back and pinned on the sides with the back strands brushed straight down, much like Christy Duke's hair.

Justine noticed that, like a bird, Mrs. Wilson didn't

look directly at them. She faced a little to the right of them, but seemed to note their every movement. She held her thin hands against the top of her small bosom and worked her fingers nervously, as though groping an invisible necklace. Although Lois had her mother's small facial features, they weren't as hard and as sharp.

"Where were you?" her mother asked, still not looking directly at her.

"Justine and I went for a short walk," she said. She looked quickly at Justine, her eyes filled with warning. "Now we're going up to her house to study. I was just coming in to tell you," Lois added. Justine noticed that Lois's voice had a new high pitched tone to it. She was straining to make a certain impression.

"All the other girls were home some time ago," her mother said, turning to face the girls. She brought her hands down to her sides. "I was worried."

"I'm sorry," Lois said.

Mrs. Wilson looked from her to Justine, then back to her daughter. "Be sure you're back in time to set the table and read to your brother."

"I will," Lois said.

The girls walked very slowly back to the street, and started toward Justine's house. Lois's mother remained in the doorway, watching them.

"She wasn't always like that," Lois said softly, so softly that Justine could barely hear her. "She used to be a lot more energetic and relaxed. Now she's like a sparrow, fluttering about, always tense, never trusting. I can't get near her, anymore. It's like trying to pet a bird.

"But I never noticed it until I stopped taking the vitamins," she added.

Justine looked at her, and then looked back at Lois's

house. Mrs. Wilson had stepped out and was picking up debris from the sidewalk: pieces of leaves, small twigs, blades of grass, pecking at them with her long fingers cupped like claws as she swept over the stones to make them immaculate.

Although Justine didn't reply, her heart began to beat faster. She looked ahead at her new house and thought about her mother. Were there any differences between what she was like in the city and what she was like here? Before she could reply to her own question, the tiny ringing began in her ears, barely audible at first, and then growing gently in intensity.

"It's happening," Lois said. Justine turned to her. Lois was grimacing through her forced smile. After a few moments, the ringing ceased. Both girls stopped and looked back over the development.

"It's a beautiful day," Justine said. "I just feel like running through the development, don't you?"

"Yes, it is beautiful," Lois said. "I can't help but agree. But we're still going to listen to some music, aren't we?" she asked, fearing Justine's change of mind.

"Sure," Justine said. "But I just love it here. I never thought I'd feel so good about a place."

"Neither did I," Lois said automatically. "Although I know you find it prettier than I do," she added so low Justine barely heard it. The words made no sense to her, anyway.

When the girls entered Justine's house, they didn't notice Elaine Freeman, for she was standing so quietly by the front window in the living room, she was like a fixture. She waited until they were all into the house, then turned on them.

"Where were you?" she demanded.

Unaccustomed to such a tone of voice in her mother, Justine smiled.

But Elaine's face didn't relax. In fact, the skin at the corners of her eyes tightened even more as she scrutinized her daughter. Elaine had been painting in her studio. She wore her sweat shirt and jeans and had her hair pinned up, revealing her small, pink ears. There was a little brown birthmark behind the right one, only now it seemed much more prominent. In fact, to Justine, all of her mother's flaws were suddenly accentuated.

"I was at school," Justine replied.

"School ended some time ago. I saw the others come home. Why weren't you with them?"

"We went for a soda," Justine said. "Didn't we, Lois?"

"Yes, we did, Mrs. Freeman. It was right near the school and . . ."

"You should tell me you're going to do these things, Justine," Elaine Freeman said, not looking at Lois. "This is a new place. I was worried."

"I'm sorry," Justine said.

For a long moment, Elaine just stared at her daughter. "For the time being," she said, "until you join something at school, you should come right home to do your homework."

"That's what we're going to do right now," Justine said quickly. "We're going upstairs to my room to listen to music and do it."

Elaine studied them again, as if to be sure they weren't lying.

"Fine," she finally said.

Justine and Lois turned and went upstairs.

"She's just like my mother now," Lois said when they

entered Justine's room. "I can see it. It's because of their meeting with Dr. Lawrence. It's starting for you."

"What's starting?"

"You'll see it better when your mind is clear. When you stop taking the vitamins," Lois replied. Justine shrugged. "You don't even know what I'm talking about right now, do you?"

"No," Justine said. She dropped her books on the bed and went to her tape deck.

"Was your mother always this worried about your every move?" Lois pursued. "Mine wasn't."

"I don't remember," Justine said, half concentrating on what Lois asked and half concentrating on her tapes. She started sifting through them.

"You will," Lois said. "We'd better really do this homework," she said, putting her books on Justine's desk. "We'll start with the biology outline of chapter one, okay?"

"Sure," Justine said. She inserted Foxy Lady, a rock group from New Zealand.

Lois smiled as the music began. "Who's that?" she asked. "They're great." Justine told her. "Never heard of them."

"Really? They've had two platinum albums and three songs in the top ten. Where have you been, Russia?"

"No, right here," Lois said. "But I might as well have been in a foreign land. Okay, I'll read and do the first five pages, and you do the next five. Then we'll pool our information."

"Good idea. Hey, if we do this all the time, we'll finish our homework in half the time."

"Now you're thinking," Lois said, smiling. "It's great to have someone to work with. Janet and I used to share homework, until one day she decided it wasn't right. We were not only cheating our teachers, we were cheating ourselves, she said. Of course, I knew she had discussed it with Dr. Lawrence at a session."

"He's such a good-looking man," Justine said. "Is his son as good-looking?"

"You'll see, and then you can tell me," Lois said, smiling, but it was a wry smile, the look of someone who already knew the answer.

"When are we going up there?"

"When you are free of the vitamin for at least twenty-four hours. I want you to be alert for this," Lois said. "What we will do . . ."

The door to Justine's room was thrust open, and Elaine stood there, her hands on her hips, her face twisted in an ugly grimace. "How can you two do any concentrating with that awful music blaring?" she asked.

For a moment, Justine simply stared at the sight of her mother in the doorway. Her mother had never barged in on her like that. Her mother always knocked, always respected her privacy, especially when she had friends over.

"It's Foxy Lady," Justine replied, as if simply identifying the music would be all the explanation necessary.

"I don't care what it is; it's terrible. It sounds like a group of people in pain. I think that kind of music might even be damaging to your mind. It certainly isn't good for your hearing. Oh, God, turn it off."

"I like it," Justine said. "You used to like it, too." She recalled how her mother had once danced to it back at their co-op, and her father had laughed hysterically. But as fast as the image came into her mind, it popped out, the memory drawn out and lost forever.

"I could never like that. Now I'm sure you are torturing your friend, who's just being polite about it." Elaine turned directly to Lois, still keeping her hands on her hips. "Lois, be honest. What do you think of that . . . that wailing?"

Justine looked at her and saw the quick change in her friend's expression.

Lois smiled and nodded. "You're right, Mrs. Freeman, but I thought if Justine liked it . . ."

"See?" Elaine said. "Lois was just being polite. Do us all a favor. Put on something beautiful. Here," she said, thrusting a tape at her. She had had it in her hands all the time.

"What's that?" Justine took the tape from her mother and read the label. Andre Previn, 'Movie Themes'?"

"Oh, my mother has that," Lois said quickly. "It is pretty."

"See?" Elaine said, smiling.

Justine stared at Lois as though she had just stabbed her in the back, but Lois simply smiled and nodded.

"It is beautiful—and perfect to play while studying," Lois said.

"Go on, put it on," Elaine commanded. Reluctantly, Justine switched tapes. The soft music began, and Elaine closed her eyes and took a deep breath. "Isn't it beautiful? That's music that makes you feel good. Enjoy," she added and walked away, leaving the door open.

Almost immediately, Justine turned on Lois.

"Wait," Lois said, holding up her hand like a traffic cop. She went to the door and looked down the hallway. Then she came back to Justine. "I had to say those things. It's expected. I would have said them and thought them if I hadn't stopped the vitamins. Otherwise, your mother might have said something to my mother, and she would have called Dr. Lawrence immediately. I've had a half a dozen sessions with him, so I know what it's like."

"You're crazy," Justine said, backing away from her.

"No, I'm not. You'll see. The other kids are the same way, all those who have been seeing Dr. Lawrence."

"I hate this music," Justine said, scowling at her tape deck.

"You won't after your first visit with him. You'll begin to hate everything else."

"That's ridiculous. No one can make me hate what I like, or like what I hate," Justine said, her eyes bright with cold determination.

"Oh, really?" Lois said, smirking.

"Really," Justine said. Lois shook her head. She went to her notebook and took out a sheet. Then she handed it to Justine.

"What's this?"

"Read it," Lois said.

Justine looked at it and then looked up. "I don't believe this."

"Isn't it your handwriting? You did it just before we walked onto the grounds."

Justine looked at it again. It was her handwriting. She looked up at Lois.

"But I don't remember doing it and I . . ." She looked down at the words. "And I love Elysian Fields. I don't understand," she said, nearly in tears.

"I don't understand it all, either," Lois said. She went to the window and looked out at the development. "Right now, all I feel is pleasure when I look at this place. It's so beautiful here. The sky is always blue; it's blue even when it's raining, and the rain is always warm and gentle."

"Yes," Justine said, coming up beside her to gaze out her window. "Everything looks so soft; all the colors are so bright. I think I could stand here and look out all day long."

The two new friends, joined by the common pleasure they were experiencing, stood silently for nearly a minute. Justine even took Lois's hand. She had never identified with any of her friends as strongly, not even with Mindy. She felt a great need to be a part of whatever it was that united everyone here. There was a great sense of community, of belonging.

Lois was the first to break the spell.

"We'd better do our homework," she said. "Otherwise they'll know."

"Who'll know?" Justine asked, that same curious smile coming over her face. It was as if she were talking to a child.

"Our parents, our friends."

"Know what?"

"That we know something's wrong," Lois said. "And if they find out, they'll tell Dr. Lawrence."

"So? What will happen?"

Lois looked out at the development again.

"I'm not sure yet, but I'm afraid," Lois said softly.

Justine felt a chill undulate through her body. However, it passed through as quickly as it had come. "But . . ." She looked out her window again. "There's nothing to be afraid of here. Here we're safe."

For a long moment, Lois didn't reply. Then she turned

to Justine, her eyelids drooping as if she were fighting great fatigue.

"Yes. As safe as animals in a zoo, secure in their cages," she said.

But Justine didn't understand, and she was caught in confusion. For now, the sweet lure to comply was irresistible, so she turned back to her homework.

Reluctantly, Lois joined her. When they were finished, she left quickly to go home to help her mother set the table and read to her little brother, explaining that these were daily chores. She reminded Justine about the vitamins again, then hurried out. Justine looked out her window to watch her new friend walk down the street.

Then she straightened out her books and papers. When she discovered the sheet from Lois's notebook again, she stared down at it with the same disbelief. It disgusted her. Finally, she tore it up into little pieces and dropped it in the waste paper basket, treating it like some profane utterance.

It's a forgery, she told herself. I could never hate Elysian Fields, she added, putting it out of her mind for what she thought would be forever.

"When you were a little boy," his father began, "there wasn't very much out there. We didn't even have a paved road leading up to the house, but it was wonderful being surrounded by the wild fields and the forest. One could think up here; one could concentrate without fear of distraction.

"Over there to the left is Sandburg Creek, which was also not half as developed as it is now. Even so, there were enough lights and traffic to make it sound like a little beehive in the distance, and at night the sky over that town had a pink glow from the lights of civilization.

"Your mother liked to sit out here on summer nights and look out at the clear, starry sky. When there was a full moon, it would almost be as bright as it is down there now."

His father stood up and motioned for him to follow. He rose so quickly, he looked as though he were his father's shadow. They were out in front of the house, looking down at Elysian Fields. His father said this was the beginning of his reorientation with reality. His father's voice was soft and kind now, a voice he had rarely heard. He was afraid to speak, afraid to move, afraid he would break the spell.

But he wasn't sure he was really out here with him. When he looked back at the house, he saw himself standing by the window, looking out. Were there two of him? Sure, that's it, he thought. There's me and there's him, the other one, the one his father was creating. Now which one of us is out here?

"Eugene," his father said, "look out there. What do you see?" When he hesitated, his father turned to him. "Go on, tell me what you see."

He peered down at the houses. The streets were so well lit that the community seemed to be housed in a giant bubble that kept night out.

"A giant bubble," he said.

"Really?" His father looked again, as if seeing it for the first time. "Yes, I see what you mean. Well, in a true sense, it is a giant bubble, Eugene. I'm keeping everything under glass." His father liked the sound of that. He laughed. "Under glass," he repeated.

"You know what I mean now when I tell you this is

my project," his father said, spreading his arms far apart
so that he resembled Christ on the mountain. "I created
all of it. And, like God, I control it. At least, that's what
I'm trying to do. Do you understand what I'm saying?"

"Yes," he said. "They're toys."

"Toys? I suppose you can say that. Yes. You have an
original way of putting things, Eugene. You always did.
As you know, your teachers thought you were very
creative, and they excused your inadequacies in other
areas because of that. A very bad mistake, I think.
Anyway," he said, turning back to the houses spread out
before him, "it's going well, Eugene. Better than I ever
expected it would. Only, there are a few hitches here and
there, trouble spots that have to be mended, problems
that have to be solved, mistakes that have to be corrected."

He nodded. He didn't want his father to stop, and he
didn't want to go back inside the house and join his other
self just yet. He always liked being out at night,
especially when the sky was clear and dotted with stars.
He remembered his mother enjoying the warm nights,
and he remembered sitting out here with her and listening to her tales about the constellations. He even
remembered his father joining them occasionally.

Doing things he used to do when she was here and
being in the places she used to be made him feel as if she
had returned, as if all that had happened since was a
long, bad dream. Perhaps now that he was waking up, all
the good feelings would come back. He turned back to
the house to see if his other self was still watching. He
was. Can't blame him, he thought. He wants to come
out, too.

"Anyway, Eugene," his father continued, turning

back to the town below, "that's where you're going to come in. That's where you're going to help me. You're going to help correct things from time to time. You don't mind doing that, do you?" he asked. "You want to help, don't you?"

"Yes," he said.

His father laughed. "You almost sound sincere—as if you have a will of your own," his father said. "But in the end, it really doesn't matter, does it? It's the same with everything down there. In the end, it doesn't matter if they do it because I tell them to do it or because they have come to the point where they, themselves, want to do it.

"When you think about it, Eugene," he said, turning back to him, "this is what it's all about—power, control—no matter if it's a church or a government or a civic organization. Someone always wants to have control. Correct?"

He nodded quickly.

"What do you feel like doing right now, Eugene? What comes to mind?"

He looked from his father to the lights below, and then back to his father.

"I want to fly," he said. "Fly over the toy houses."

"You can't fly, Eugene. You're not a bird, and, anyway, I don't want you in the light. Remember that. The light is bad. You know what the light can do to you?" He shook his head. "It can turn you into a blob of protoplasm, a pool of human jelly. It can melt you. Never go in the light. From this day forward until I tell you otherwise, you are a creature of darkness. Understand?"

He stared at his father, then looked back at the house.

"What about him?" he asked. His father looked back at the house.

"Who?"

"Him. The other me."

"Oh, him. He can't come out of the house."

"Never?"

"That's the way it has to be, Eugene. He stays in. You come out, but only at night, and never do you go in the light. Got it?"

"Yes."

"You were always a very bright boy, Eugene. You saw your IQ scores, your aptitude tests. You have high native ability, great conceptual capacity. Your failure to do well in school was the result of other things, not your lack of intelligence. Now, Eugene," his father said, turning him back to the development, "I'm going to number the houses below so you will be able to identify them. You don't have to know the names of the people in them, just the numbers, okay?"

"Like painting by numbers?"

"Exactly. I'm going to paint the development in your mind by numbers. I have reasons for this. You don't have to know the reasons right now, but later on, I'll need you to help me. Think you're ready?"

"I'm ready," he said. He looked back at the house. Too bad about *him,* he thought. He'll never be ready. He'll have to stand in the window and watch me.

"Okay. Right below us, you see house number one. I want you to go down there, staying in the darkness all the time. Go into the back yard, and get that potted plant on the small, round metal table. Understand? Get it and bring it up to me without being seen by anyone in the house. Go on," his father said and pointed.

He shot forward like a golden retriever and scurried down the small slope, sliding over the grass, running, it seemed to him, on air. He suddenly realized why. He had been turned into a shadow. When he reached the bottom of the hill, he looked up and saw his father's silhouette. His father was a shadow now, too. He was the son of a shadow. It was easy to become one with the night. It also explained why his father told him to avoid the light. Light burned away shadows. Light was deadly.

When he reached the rear patio of house number one, he crouched into a ball. Then he rolled himself to the edge of the patio. He flowed over the stone until he reached the small metal table and seized the potted plant in his dark hands, hands he, himself, could not see.

But just before he started away, he saw her through the patio door. She had a glass in her hand, and she wore a diaphanous nightgown. The outline of her breasts and her small, flat stomach was vivid. He was fascinated because of the way the light passed through her body. She didn't melt, nor did she disappear. She absorbed the light; she even seemed nourished by it. He watched her until she was gone.

Then he turned and rushed back into the night. He scurried up the hill, clutching the plant to him. When he reached the top, he paused, and then moved to the patio and joined his father's shadow.

"Good," his father said. "That was very good, Eugene." He took the plant from him and handed him a tiny chocolate bar. "Go on, eat it," he said. "You earned it."

He stripped away the wrapper and put it in his mouth. The taste was fantastic, and with that taste came a whole rush of memories of delicious things he had not had for . . . forever. Unfortunately, the tiny chocolate bar was gone in seconds.

"Want another?" his father asked.

He nodded.

"Take this plant back and put it exactly where you found it on that table," he said. "Go on," he said, handing him the plant.

He responded instantly, moving swiftly through the darkness. He looked through the patio door again, hoping to see the creature of light, but she wasn't there. He put the plant back and rushed up the hill where his father waited with another small chocolate bar. He seized it greedily and shoved it into his mouth, forgetting to take off the wrapper.

His father laughed. "Ye old carrot and stick method," his father said. "Eugene," he said, putting his arm around him, "you're going to be all right now. You really are going to be my assistant, okay?"

He nodded, and his father led him back to the house. The other backed away from the window and retreated to the darkest corners of his bedroom to wait.

When he reached his bed and undressed, he lay back expectantly, but his father came to the door to stop the nurse.

"Mildred, forget the straps. He doesn't need them anymore," he said.

"You sure?"

"I think I know when I'm sure," his father said sharply.

"Nevertheless, I'm locking my bedroom door," she said.

His father laughed. "I should have him lock his

instead," he said. "Good night, Eugene. Welcome back."

"Thanks," he said. "But I forgot where I was."

"You weren't here, that's for sure," Mildred said. He watched her walk out behind his father. She closed the door and left him in complete darkness.

It was then that his other self emerged, approaching the bed. When he looked up into the darkness, he could just make out his image.

"How was it?" he asked, envy dripping from his voice.

"It was . . . good. I felt free and I was able to fly. As long as I stay in the darkness, I can fly."

"It's not fair. I should be out there with you."

"I can't do anything about that. Don't make me feel bad. I feel good now," he pleaded.

"He gave you chocolate. I saw him."

"So?"

"You ate it all?"

"It was just a small piece," he explained.

"You could have saved a little for me."

"I didn't think of it. Next time, I will. I promise."

"Sure." He could almost see him smirking.

"I mean it."

"I won't hold my breath. I'll tell you this—I'm not staying in here forever."

"Listen to me," he said, sitting up. "If you go out there into the light, you'll disappear. Don't be stupid."

"I'm not staying in here forever," his other self repeated, then stepped back into the darkness.

"Hey," he called. "Hey." He wouldn't return. "Don't do anything stupid," he whispered, but there was no response. He listened for a long time, then turned over and closed his eyes.

He had been flying, floating over the land. He couldn't wait to do it again. It wasn't only that the movement felt good, either; it had also pleased his father.

He was forgiving him. He really was. That was why he had spent all this time working with him and why he was now permitting him to help him with one of his important projects.

Maybe, if he worked hard enough and was good enough, he would be able to find a way to put her head back, too.

And then, they would be all together again, sitting on the front patio, looking up at the stars, listening to her talk about the constellations.

It would be so good, even if the three of them were only shadows and could live only in the darkness.

He turned over and called to his other self.

"Hey, listen," he said. "I just thought of something that is going to make you very happy." He waited. After a long moment, he heard his reply.

"What?"

"If this works out, you and I will become one again. And you'll be out there with me, and you'll get the chocolate, too."

"You'll screw up; you always do."

"No, I'm going to really try this time. I promise. No screw-ups. Trust me."

He listened. "Well?" he asked.

"You'll go into the light and die and leave me here, lingering in the darkness," his other self finally said.

"I won't. You'll see," he said, trying to fill his voice with the sound of confidence.

There were no more words between them. He sensed that his other self had gone to sleep, so he turned over again and closed his eyes. Almost immediately, he saw the translucent creature of light, her body sparkling as though it had been carved out of diamond. Instinctively he understood that she was temptation, that she would draw him out of the darkness and to his own death.

He kept her image locked inside his eyes so his other self wouldn't see it, because he knew if he did . . .

He would go down there again and again until she saw him and drew him into the light. And he knew that if his other self died, he would die, too.

There was only one safe solution, and that was to draw her into the darkness before she could draw him into the light. Then he would be safe, as safe as a shadow locked in a coffin.

He even imagined being in it now. He reached up and pulled the lid down over him and then . . . he fell asleep.

7

SHE REMEMBERED. THE homework she and Lois had done together had been left neatly on her desk and it helped trigger her memory. As she showered and dressed for school, she kept thinking about not taking the vitamin. In fact, she concentrated on it as if it were information for an exam. She repeated it to herself as she walked down the stairs and toward the kitchen, where her parents were already seated at the dinette having breakfast. Instinctively she sensed that if she didn't keep conscious about it, she would automatically take it.

Her mother had left the vitamin out, next to her glass of orange juice. Her parents smiled at her as she entered, both of them looking bright and cheerful. Her mother wore her beige blouse, the one with the tie painted on it, and her dark brown skirt. It had an accompanying jacket, an outfit Justine thought of as her mother's business outfit.

She had her hair pinned back, the way Lois's mother had worn hers yesterday, and she wore only a touch of lipstick. Tiny diamond earrings glittered in her pierced ears. She was so fresh and alert, Justine thought she looked as if she had been up for hours.

"Good morning, honey," she said, the musical tone in her voice so emphatic, she almost sang it.

"Morning, princess," her father added.

"Morning. Where are you going, all dressed up?"

"Christy and I are going into the city to an art gallery on Sixtieth."

"An art gallery?" She smirked. "You never used to dress like that to go to an art gallery."

She remembered the outfits her mother usually wore to galleries. Her father had always teased her about them, calling them "artsy-fartsy." She'd looked more like a resident of Soho than an upper-middle-class housewife who lived in an exclusive section of Manhattan. Her hair was always loose and carefree. She wore dangling, handmade earrings, faded jeans and an over-sized shirt.

And anyway, her mother was never one to put on airs, despite the fact that she came from a rather wealthy family. Justine's maternal grandfather was a highly successful broker on Wall Street and, before she died last year, her maternal grandmother was very active in New York high society, always on this committee or that, organizing charity balls. And yet, Elaine had rejected that life and at times seemed determined to express it by dressing casually.

"Well, this is the proper way to dress for a gallery on Sixtieth," her mother said quickly. "Take your vitamin. Do you want eggs this morning or cereal?"

"Just cereal," Justine said. She eyed the vitamin for a moment, then looked at her parents. They were watching her like hawks.

She plucked the vitamin off the table and put it in her

mouth, working it under her tongue the way Lois had demonstrated in the luncheonette yesterday, then lifting the glass of juice to her lips.

"Isn't it a wonderful morning?" her mother said. "I sleep so much better here than I did in the city."

"Me, too," her father said. "It's the clear air and the silence."

"Yes, I love how peaceful it is at night," Elaine Freeman said. Justine stared at her mother. Weren't they both complaining about how hard it was to get used to that silence just the other day? Her mother had even joked about recording the city street noises.

She looked out the window. The sky was completely overcast. In fact, it looked as though it might rain. Yet neither of them seemed to notice the dreariness.

She brought a napkin to her mouth and pressed the vitamin out and into it. Then she crumpled it up quickly and dropped it in the wastebasket on her way to the cereal cupboard.

She listened to her parents making plans to meet for lunch in New York, heard the happy, almost musical tone in their voices as they spoke, and studied the enthusiasm in their faces—the way their eyes widened and their smiles flashed. It was almost as if they were being phony with one another, putting on an act to impress each other. She was a little disgusted by it, but she said nothing.

She ate quietly and listened. Finally, her silence caught her mother's attention.

"Why so quiet this morning, Justine? Aren't you feeling well? Didn't you sleep well?"

Her father stopped sipping his coffee and studied her,

waiting for her answer. She looked from one to the other and sensed they were very interested in her response. They wanted reinforcement; they wanted to know all was wonderful. She recalled Lois telling her how she pretended now, how important it was not to let anyone know she was different.

Her words echoed through Justine's brain. *Our parents, our friends will know something's wrong, and if they find out, they'll tell Dr. Lawrence . . . I'm afraid.*

"Oh, yes," Justine said, imitating their enthusiastic expressions. "I had a wonderful sleep. I was just listening to you. Sounds like you're going to have a nice day."

"Hopefully," her mother said. "Already I feel so secure here, so relaxed, that the thought of leaving it, even for a day of pleasure in the city, makes me nervous." She giggled.

"I'm sure you'll have fun in New York," Justine said, unable to keep the envy from her voice. She had wanted to go to the city. She wanted to now; she wanted to spend time with Mindy and some of her old friends. It was all coming back to her.

"And you'll have a nice day in school. I'll be home before you," she added, "so don't worry."

"Oh, that's all right. You don't have to rush back. I . . . I'm thinking of joining the school newspaper," she said quickly, "and there's an organizational meeting after school."

"That's wonderful, Justine," her father said. "You were never interested in such a thing before, though I always thought you had some writing talent."

Justine shrugged. She couldn't remember her father ever saying such a thing.

"It doesn't matter what you do after school, honey," Elaine said. "It's important that you find someone here when you come home. We're not going to be one of those latchkey families," she added, and she and Justine's father laughed as though she had just delivered the punch line to a private joke.

"I used to come home to an empty apartment often in the city," Justine said. Her words broke their mood, and she regretted them immediately.

Her father's smile evaporated and her mother looked as though she had cursed her.

"I mean . . ."

"You don't have to remind us about our past mistakes," Elaine said. "It was wrong then, especially considering where we lived."

"Where we lived?"

"In New York!" her mother said, her eyes even wider. She looked like someone under electric shock treatment. Her entire face was distorted, her nostrils widening, her mouth stretching.

"But we lived in a good neighborhood," Justine protested.

"No neighborhood in New York is safe," her father said. "I didn't need Dr. Lawrence to remind me of that."

The mention of the doctor triggered Elaine.

"And the doctor's right. Why are so many young people lost today? Because they don't have a sense of family, a cohesion at home," she replied. "Children should know when their parents will be home, when they'll eat, when they have to do chores, and when they can talk about things with their parents. There should be no confusion and no doubt. You'd be surprised at how important this is for young people today," she added.

Justine thought her mother sounded like a tape recording. She just stared at her.

Suddenly, her mother's face started to crumple. "How many times have I failed to plan dinner because I was off to a matinee or out with some friends to see a new art exhibit? What about all those nights I left you and Daddy home alone? Have I ever sat down with you and planned out your work schedule, the way Christy Duke does with her boys?"

"Now, now, Elaine," Kevin said, reaching across the table to put his hand over hers. "Don't be too hard on yourself."

"I expected your father to do many of those things," she said, refusing to be interrupted, "but it was an unfair expectation. He's worked hard to build his career and provide a good life for us."

She paused and took a breath, pulling herself up in the chair. Then her gaze turned to her daughter, but Justine saw no warmth in her mother's pale blue eyes.

"As Dr. Lawrence says, most of the problems with teenagers today come about because parents don't define their roles. Their children get confused and disorientated, set adrift in the world," she added.

For a moment, no one said anything.

Then her father sat back, smiling.

"Well," he said. "This is going to be a wonderful day. The weather's great; we're all up, and there's a smile on my face for the whole human race."

Her mother laughed, and the mood swung back to the cheerful family breakfast. The radical change in moods was frightening. It was as though her parents had become a pair of schizophrenics. She watched them for a few moments, took some spoonfuls of cereal, then brought her dishes to the sink.

"I'll take care of that," her mother said. "You go finish getting ready for school. You don't want to be late."

"Want me to drive you, princess?" her father asked. She looked at him. She did want him to drive her, but she knew the other kids would be waiting at the bottom of the hill and none of them got rides from their parents. Also, she realized Michael Duke would be with her father; she couldn't talk to him alone.

"No, we all walk to school together," she replied.

"That's right," he said. "I forgot. What a great idea."

"Wonderful children," Elaine said. "Sticking together like that, giving each other a sense of identity. Everyone isn't obsessed with himself as people often are in the city," she added.

Kevin nodded. "Amen to that," he said.

Justine excused herself and went up to her room to get her books and brush her hair one last time. Her hand was shaking as she did so and for a moment, she thought she would start to cry. Then, she suddenly heard that tiny ringing in her ear again. What was that? she wondered.

She looked out the window to see if there was anything out there that could have caused it—men working on electrical wires or telephone lines. But there was no one outside. It was as quiet as ever, only . . . only didn't it look a little more dreary this morning? It was probably because of the overcast sky, she concluded.

She took a deep breath and went back downstairs. Her

parents were saying good-bye to one another, acting as though they wouldn't see one another for months.

She interrupted them with her good-bye, then hurried out to meet the others at the gate.

Janet Bernie looked up approvingly, noting that Justine was on time this morning. Although Justine sensed that Brad wanted her to walk alongside him again, she held back, hoping to make contact with Lois. She saw Brad's disappointment as he started walking, and the group followed.

Lois studied her out of the corner of her eyes, looking for some sign. Justine did not forget the secret they shared. She did sense that she had more control of herself and her thoughts. Memories weren't as vague as they were yesterday. She felt more like she did the day she'd arrived.

Finally, she pretended to drop a book, and Lois stopped to wait for her as she picked it up. They had a brief moment without the others around them.

"I didn't take it," she whispered.

Lois smiled and closed her eyes.

"And I'm beginning to see what you mean," she added.

They quickly joined the others. Janet had already stopped to see what was holding them up. When Justine stole a quick glance at Lois, she saw her face beaming with hope, but she also caught her look of warning.

"Isn't it a wonderful day?" she asked Brad, whose face lost its look of disappointment instantly. "I can't wait to get to school," she added, and everyone around her began to chatter about their homework, their classes, and their teachers.

Their conversation reeked of sweetness and purity. Despite Justine's effort to indulge them, inside she was sneering. Every word rejuvenated her former dissatisfaction with these new friends. As they all walked along, the conversation and the laughter of the kids from Elysian Fields seemed stupid, inane.

Lois caught the change in her face. She stepped closer to her, subtly leading her a few feet away from the others. The only one who seemed to care at the moment was Brad, who kept glancing back at Justine.

"Don't say anything. Just nod," Lois said. "You feel different this morning, don't you?" Justine nodded. "And you dislike these kids even more than you remember." Justine nodded again, more emphatically this time. "You won't want to hurry back as much after school," Lois said. "But we've got to be careful. Just do what you did yesterday. Don't give them any idea you feel differently about them."

"But . . ."

"We'll talk later. But we can't arouse suspicion," Lois said quickly and stepped forward to move up beside Janet Bernie.

"I can't wait to see how Mr. Borris likes my diagrams. I've got every one right," she bragged to Janet and the others.

"So do I," Janet said.

Justine dropped a few steps farther behind. Lois's abrupt change in behavior was unnerving, but she understood her motives. She looked back toward Elysian Fields, thinking about her parents again. She shuddered in anticipation of what it was going to be like when she returned home.

Although she was more in control of herself, she was more confused than ever. She couldn't deny the vague fear that maybe the vitamins were good, that perhaps she shouldn't have stopped taking them.

Where was all this danger that Lois kept suggesting? Did Lois really know what she was talking about? she wondered.

He was surprised to wake up and find himself unbound. If fact, it took him awhile to realize where he was. He was like someone who had been away for a very long time, so long that once familiar surroundings were now strange. He rose slowly and sat at the edge of his bed for a few moments, looking down at his legs. He had the impression that they had been sewed back on. He raised his arms to test his control of his limbs. Even his arms felt as if they had been reattached. And yet, a memory lingered: a vision of himself armless and legless.

It was all too vivid to just have been a nightmare. He could clearly recall someone coming into his room and putting him in a flat, rectangular basket with handles on the sides. She carried him from room to room. She washed him, dressed him, fed him, and then put him back in the bed.

Or was it a crib?

Could it be that he remembered being a baby? What about all the rest of it? The stuff that happened afterward, up until now? Why couldn't he remember any of that?

The nurse stepped into his room, her arms folded under her bosom, her hands under her elbows. She stared at him a moment, and then bit on the inside of her left cheek as she shook her head.

"Why did you take off your pajama top and tie it around your waist, and why did you take off your pajama bottom and put your arm through the leg?" she asked. He looked down at himself. She was right.

"I don't know," he said.

"Must have been some night," she said. She came over to him and pulled the confused garments off his body.

"I forgot what happened to me since I was a baby," he said.

"You didn't forget. You just don't want to remember. You're reading about it all and you're trying not to think of yourself as 001. The doctor expected that."

"The doctor?"

"Your father, or don't you remember you still have a father?"

"My father," he repeated and turned to his television set. "Sure. He's on channel three, right? Turn him on."

"He's not on television this morning. This morning he's making a live appearance," she said dryly as she threw an armful of clothes at him. "You remember which part goes where, or do I have to dress you?"

He looked at the underwear. It was coming back to him slowly. Carefully, he put on his briefs, and then pulled the T-shirt over his head.

"Wonderful," she said. She looked at the hospital gown hanging on the inside of his closet door, and then shook her head. "Today you will get dressed like a normal person. Your father wants to take you out again."

"Take you out again," he repeated. Or was that his other self who said it, said it out of envy? He looked around, but there was no one else there.

He held up a pair of gray slacks and a short-sleeved,

light blue shirt and she nodded. "What he expects to do with you, I'll never know," she said. "Your brains are scrambled eggs."

"Scrambled eggs?"

"Oh, never mind."

He stood up to dress himself. But when he put his shirt on as though it were a straitjacket, she had to reverse it.

She gave him a pair of dark gray socks. He studied them for a moment, and then put them on his feet, pulling them vigorously over his toes. She stood by, smiling. He stepped into his black, soft leather loafers and looked up proudly.

"I'm hungry," he said, somewhat confused. "I mean, I'm supposed to be, right?"

"Considering it's morning, yes. That's quite normal. You'll have breakfast, and then your father's taking you out."

He nodded and followed her to the kitchen.

When she brought the food to him, the definition of hunger came roaring back over him. He literally attacked his food, stabbing and poking the eggs, crushing the bread in his fist before stuffing it into his mouth. With an expression of amusement on her face, she watched him.

After a while, he began to handle the food and utensils in a more mannerly fashion. "It's coming back," he said. "Everything's coming back."

"You don't want that," she said. "Take my advice, pick and choose carefully."

"All right. How old am I?"

"You're twenty."

"And my name is Eugene?" She nodded. "Eugene . . . what? Don't I have a second name?"

"You do, but maybe you don't want to remember it."

"I do."

"All right. Lawrence. Eugene Lawrence."

"Eugene Lawrence," he repeated, and then turned to the right and stared as if a ribbon of memories were floating by. There were voices, voices in an echo chamber.

"Eugene," he heard. "Eugene . . . let go now, boy. You've got to let go. Eugene."

"Easy with him."

"Eugene, you've got to let go."

"I've got to let go," he said to the nurse.

"Oh, shit." She grimaced. "Don't tell me what you're talking about now."

"Let go, Eugene."

"I can't."

He turned to the nurse.

"I can't let go."

"So, don't let go. Jesus. Where is your father? He's never late."

"Eugene, you can't keep holding on," he heard. He needed to find the source of the voice. Suddenly there were more voices, coming at him from every direction. He spun around in his seat, turning in the direction from which each statement originated.

"Just get him out of there."

"Don't worry about it, just get him out."

"Eugene, we're taking you out. Don't you want to let go?"

"Eugene, move your leg just a little more."

"Try to let go."

"Eugene."

"Eugene Lawrence, can you hear what I'm saying?"

"Eugene."

He put his hands over his ears. "Tell them to shut up."

"Oh, great," the nurse said, slamming down her coffee cup.

"I can't stand it," he said.

"This is great," she repeated. She rushed out of the kitchen and returned quickly with a syringe.

He clasped his hands on his lap, squeezing the fingers against one another so tightly, he nearly snapped his wrists. He saw her approaching.

"No!"

"Eugene, take it easy."

"Let go."

"Move your leg just a little."

"We're taking you out."

"You've got to let go."

"Christ, what are we supposed to do?"

"Easy," the nurse said. She rubbed his arm with a wad of cotton soaked in alcohol.

"No! Don't cut off my arms. I'll try to let go."

"You've got to let go."

"Move your leg just a little."

"Lift him out. Forget it."

"You lift him."

"Eugene Lawrence, can you hear us?"

"Relax," the nurse said. She poked him with the needle and his arm fell off, but the hand wouldn't let go.

"He's still holding on."

"Christ, they don't pay me enough for this. His arms are like vises. Help me, will ya."

"Move your leg just a little."

"Stand up now," the nurse said. "You've got to lie down for a while."

He stood up. Then she started to lead him out of the

kitchen. He looked back and saw his arm lying on the floor. In his hand was a fistful of his mother's hair.

She took him back to his bed and helped him stretch out. His eyes were getting heavy, and his body felt as if it were floating away from his head. It was happening again. He was losing all of it. And just when he was getting it all back.

"I . . . tried," he said.

"It's all right," the nurse said. "You'll try again. This is expected."

"Can you sew my arm back?" he asked, but he didn't hear her response. The darkness was flooding in too fast, roaring like ocean waves, drowning out the light and any other sounds. Then, it suddenly became peaceful and still.

He could hear voices very far off, tiny telephone voices like when the receiver is on the table and you're standing a few feet away.

"What happened?" he heard his father ask.

"He got up all right and got dressed and even started eating breakfast."

"And?"

"He asked questions about himself."

"Like what?"

"His age, his name, and then suddenly he started with that business of not being able to let go. I had to give him a sedative. It was getting out of hand. Why were you late?"

"I ran into a problem. There's been a breakdown. All right, we'll wait until he wakes. These reoccurrences are expected. It's very similar to someone who has taken LSD and suffers from hallucinations. Months later, the hallucinations can reoccur anytime, anywhere. I told you about the man who thought he was no bigger than an ant. One day they found him clinging to a lamppost because he was terrified of being stepped on."

"I know, but these reoccurrences are always more frequent when you try to cut the dosage."

"I've got to cut the dosage if he's ever going to have any practical use."

"So, why use him?"

"I want to use him."

"That's revenge talking. You're not being rational, Doctor."

"Skip the comments. Let me know when he regains consciousness."

"You're still taking him out?"

"If I can," his father said.

When Justine entered the building, she felt as if today were the first day she had attended this school instead of yesterday. As Lois had promised, she and Justine took advantage of every opportunity they had to converse with one another without the others listening in. They walked together in the halls; they went into the bathroom together, and they sat together at lunch. Although at lunch, Janet, Stacy, and Martha sat with them, so it was impossible for them to talk freely.

Lois repeated her warning that Justine should try to behave like the others and not be unfriendly toward them. However, for Justine the task grew more and more difficult as the day wore on. For one thing, she couldn't tolerate their pompous criticism of other students— students she liked. She was even frustrated by Lois. She wanted Bonny Joseph to join her and Lois, but Lois refused to permit it.

"I've never been friendly with her, and I can't just become friendly with her now."

"You're making me nuts with this paranoia," Justine said. "What can they do to us?"

"I'm not sure," Lois said sadly. "I told you—I don't know everything."

"So, screw them," Justine said angrily.

"You're going to be sorry," Lois told her. "I just know it." But Justine's sense of emancipation continued to develop until Lois spoke with a sense of desperation.

"I'm not afraid of these nerds," Justine finally responded. She had regained most of her former spunkiness and self-confidence.

"It's not *them*," Lois said, "not exactly. We'll talk more after school, okay?"

"I'm going for a ride with Tad after school," Justine revealed. "He asked me in class."

Lois's eyes bulged with exclamation. "No! You can't! We would never go with him. He's not from Elysian Fields."

"So? That's stupid. Why hang around only with kids from Elysian Fields?"

"Look at them. Do they hang around with any others?"

Justine thought about it. It was true. The kids from Elysian Fields sat beside one another in class, walked with one another in the halls, sat with one another in the cafeteria, belonged to the same clubs or teams. As she watched them walk and talk to one another throughout the day, she noted how they did avoid and ignore the other students. It was as though everyone else in the school were invisible.

"I'm not going to be like that," she told Lois.

"And then they'll know you're not taking your vitamins."

"I took the vitamins and I wasn't like that," Justine responded. "Right?" She wasn't sure now, recognizing the vulnerability of her own memory.

"That's because you haven't had your session with Dr. Lawrence. Once you do—"

"I don't care. If I don't want to take the vitamins, I won't. I'm going to tell my parents so. I don't see the point in hiding everything."

"But you told me yourself how different they were today. Don't you see? They won't be on your side. If they think something's wrong with you, they'll involve Dr. Lawrence faster, before you and I have a chance to . . . to learn what's happening. Something's not right. We've got to get help, but we can't let on what we know. Not yet. Please," she pleaded.

Justine acquiesced, agreeing not to go for a ride with Tad Donald, but only because Lois promised to move up the timetable and take her to spy on Dr. Lawrence's son.

"You'll tell your mother you're coming to my house to study, and I'll tell mine I'm going to yours. We'll meet in front of your house at seven. Of course," Lois said, "it might be wiser for us to wait until tomorrow night, like I originally planned. Our parents will be going to the meeting."

"Another meeting? What do they do at those meetings?"

"I don't know exactly, but that's something else we're going to have to find out," Lois said. "I know that when they return, they criticize me more and add more rules and restrictions. The only thing is, everyone has the same restrictions."

"Like what?"

"Curfews, places we can't go, things we can't wear, people we can't see. You name it, it's on the list. But I never seemed to notice it or care until I stopped taking the vitamins. The others never complain."

Justine nodded. Lois's observations were beginning to sound frightening.

After school, at Lois's insistence, she did go with her to the newspaper club meeting, even though she hated every minute of it. But they had to walk back to Elysian Fields with Brad and Janet.

Although Justine didn't contribute much to the conversation because it revolved around the newspaper, Lois was loquacious enough for both of them. Justine noted Lois's sense of desperation, her energy and eagerness to sound and act like the others. She couldn't help feeling Lois knew something else, something more that put all this fear of discovery into her. Justine concluded it had to have something to do with Dr. Lawrence's son.

Janet was the first to part company, since her house came up first. When they reached the Wilsons' house and Lois left them at the top of the hill, she gave Justine a look of warning and nodded at Brad.

Justine mouthed a "Don't worry." She was sure she would have no problem handling him. She knew he had a crush on her. Throughout the school day, he had taken advantage of every opportunity to talk to her or be near her. She sensed how jealous and annoyed he was whenever she spoke to Tad.

"So how do you like your classes so far?" Brad asked as they continued walking toward home.

"They're all right," she replied and quickly wondered

whether that was enthusiastic enough. Lois had made her paranoid, she concluded. This was ridiculous.

"Was I right about Mr. Spiegel?"

She had forgotten what he had told her about him.

"Oh, yes," she said. He seemed pleased. She looked back. None of the other teenagers and kids from Elysian Fields were outside. There were no younger kids riding their bikes or skate boards, and no older kids just hanging out. All the kids had been sucked up into their homes so quickly, it made her think of vacuum cleaners. She sensed an absence of spontaneity. Each kid rushed home to start on his or her homework or help with the household chores. Where was the individuality here?

Brad walked along quietly for a while, a soft, thoughtful smile frozen on his face. He had that same far-off look in his eyes she had noticed in the eyes of the others whenever they were quiet. It made her wonder about Lois's fears. Why was she so afraid they'd sense that something was amiss? They all looked too preoccupied with their own thoughts, their own activities. They were just nerdy teenagers, that's all, she concluded. She couldn't imagine being afraid of them. Why, if Mindy were here . . .

Mindy, she thought. She should call her this afternoon and find out what was new.

"Do you like living here?" Brad asked. She realized he was struggling to make conversation. Despite his age and his good looks, he was as awkward around girls as a twelve-year-old. She thought about loosening him up again, having some fun.

"It's nice," she said, "but some of the kids are unreal."

"Unreal?"

"Yeah. You know—nerdy."

The smile left his face. "They're not nerdy," he said. "They're just trying to do the right things. Dr. Lawrence says the world today is different, more dangerous than it was when he was my age. There are so many things out there that can destroy you . . . people, drugs, violence. You've got to be on guard, make yourself strong . . . physically, mentally. Why defeat yourself? That's what you do when you don't try your best."

She was nearly overwhelmed by his outburst. His face was flushed with the effort.

"You sound like some kind of a preacher," she said.

"Me?" He laughed nervously.

"You don't think so?"

"No."

"Well, I think so." Lois would probably become hysterical if she heard and saw me do this, she thought, but she decided to continue. "Tell me you drink booze."

"I . . . I've had it, but I don't drink."

"And you've never done pot, right?"

"I didn't say never. I just don't do it now," he said, growing angry. Was this what Lois meant by riling up the other kids? Make them admit that they were normal, that they had normal desires and made the same mistakes? They all acted as if they were so perfect. Nerds. She didn't want to stop now. She wanted to continue to explore, to test.

"Never want to, never get the urge?"

"No," he said, and then he turned to look up. She saw that he was gazing at Dr. Lawrence's house.

"Why do you like Dr. Lawrence so much?"

"Why?" He smiled at her as though her question were

childish. "Because he's a great guy. You can trust him," he said, growing serious.

"More than you can trust your parents?"

"Of course," he said. "A lot more." He was so intense now that she couldn't look away. Her heart was beating quickly. She looked back to be sure no one else was watching them. Maybe she could find out more, especially about Dr. Lawrence, so that when Lois and she met later . . .

"You want to come over for a while?" she asked.

The question took him by complete surprise. "Huh?"

"Listen to some music, talk."

He looked back at his house.

"Go tell your mother," she said, anticipating his problem.

"I don't know. I . . ."

"Don't you like me?" she asked, pursing her lips in a pout.

"Yeah, sure."

"Good," she said, "because I think I could like you." She let her books slip, and he picked them up quickly. When he handed them to her, she squeezed his hand. "Thanks. So come over," she repeated. As she took her books from him, she leaned forward so the tip of her breast grazed his knuckles.

He pulled his right hand back as if he had placed it on a hot electric burner.

"Sorry," he said. "I didn't mean to . . ."

"That's all right," she whispered. "I liked it. Didn't you?"

She stared into his eyes and saw the struggle in his face.

He looked up at Dr. Lawrence's house again, then

back at her. "I gotta go," he said. "I gotta do my homework."

"What?"

"I gotta go," he repeated. He turned and hurried to his front door. He looked back at her once, then rushed inside.

"Jesus," she said. She vaguely remembered him running from her the day she had gotten into her bikini to go with him to the pool. Only that seemed ages ago. What was wrong with him? She made a mental note to ask Lois about him later. Maybe she had had a similar experience with him. Now that she thought about it, none of the boys in Elysian Fields were aggressive when it came to girls. Maybe they were all homosexuals, she mused, laughing at the idea. Maybe the vitamins turned them into homosexuals.

Later that afternoon, just before dinner, Christy Duke called her mother to tell her about the excitement at their house.

When Justine came in to help with the dishes, she heard the tail end of the phone conversation. Her mother kept saying, "Oh, no, how terrible. Oh, no."

"What happened?" she asked after her mother cradled the receiver.

"Brad had an accident with the car," her mother said. "I feel so sorry for Christy. She's a wreck. They just got back from the hospital emergency room. Poor thing. I'll have to go over later and comfort her."

"He cracked the car up?"

"Cracked it up?" Her mother turned to face her, a confused expression on her face. "Oh. No, not that serious, thank God. He burned his right hand while working on the engine. The doctor said it was burned so badly, it couldn't have been worse had he held his hand against the hot engine block.

"Imagine that?" she said, then went back to her work.

And suddenly, Justine understood why Lois felt such intense fear.

8

LOIS WASN'T WAITING in front of the house, and Justine was nearly ten minutes late. She had called Mindy and talked longer than she'd planned. Mindy was a lot friendlier, telling her she sounded more like her old self and not like a stuck-up rich kid. After they'd hung up, Justine had hurriedly explained to her mother that she was going to Lois's house to study, and slipped out the door.

But the street was as quiet and as deserted as ever. What's more, the bright lights illuminated the road all the way down to the top of the hill, so she could see that Lois wasn't on her way, either.

She debated going back inside to call her. Of course, her parents would want to know why she was calling her friend if she was on her way to her house, anyway. And it might make Lois's parents suspicious, too. If she was late, it had to be for a good reason, Justine thought as she backed into the shadows of the hedge.

At least she wasn't uncomfortable. It was a warm night, even though there were low clouds blocking out the half moon and stars. But she had to stay out of sight.

The pervasive quiet amazed and unnerved her. There wasn't a moving car or a strolling person in sight. Windows glowed, as though lit by stage lights, but she saw no one move behind them. It was as if the houses were only shells, facades, and no one really lived inside.

The only sound she heard was the heavy hum of those streetlights. They were so bright, she couldn't look directly up at them. Funny, she thought, that humming sound had never bothered her so much. Why didn't other people complain? It was such a monotonous and intruding noise. It couldn't be that others didn't notice it. Perhaps they were willing to put up with it because of the great illumination the lights provided.

Suddenly she heard something off to the right of her house. She stared at the pitch-black darkness there, for the streetlights did not intrude upon the shadows that lingered around the homes. Their rays were directed with precision, cutting a sharp corridor of light along the streets.

She thought she saw a shadow move. It was hunched over like a stalking animal. Could Lois have snuck up to her house, afraid she would be seen coming here? Justine wondered. Nothing would surprise her, anymore. She moved in that direction, trying to get another glimpse of the shadow.

"Lois?" she called softly. "Is that you?"

There was no response. The shadow seemed to merge with the darkness and disappear. Perhaps it was just her overworked imagination, she thought. Damn this delay. Maybe Lois had decided to back out of their plan. Sure, she thought. She just wanted to keep me from Tad. Maybe she likes him herself after all, she thought suspiciously.

There was only one thing to do—go to Lois's house, just as she'd told her mother she was going to do. If Mrs. Wilson seemed suspicious, she would just say it was a mix-up, her fault. Anything was better than waiting in the dark, wondering what had happened to her friend.

She started down the hill. It wasn't until she was nearly halfway to Lois's house that she saw the black Cadillac parked in front of it. So that was it, she thought. Dr. Lawrence was visiting the Wilsons. That was why Lois couldn't leave. What should she do now? She couldn't go home and tell her parents she and Lois were unable to study because Dr. Lawrence was there. The only thing to do was to wait for him to go, then see if Lois would come out.

She stepped off the road under a large oak tree and backed into the shadows. Once again, she heard a scuffling noise off to her right, and turned quickly to see a shapely shadow slide along the perimeter of light. Was it a dog? A deer? Could it be one of the other kids playing some kind of a joke on her? she wondered. Somehow, she didn't think them capable of practical jokes.

"Who's out there?" she called in a loud whisper. There was no response.

Then her attention was seized by the sound of the door opening at the Wilsons' house. She saw Dr. Lawrence step out, talking to Lois's parents in the doorway. He put his arm around Mrs. Wilson as if to console her, and then he shook Mr. Wilson's hand and went to his car. Justine hid behind the tree, watching as he drove up the hill toward his home. Then she waited outside Lois's house.

A good fifteen minutes went by, and yet Lois did not emerge. At this point, Justine didn't know what to do.

What would she say to her parents when she went back home? Maybe Lois's parents just wouldn't let her out now. At least she could find out the reason if she knocked on the door.

Emerging from the shadows, she walked to the Wilsons' front door. She looked around, once again sensing that she was not alone, and then pressed the buzzer. A moment later, Lois's mother came to the door. Her looks were unchanged from the previous day, but she wore an expression of deep sadness and concern. There was no smile on her face, no friendliness in her eyes.

"Good evening, Mrs. Wilson," Justine said. "Is Lois home? We were supposed to study together."

"She's home," Mrs. Wilson said, "but she's not feeling very well."

"Oh. What's wrong?"

"She's sick," Mrs. Wilson said, obviously reluctant to elaborate. What could it be? Justine wondered. "She can't see anyone tonight," the woman added.

"I'm sorry. Please tell her I came by. I hope she feels better," she added quickly.

Mrs. Wilson was already starting to shut the door. "I will," she said, and the door closed in her face.

Justine stood there for a few minutes, her heart beating madly. Mrs. Wilson seemed weird. Something was going on; something she couldn't talk about, Justine thought.

She wondered if there was some way she could contact Lois. Where was her room in the house? Could she tap on a window and get her attention? She looked around again to be sure there was no one watching, then started around the house. The north side was mostly dark, with light only in the downstairs windows of the living room and kitchen. Lois's bedroom had to be upstairs.

Was Lois asleep? Maybe she was really sick. It was the only explanation, Justine thought. She was about to start around to the south side of the house when she heard footsteps in the darkness behind her. She spun around and saw a large shadow, the shadow that was hovering at her house, move across the wall of blue-black darkness behind her.

Who the hell was that? She debated challenging the shape, then decided that if she made noise, she would attract attention to herself snooping around Lois's house. So she continued around to the south side.

She stopped by the living room window and peered through the sheer curtains, hoping to catch sight of Lois. But all she saw was Mr. and Mrs. Wilson sitting stiffly on their couch, staring at the television set. That wasn't so unusual. The unusual sight was the man on the TV screen.

It was Dr. Lawrence. His face took up the entire screen. She watched for a few moments to see what was going to come on next, but the image never changed. The doctor lectured on and on, staring out at his captive audience.

When Justine heard movement behind her again, she rushed away from the window to the safety of the illuminated street. Once there, she hurried up to her house, still sensing that she was being pursued by someone in the night. The relative silence and the absence of other people all intensified her feeling of vulnerability. Angry about being chased back to her house, she was tempted to turn around and confront her pursuer.

But she didn't pause. Maybe Lois would try to call her

later, she thought. Frustrated and confused, she went in, expecting her mother to question her about her quick return. She would tell her the truth—Lois was sick.

However, when she entered her house, no one called out. She paused in the doorway. Someone else was here; she recognized the voice. It was Dr. Lawrence. But his car wasn't outside. Had he walked down from his home?

She went farther into the house and came to the living room. Her parents sat side by side on the couch, much like the Wilsons, and watched a videotape of Dr. Lawrence. Her parents either didn't hear her behind them, or else they didn't care. They never broke their concentration.

Dr. Lawrence was talking about the problems involved with bringing up children today. He was explaining why children need strict discipline. Justine thought his speech was boring and dry. How could her parents be so entranced?

"I'm back," she announced, but they didn't acknowledge her. "I said, I'm back. Lois is sick," she added. Still, they didn't respond. "Jesus, what's the big deal? It's not Tom Selleck," she added. Her mother just adored Tom Selleck, but her mother did not turn around. "What, are you two getting tested on this?" she quipped. Their silence unnerved her. "Jesus," she repeated, stomping up to her room.

She sat on her bed for a while, thinking. Why didn't Lois call? Maybe her mother didn't tell her that Justine had come to the house. Her mother must have gone right to the living room to watch that videotape. Why were Justine's parents watching the same tape? And at the same time? And who was that in the shadows? It was all starting to get to her now. Justine was very upset, and she wanted some answers.

She put on one of her tapes and lay back on her pillow. Now, more than ever, she wanted to leave Elysian Fields. Everyone here is screwed up, she thought. Even my own parents.

Nearly a half an hour later, after she had turned off her tape deck, she heard them moving about downstairs. Curious, Justine went down to see what was so great about watching Dr. Lawrence on television.

Her parents were having coffee in the kitchen, discussing the doctor's speech. They recited his theories, like students studying for an exam.

She nearly laughed. "Hello, zombies," she said.

Somber expressions darkened their faces as they turned and looked at her. "Jesus."

"Watch your language, young lady," her father snapped.

She stared at him. "My language?" She glanced at her mother, but there was no sympathy in Elaine's face. "What were you two watching on television?" she asked.

"When?" her mother replied.

"When I came home."

"When you came home? Didn't you just come in?"

"No. I came in before, and you were sitting in the living room, watching Dr. Lawrence on television."

"What?" her father said, a look of amused confusion on his face.

Her mother smiled. "We didn't watch anything on television, Justine. We've been sitting here talking since you went to Lois's. How was your studying?"

"We couldn't study together. She was sick. I came

right back," she said. "Don't you even remember me coming home?"

They stared at her as if she were crazy.

"What's going on here? You two are freaking me out."

"I wish you'd start talking like an adult," her father said with a tired voice. "You're not a kid, anymore. You're a young woman, and you've got to start behaving like one. Adulthood requires responsibility."

"I'm only a sophomore," she proclaimed.

"Your father's right, Justine," her mother said. "It's time you realized you're going to be held accountable for your actions."

"What?"

"Your homework all done?" her father asked. She stared at him. He looked so different, so strange, so cold. Where was the familiar warmth in his eyes? No matter what she did, he always had a loving look. She was his princess. He never stopped telling her that.

"I told you," she said. "I came back because Lois was sick."

"So then you'd better get yourself upstairs and do what has to be done. It's getting late, Justine," her mother said.

"I don't know where I am, anymore," she said out of frustration. She didn't know what else to say.

Her father's eyes widened, and her mother tilted her head as if she had said a remarkable thing. "You're home, Justine. You're in Elysian Fields, and you're safe."

"Huh?"

"Safer than you've ever been," her father added. "Be grateful for that."

"Je—" She bit her lower lip as tears stung her eyes, threatening to emerge. "I can't stand this," she said and turned to run up the stairs.

When she got to her room, she slammed the door. For a long time, she just sat on her bed, staring at the stuffed stark white Gund cat her father had bought her last month. Instinctively, she embraced it, pressing its soft fur against her cheeks. She wiped away her tears and took deep breaths.

"I wish you had come out, Lois," she whispered. "I need to talk to you," she muttered. "Only you seem to know what's going on here."

She got ready for bed, eager for the coming of morning when she and Lois would meet and she could tell Lois some of the things that were happening. Lois would understand. Lois could explain.

One thing was for certain, she thought. She could not take that vitamin in the morning.

She was already in bed when her parents came upstairs. Her father opened her door softly and peered in. She pretended to be asleep.

"She's in bed," Justine heard him say. Her mother was standing right behind him.

"Sensible," her mother said. "Early to bed, early to rise . . ."

"Makes a man healthy, wealthy, and wise," her father said and closed the door softly.

She heard them walk off to their own bedroom, and then she fell asleep with an ache in her chest from the effort required to restrain her tears.

"Where were you?" he asked. He saw the smirk on his other self's face and knew he had been somewhere.

"You went out, didn't you? While I was asleep here, you went out."

"Maybe."

"No maybes. You went. I can smell it on you. I can smell the grass and the cold, night air."

"So?"

"Why did you do it?"

"I'm not going to linger here forever in the shadows while you sleep."

"Where did you go? The lights are so bright. It's so dangerous."

"I think, after all this time and practice, that I know how to stay safely in the darkness."

"But where did you go?" he asked insistently.

"I went down the hill, exploring. And guess whom I saw?"

He sat up as quickly as he could. The nurse was in the living room watching television. He could hear the set, and he could see the flashes of light on the corridor walls outside his room as figures moved on and off the small screen. As she was occupied, there was no danger of her coming in here and discovering his other self.

His father was working in his office with the door closed.

He took a deep breath. "Who did you see?"

His other self stepped forward, out of the shadows, so they could confront one another. They looked so much alike that no one but him could tell the difference, and even he had trouble doing that sometimes.

"It's whom, *whom* did you see. People who are organized and have confidence in themselves care about speaking correctly."

"All right, whom?"

"Well, at first I thought it was her as a young girl. I thought, look what the doctor has done! He has turned back time. His project is an experiment involving time. He should call it The Fountain of Youth Project instead of Elysian Fields. But then I got a closer look, and I realized what he had done."

"What has he done?" he asked. He was growing short of breath and had to breathe deeply to keep himself conscious.

"He put her head on a young girl's body. It's not unexpected. That's what he does, you know—plays with people's heads. He made certain repairs, made it youthful, and put it on her body. A young girl is walking around with her head."

He stared for a long moment. "No, he wouldn't do that, would he?"

"Why not? It's an experiment, isn't it? And you know what he can do, what he is capable of creating. He can change their heads around any time the wants to. He's done it to you, on and off. He's still doing it to you."

"But that wasn't right. That shouldn't have been done."

"No one tells the doctor what's right and what isn't. Least of all, you."

His other self started to back away.

"Wait."

"What?"

"Did she see you?"

"Not exactly."

"What's that supposed to mean?"

"She heard me, but she didn't see me. Why?" His other self stepped forward and looked down at him suspiciously. "You're planning something, aren't you? Come on, own up to it."

"Yes, I'm planning something."

He looked at the doorway because he heard the nurse get up and walk about out there. He knew that his father would be coming in to see him soon.

"What? What are you planning? You can tell me. You've got to tell me. I've answered all your questions. You've got to answer mine."

"It's simple," he said.

"What is?"

"What I have to do."

"Then tell me, damn it."

"I've got to get her head back," he said, then fell back against his pillow. He was tired, as if he had run up and down the hill and scurried around the development. His other self stood there in silence, then backed into the darkness again.

And not too soon, either. A moment later, his father entered, flicking on the lights. The room exploded, the illumination burning away the skin of silky darkness that had covered the walls and ceiling. His father glowed like a hot coal as he strode into the room. He was terrified his father would touch him and sear him right to the bone. His flesh would melt under his father's fingers.

"How do you feel, Eugene?" he asked. Little puffs of smoke followed the words from his mouth. He could even hear the roar of the furnace within him.

"Fine. A little tired, but fine."

"That's good. You sound fine. Still worried about losing your body?" his father asked him.

He couldn't see his other self now, because he had retreated into the walls to escape the light, but he could imagine the smirk on his face. He could almost hear him say, "See? What did I tell you? He talks about losing bodies."

"Sometimes," he said. "Sometimes I can't help but worry."

"Well, I don't want you to worry about that anymore, Eugene. The fact is, you've become a part of me, an extension of me, so you don't have to think about your own body anymore. I see you don't understand," his father said, staring down at him.

He could feel the intense heat from his eyes. It was like two rays burning little holes in his head. He wanted to bring the blanket up over himself, but he knew it would do no good.

His father stepped closer and held his arm over him. He cowered as the heat from the arm made the skin on his face tingle.

"See my arm, Eugene. Well, when I want you to, you will be my arm and thus, this arm will have a greater reach. You won't think of yourself as Eugene. You will think of yourself as my arm. Now do you understand?"

He didn't, but he nodded quickly.

His father smiled. All of his teeth had become tiny, bluish-white flames, and his eyes glowed like two hot coals.

His father stepped back and went to the window. As he walked, charred air dropped to the side. The whole room now had the odor of burnt electrical wires. It made him nauseous, but he was afraid to complain.

"Actually," his father went on, gazing out the window, "everyone down there is becoming a part of me. I am expanding in leaps and bounds, growing longer, taller, wider every day. I'm like an octopus with ever-growing tentacles, a spider who continually adds legs.

"And do you know how that makes me feel, Eugene," he said, turning back to him. He was smiling widely. Tiny surges of lightning sizzled on his forehead and cheeks. "It makes me feel like God, because I've come to the conclusion that God is protoplasm, ever-increasing protoplasm."

He was replaced by an intense gaze. The lightning stopped, but his face took on a metallic glow.

"It's good to have someone to talk to, Eugene, someone who understands, someone who won't laugh. So few people have the vision you have now, Eugene.

"It's ironic that what has come about suggests the Trinity, isn't it? I mean, here you are, the son, and I am the Father, and what I have created is the Holy Ghost."

His father laughed.

"In time perhaps, even those religious fanatics will come to believe in me and in what I have accomplished, huh? Those who think that science is the work of the devil.

"There's only one thing, Eugene, one sad thing," he continued, walking back toward the door, his voice taking on a heavy, troubled tone, "eventually, I will have to send you into the world. And you know what they'll do to you, don't you? They'll crucify you." He stared at him.

Suddenly, his father laughed.

"And then, I'll resurrect you, just as I resurrected you before, and we'll create an army of disciples.

"Sound good?" He clapped his hands together, rubbing the palms. "Okay, I've got to go back to work. We had a little problem, but I've fixed it, I think. If not, well . . . then my reach must be extended, and that's where you come in, Eugene. You will truly be my right-hand man.

"Rest up. In the morning we'll continue the good work."

He snapped off the lights, and the fire was sucked back into the light fixture. Almost instantly, the room cooled down, and the odor of burnt wires disappeared. His father stood in the doorway a moment, now a charcoal silhouette. And then, he walked away.

As soon as it was quiet again, his second self came out of the darkness.

"You don't have to say anything," he said. "I don't want to hear 'I told you so.' "

"I told you so," his second self taunted.

"I don't care what he says. He shouldn't have used her head. God or no god, he had no right to do that."

"You gave him the right."

"I did not. I did not!"

"Quiet, you fool. You'll bring her running in here. All right, you didn't give him the right. But you did give him the opportunity. Isn't that so?"

Reluctantly, he nodded.

"But just because he had the opportunity, doesn't mean he had to go out and do it."

"No. Listen, I agree with you. I didn't say you were wrong. I only wanted to know your plans, that's all."

"Then you're willing to help me?"

"Yes, of course."

"Good, because you know your way around down there, and you know where she is and when it would be best to . . . to do it."

"Uh-huh."

"Okay." He closed his eyes when his head touched the pillow. "I'll rest now. Then we'll think and we'll plan."

"Fine. Rest. I'm tired, too."

"Did you see him? Did you see the fire and the light?"

"Yes." His other self's voice was dwindling.

"Did you see how he glowed? He doesn't have to be afraid of the light; he is the light."

He opened his eyes and sat up again, a realization coming.

"He would destroy you if he saw you. Do you hear me? He would burn you away, and I need you. I need you more than ever. Are you listening?"

"I know," his other self whispered.

"He knows about you, so be careful."

He closed his eyes again.

"Be careful," he muttered.

Before he fell asleep, he imagined himself going down there, and then he saw himself coming back up the hill toward home. He was smiling, and he felt so light and happy.

He was holding her head in his hands, bringing it back to where it belonged.

9

JUSTINE WAS ALMOST late. By the time she had gotten dressed and left her room, her parents were already down in the kitchen finishing their breakfast and chatting happily, their smiles as bright and excited as the faces of children on Christmas morning. Why didn't she share their optimism and energy in the morning? Maybe she should be taking the vitamins, she thought. For a moment, when she held it in her fingers, she debated whether or not to actually swallow it.

She didn't. Once again, she went through the ruse Lois had demonstrated, and then she sat down and had breakfast, intrigued with her parents' topics of conversation.

He mother had never been a traditional housewife. Occasionally Elaine had tried a new recipe published in the *New York Times*, but her cooking was often a subject of humor. Her father often teased that her mother's favorite meal was "Let's make reservations." It was understandable. Neither Justine's maternal grandmother nor her mother had been at home in a kitchen. They'd had maids and cooks. Justine's grandmother was always too engrossed in her charity foundations to devote time toward running a household anyway.

Elaine Freeman had never felt guilty about her lack of interest in household matters. She was an artist, an intellectual, a sophisticated woman—everything the wife of an up-and-coming corporate lawyer should be. In her mind, these things more than compensated for her failures in the domestic arena.

But suddenly she was sitting here talking about the dinner menu as if it were going to be an art gallery opening, and Justine's father . . . he was actually showing interest. Justine thought they would never stop talking about it. Finally, when there was a break in their conversation, she asked about the MTV hookup.

"We're not getting it," her father said, his happy-go-lucky tone of voice disappearing and his hazel eyes darkening.

"Not getting it?" She looked at her mother, who nodded approvingly. There was something almost comical about her look of agreement. It reminded Justine of the exaggerated expressions on the Dukes' faces when Justine and her parents first arrived. Their reactions were so dramatically sad or angry, they looked farcical. Her mother pursed her lips and closed her eyes as she nodded. "But why not? You told me we could get it here."

"It's not a matter of the technology," her father said, somewhat pedantically. "This community is just as up-to-date as any in America. More so, probably."

"Then why not?" Justine asked, her tone almost demanding.

Her father sat back in his seat, his arms folded across

his chest, and stared blankly for a moment. "MTV is not a good influence."

"Huh?" She looked at her mother again. How many times had the two of them sat and watched MTV together in New York?

"It encourages kids to be rebellious because most of the rock videos show punk rock or drugs. And the costumes these singers wear," her father continued as if he were reciting the gospel, "outrageous. What do they expect from young people today?" he asked, turning to her mother for support. She was nodding again, her head bobbing like a puppet. "Considering what someone like that Madonna wears, everything goes. Nowadays, even prostitutes are held up as cult heroes."

"But Mom . . . you like Madonna," Justine protested. "You never complained about her costumes."

"How utterly ridiculous," her mother said and laughed. "Can you imagine? Please, Justine. Just because I didn't voice my criticism doesn't mean I approved." She laughed again, a thin trickle of a laugh that trailed off, then lingered like an echo.

Her father sat forward. "Don't go around telling people, *especially* people here, that your mother likes such things."

"But she *did*," Justine insisted.

For a moment her parents just stared at her, their eyes blinking rapidly. She felt her face redden, and her heart began to beat rapidly.

"At least, I thought she did," she finally said. That seemed to please them.

"Well, you were mistaken. Now everything's straightened out," her father said and smiled.

"Just a few days ago, you bought me one of Madonna's tapes," Justine said softly, reluctant to let go.

"What?" her father asked. He smiled at her as if she were talking in her sleep. "I did no such thing. And don't go around saying I did," he added.

"Well," he said, slapping his hands together, his happy-go-lucky expression rapidly returning. "I've got to get on the road. My turn to drive Michael. God, you look good this morning," he told Elaine. "Doesn't your mother look healthier? I can't believe how she's blossoming."

"Oh, Kevin."

"Doesn't she?" he asked Justine.

She looked at her mother. As far as she could see, she didn't look any different from the way she'd looked in New York. In fact, she looked a little more peaked and less robust. There were wrinkles in her brow as if she were weighed down with troublesome thoughts.

But it seemed important to her father that she agree. "Yes," she said.

"Oh, I'm not," her mother said. "But you know what . . . I'm going to sit out in the sun today and get a tan before it gets to be too late. Christy has such a beautiful tan, don't you think?"

"Yes," Justine said. She felt like some kind of stooge, there to reinforce everything her parents said.

"All the women I've met in Elysian Fields look so tan and healthy. They make me feel sickly white and puny beside them," her mother confessed. "When we were living in the city, I didn't think much about having the healthy, outdoor look."

"Well, soon you'll have it, too," Kevin Freeman said

as he got up from the table. "You ladies will excuse me. I'm off to do battle in the jungle."

"I'll see you off," Justine's mother said, and escorted her father to the front door where she kissed him good-bye. In New York, Justine recalled, her father often left for work before her mother had even risen from bed.

"Now then," her mother said, returning, "you'd better get a move on, too."

"Ma," Justine began, sitting back, "do you really like it here as much as you claim, or are you just putting on for Dad?"

"Putting on? How could you say such a thing, Justine? Putting on?" She grimaced as if Justine had uttered a blasphemy, but Justine often recalled times when she and her mother shared little deceptions, especially about people her father liked and her mother really didn't. "I wouldn't deceive your father like that. How can you expect a marriage to succeed if one person deliberately deceives the other? That's what's wrong with so many marriages today," she went on, speaking as if she were standing in front of a classroom of potential wives. "Husbands and wives don't trust one another and are not honest with one another. As well as with their good friends," she added.

"You like these people?" Justine pursued.

"Of course. They're . . . together. Their lives are organized and, they're quite active. I have no regrets," she added, smiling as she went to clearing the table.

Justine watched her mother work for a few moments. There was something so different about her, even about the way she moved. She noticed how careful she was, how she seemed to be following a prescribed plan— taking pains to organize the dishes carefully in the dishwasher, picking up the silverware with a sense of organization, forks first, spoons next. Never were the domestic chores treated with such respect.

Justine was nearly hypnotized by her mother's behavior. She had to rush to get her things together to meet the other kids at the bottom of the hill. She was eager to get there to talk to Lois and find out what exactly had happened the night before.

When Justine arrived, Lois was standing beside Janet. Everyone was listening to Brad describe how he had accidentally burned his hand on his car engine. When she appeared, he hesitated, and the others looked up expectantly.

"Morning," she said. "I'm sorry about your hand," she added quickly. "Your mother told my mother."

"Just one of those things, those stupid things," he replied.

"Now that Justine is here, we can get going," Janet announced with a smirk, and everyone started for the front gate.

Lois looked at her and smiled. Justine maneuvered herself next to her, hoping they'd have the chance to talk freely for a few moments. Like yesterday, the topics of conversation ranged from homework assignments to club activities. Lois contributed, and Justine winked at her as she, too, added something to the discussion.

Just before they reached the school grounds, Justine, growing frustrated with their inability to talk privately, deliberately dropped her notebook, causing pages to scatter.

"Lois, can you help me pick this up?" she said before any of the others could offer. "It's all right, don't wait," she told them when they stopped and turned. "We'll be right with you."

"Hurry, or you'll be late for homeroom," Janet said.

Lois and Justine began to scoop up the pages.

"Figured that would work," Justine whispered. "So what happened last night? Why didn't you come out?"

"Come out?" Lois handed her the pages. "What do you mean?"

"To meet me, stupid." Justine spoke rapidly, one eye on the others. "I was waiting and waiting, and then I saw Dr. Lawrence's car. Your mother told me you were sick. Didn't she tell you I came to your house? I didn't want to get you in trouble, but . . ."

"She didn't tell me, but that was probably because she was concerned about me."

"You really were sick?"

"Yes, I was," Lois said with an idiotic smile on her face.

"Well, what was wrong with you?"

"I had . . . problems," she said, "but Dr. Lawrence helped me, and I feel much better today, thank you." She started away.

"Wait a minute. What the hell . . ."

Lois turned around sharply and stared at her, her eyes blinking rapidly the way Justine's mother's and father's eyes had blinked during breakfast.

"What about our plans?"

"Plans? Really. I don't know what you're talking about, and we're going to be late for homeroom. I've never been late for homeroom," Lois added. Pulling her shoulders back with pride, she started walking quickly toward the front entrance of the school, where the other kids from Elysian Fields waited impatiently.

Justine stood there for a moment looking after her. Then she hurried to the building herself.

After homeroom, Justine was able to get a hold of her friend while the others rushed off to their first period class. She pulled Lois aside by the water fountain.

"Lois, did you take your vitamin today?" she asked with incredulity.

"Of course," Lois said. "I always take my vitamin. Don't you?" Lois sang and moved on to her first period class, leaving Justine to stumble over her own confusion.

All that day, Justine felt like someone who had been struck dumb. In a daze she moved from one class to another, watching Lois, studying her behavior toward the others. What had once been an act, now looked authentic. Lois had been returned to the fold. She was one of them again.

What frustrated Justine most was she had no one to turn to, no one in whom to confide or seek advice. She felt a natural need to turn to the other students, the ones who were not from Elysian Fields, especially Bonny Joseph and Tad Donald, but every time she spoke to them, she felt the eyes of the kids of Elysian Fields on her. They were watching and listening, and she remembered Lois's warnings from the day before.

She found she was actually afraid, more afraid than ever, because of Lois's apparent desertion. She was alone with the strange and incomplete knowledge that something odd was happening at Elysian Fields.

She considered calling Mindy after school, but when she reviewed what she would tell her, she grew even more distressed. What would she say? That her mother cared more about household duties? So what? She could tell Mindy that her father didn't approve of MTV or her mother changed her mind about it. Some complaint.

She could tell her that they wanted her to take vitamins, vitamins that made kids act differently. She could tell her that the boys were unusually shy, naive. But Mindy wouldn't be impressed with any of those complaints. Who would?

Mindy wouldn't understand. Mindy wouldn't care, and Justine couldn't make her care because she couldn't formulate her own feelings clearly or dramatically enough to interest her. She had to discover something more, something that anyone would understand.

Her mental turmoil left her withdrawn and quiet for the rest of the day, but the other kids didn't notice. They mistook her stillness and vacant look simply for attentive behavior. They didn't detect anything critical in the way she observed them. They smiled at her and hovered about her. The only time she seemed to draw out their suspicions was at the end of the day when she told Lois and Janet she wasn't going to attend the school newspaper meeting.

"I have a bad headache," she said. "I just want to go home and lay down."

"You shouldn't give into it," Janet said. "Occupy your mind and it will pass."

"I think I just need some rest," she insisted.

"Dr. Lawrence always tells us to avoid excuses for not doing the right things, to live as though we had no alternative," Janet responded. "Right, Lois?"

"Yes," Lois said softly. "Rationalizing weakens the individual. Your personality has to be built up just the way you would build up your body," she recited.

"I've got to go home," Justine said. She didn't wait to

hear any more slogans and platitudes. She hurried off without looking back. A fluttering rippled in her chest, as if a baby bird were trapped beside her heart.

She practically ran all the way back to Elysian Fields. Twice tears came, and she had to wipe her cheeks. The security guard looked up with surprise as she burst through the gate and charged up the small hill. She was determined to talk to her mother, to tell her everything that had happened, everything Lois had told her. She would make her understand, and together, they would make her father understand. Her parents would care. They were her parents; they had to care.

Hope lifted her, carrying her up the street. But as she ran, she was like a horse wearing blinders, refusing to look left or right, her attention centered and locked on her home. She had become afraid of the development, afraid of its charm and its beauty. She feared looking at the colorful flowers and the facilities. The pretty houses, the elaborate landscaping, the clean, wide streets reminded her of the sirens from Greek mythology.

She had always been impressed with that tale about Odysseus, the episode when he was sailing home and he asked his men to tie him to the ship's mast after he had filled their ears with wax so they couldn't hear the song of the sirens, beckoning them closer, tempting them so they would crash on the rocks. He wanted to enjoy the beauty, but he knew if he did so without being tied, he would succumb to the evil call.

So, too, would the development beckon her to crash on the rocks, she thought. It would confuse her and soften her opposition. She would be lost. She anticipated that slight ringing in her ears, but it didn't come before she reached her house. Encouraged and determined, she charged through the front door.

"Mommy!" she screamed. "Ma!"

She dropped her books on the small table in the hallway and raced into the living room, then into the kitchen.

"Ma!"

She went directly into the studio, expecting to find her mother involved in her work. But the room was empty.

"Ma!"

She turned to go upstairs, but stopped to look at the painting her mother had been working on, the one depicting the view from the rear of their house. It wasn't completed, but enough had been done for Justine to understand her mother's viewpoint and perception. The oils were brighter than the colors Elaine usually used. In fact, the painting screamed out at Justine. It was like looking directly into a high-wattage light bulb. There was something blinding and mesmerizing, as if the painting were casting a spell. It turned her into a moth, magnetically attracted to the light. She stepped closer to view it.

Justine was struck by the way her mother had painted Dr. Lawrence's house. The house was enormous in relation to everything around it, and that enormity was heightened by the particular shade of shiny black. The house rose off the canvas, in a three-dimensional manner.

Her mother had placed the sun behind the house so that the building cast a giant shadow over everything, and the shadow seemed to be in the shape of a hand. It was as if it held the entire community in its grip.

A figure was hidden within the shadow. Right now it

resembled some kind of animal, almost like an ape. A tiny part of it had been painted in a slightly darker shade of black so that it seemed to be gradually emerging out of the darkness.

Justine couldn't help but reach out slowly and touch it. The moment she did so, she pulled her finger back as if she had touched the tip of a burning candle.

She stepped back from the painting, unable to turn away from it, and yet terrified of it. Finally she groaned, closed her eyes, and rushed out of the studio. She hurried upstairs, calling as she took two steps at a time.

"Ma! Mommy?"

The bedrooms were empty. Puzzled, Justine went back downstairs. Her mother's car was in the garage, so she must have gone off with someone else, she thought. Yet, she had been making such a big deal about being home when Justine returned from school.

The answer was in the kitchen. She had rushed through so quickly she hadn't seen the note on the refrigerator.

"Next door at Christy's. Come over if you get home before I do. Mom."

She decided to go over and see if she could get her mother to come home with her so they could talk before her father returned from work. She needed to convince her mother of the validity of her fears first.

Dressed in an oversized, dark blue sweat shirt and a pair of jeans, Christy Duke greeted her at the front door and insisted she come in.

"Your mother's in my studio. We've been discussing art all afternoon. I'm so glad she's here. I've got a fellow conspirator," she said and winked. "Come in. You look lost. Is something wrong?"

"No, I just have a headache."

"Oh. Well, we'll fix that. Come in," Christy said, her voice so cheerful and her smile so warm, Justine couldn't help but relax. How could anything be wrong with someone like her? Maybe . . . maybe she should confide in her, too, Justine thought. Christy wasn't like the other parents she had seen here. Christy would be sympathetic. Perhaps she should even tell Christy why she thought Brad was acting odd. Then Mrs. Duke would really become involved. "Everything all right at school?"

"Uh-huh," Justine said, entering.

"Good. It's a great school system. You're really going to like it here," Christy said. "All the kids do."

Justine kept her reaction down to a slight smile.

Christy studied her for a moment. "You don't suffer from sinus headaches, do you?"

"No," she said quickly.

"Because there's something about Dr. Lawrence's vitamins . . . you've been taking them, haven't you?"

Justine hesitated. She thought it would be best to talk to them both at the same time.

"Where's my mother?"

"Oh. Let's go in the studio." She led Justine through the house. Her studio was practically in the same place—off the kitchen, with a window facing the rear.

Elaine stood up the moment Justine entered. She, too, was dressed in a sweat shirt and jeans. For some reason, the resemblances Justine had seen between the two women seemed to be stronger than before. Both had their hair tied back in the same way. Neither wore any makeup, not even lipstick. They looked like the co-conspirators Christy had jokingly suggested they were.

It bothered her, but for a moment Justine wondered if she wasn't just envious of her mother for developing a warm and close friendship so quickly, while she was unable to find anyone with whom she could share intimacies.

"Hi, honey," Elaine said. "Home so early? I thought you had a newspaper club meeting."

"I have a headache," she said. She looked at Christy again. "So I came right home."

"Oh, that's too bad. Maybe you should take a couple of aspirins and lie down for a while. I'll come right home," she added.

"Maybe she's developing an allergy," Christy said. "It can come on suddenly." She smiled and stroked Justine's hair. "You look good, honey."

"Thank you." They both call me "honey," and they say it the same way, she thought.

"Doesn't Christy do beautiful work?" Elaine said.

Justine looked at the paintings on the walls. There were various landscapes, the usual fruit stills, a portrait of Brad and Steven when they were much younger.

"Yes," Justine said.

"And I just love her latest," Elaine said, gesturing toward the easel.

Justine stepped forward to take a look.

The little bird that fluttered beside her heart closed its wings slowly. She felt its head lower and its heart stop while hers pounded.

Christy Duke was painting a landscape, too—the view from the rear of her house.

And it was exactly like the one her mother was doing, down to the dark and grotesque shape emerging from the shadow cast by Dr. Lawrence's overwhelming house.

* * *

Still as a statue, he hovered near the rear window. The only part of his body that had moved during the last half hour was his eyes. They went from side to side slowly, searching the scene below like a radar device, recording all movement, studying every change. He was waiting for her, waiting to catch sight of her coming up that hill. He was obsessed with the need to see her. Even the nurse was impressed with his intensity every time she came in to check on him.

"You're in deep thought today," she told him just before she left his room the last time. "What's on your mind?"

She looked into his eyes, gazing into his dull blue pupils as though they were literally windows through which she could see into his head.

He was afraid she could, so he closed them. "I'm just tired," he said, but she didn't move away from him. It had been so long since he had successfully deceived anyone.

He opened his eyes again and saw her scrutinizing him, her puffy cheeks even more blown out, her eyes shrinking into probing microscopic lenses. Her nostrils moved like a rabbit's, and her lips writhed up in the corners like worms, revealing just a little bit of her nicotine-stained teeth.

He couldn't let her know what he was thinking; he couldn't let her know what he was planning. If he did, she would rush off to call the doctor, and they would do something to stop him. And they wouldn't let him sleep without being strapped in.

He gazed quickly at the shadow in the corner and saw his second self watching with anticipation.

"I'm waiting for her to come home," he said. "She's bringing me a surprise."

"Oh, shit," the nurse said. Instinctively now, he knew what bothered her. "I don't want to hear about it. Your father has the patience for this, but I don't," she added, then left the room.

"Good work," his second self said. He stepped up a little, but stopped short of the lighted area. "Didn't think you could think that fast, anymore."

"I didn't lie to her, did I? I am waiting for her to come home."

He turned back to the window and peered down. A car had turned into the development, then continued on toward the west end. Everything below seemed to move in slow motion. Now his concentration was so strong that he didn't even feel the fly settle on his forehead. It pranced over his skin, then dropped down to the tip of his nose. It even walked over his puffed lips before it grew disinterested and flew away.

His tongue stirred, and the tip emerged like a red ant coming up from a tunnel. There was an increase of activity below. Younger kids were coming home from school. Cars turned into driveways as others wove their way through the development. Threads coming back to the eye of the needle, he thought.

And then, he saw her. She was walking very quickly, so quickly that her head, somewhat loose, he thought, bounced precariously on her neck. For a moment he envisioned it falling off and bouncing on the road as it rolled down the hill toward the front gate. He saw the decapitated torso turn as if it could watch the head spin away. At the gate, the security guard knelt down and scooped it up gracefully, moving his arm with the follow through of a bowler after he had just thrown a perfect strike.

He carried the head back up the hill and returned it to the awaiting torso.

"You want to be more careful about this," he said. "Can't go around losing your head."

She thanked him and continued on to the house. When she drew closer to it, he could see her features more clearly, especially now that he was looking at her in daylight.

He gasped.

"What?" his second self asked. "Come on, this isn't fair. You can stand there in the light and look. I've got to lay back in the shadows."

"It's her; it's her; it's definitely her."

"I told you that. Is that all?"

"Being told and seeing for yourself is not the same thing."

"So?"

"Her head—it's not even on that well. To tell you the truth, I don't think there'll be any problem. I'm surprised at the sloppy work my father did."

"Hey, he's a pioneer. He's just starting out. It's not fair to judge his work like that."

"I know; I know."

When he saw her go into the house, he didn't step away from the window, anticipating her reappearance. He watched her come out and go into the house next door. Then he turned from the window and went to the desk. He sat down and began to sketch her face. He was never good at art, but this was important. After only a few minutes, he had what he considered to be a perfect likeness. He lifted it up to show his second self.

"Not bad."

"Not bad? I'd say, rather good."

"So say it."

A few moments later, the nurse returned. It was time for his sedative. He didn't want to take it, but he knew there was no way to avoid it. And, anyway, it was better not to stir up any suspicions.

"Oh, good," she said, seeing him at the desk, "you've done some writing. The doctor will be happy."

"It's not writing," he said. "I drew a picture." He plucked the pill from her fingers and chased it down with the cup of water.

"A picture, huh?" She leaned over him to look. "So?"

"What?"

"Where is this picture?"

"Right there in front of you. If it were a snake, it would bite you," he said, and his second self laughed. She turned to look into the corner, but he had retreated into the darkness sufficiently.

"Is that so? A little frisky today, huh?"

"Yep."

"But you're nuts, nuttier than ever, in fact." She held up his sheet of paper. "There's nothing on here. Just a pencil dot in the center."

He smiled. She couldn't see it.

"Jesus, you're a lot of laughs," she said, dropping the sheet of paper. "You'd better go and lie down."

"Anything you say," he said. He winked at the shadows, and then looked down at the sheet.

His mother's head couldn't be any clearer. As he looked at the picture, it began to grow a body beneath it. There was already half a neck.

She's coming back, he thought. In every way. It won't be long, now.

His thoughts were so vivid, he spoke them aloud.

"What's that? What won't be long?"

"Nothing."

"You don't mean your pecker, do you?" she asked and laughed.

He laughed, too.

"You're getting good at this," his second self whispered. "I think you're going to succeed."

Filled with hope and anticipation, he followed her back to his bedroom where he would drift into an easy sleep. His rest was very important now. He needed all his strength and wits about him when he went down there.

Maybe he would go tonight.

And then, in the morning, he would wake up and find her head on the table beside him, smiling, happy he had brought it back to where it belonged.

10

JUSTINE COULDN'T WAIT to leave Christy Duke's house. Christy's warm smile had become eerie, frightening. She wanted to get out of there before Brad and Steven returned from their after-school activities, and certainly before Michael Duke returned. This family next door, as well as most of the other families in the development, were part of a conspiracy. At least, that was the way she saw it.

Even more frightening was the fact that her parents could not see the problem. It might very well be too late for them, she thought, and if it was too late for them, it was certainly too late for her. Who else could she turn to at this point?

When she and her mother returned to the house, Justine tried to make her mother see what was happening, even though she was not quite sure about the source of the evil. It was something terrible, that was for sure.

"Let's get you a couple of aspirins," her mother said as soon as they walked in the door.

"No, Mom. I don't have a headache. I just wanted to get you home."

"What?" Elaine tilted her head and smiled. "Whatever for? And whatever it is, why couldn't you tell me at Christy's? She's my closest friend."

"Closest friend? Mom, you've known her only a short while. How can she be your closest friend?"

"We've known each other for more than a short while, Justine. What in heaven's name are you saying?" her mother asked, maintaining that light smile.

Justine thought she looked clownish. "But before we came here, you only saw her a few times, and . . ."

"We've been here quite awhile."

"No we haven't. Oh, God, this is all part of it," Justine said, recalling Brad's inability to remember exactly when his family had moved to Elysian Fields. All of the Dukes had been confused over how many years they had been living here. She shook her head, her eyes filling with tears.

"Part of it? Part of what?" Elaine asked.

"Of what's happening!"

"I don't understand, honey. What's supposed to be happening?"

Instead of responding, she took her mother's hand. "Come with me, quickly," she said, leading her through the house to the art studio. She stopped when they stood in front of her mother's painting. To Justine, it looked as though that small, dark, ominous figure had emerged even more out of the darkness. "Look," she said.

Her mother, still wearing that incredulous smile, turned to the painting, then looked at Justine.

"So? Don't you like it?"

"Like it? Mom, it's the exact same painting Christy is doing. Can't you see that?"

"Well, we're both doing a landscape of the development, but . . ."

"It's exactly the same!" Justine protested. "Down to the smallest detail. It's as if you two were painting by numbers and doing the same picture."

"There are some similarities, but to say it's exactly the same . . ." Her mother's smile faded quickly. "I think I have some originality, and I didn't even see Christy's painting until I had been well into mine, Justine. I don't appreciate your implication that I'm copying someone else's work."

"Mom, I'm not talking about your artistic ability. This is . . . this is eerie. Don't you see!"

Her mother glanced at the painting again, then shook her head.

"I don't see, no." She started to turn away.

"And what is this supposed to be?" Justine demanded. She put her right forefinger on the dark figure.

"Don't touch it!"

Justine pulled her hand back quickly.

"Never touch a painting like that," her mother chastised.

"But Mom, what is that?"

"It's just a shadow. Now, do you want some aspirin, or don't you?"

Justine just stared at her mother. She looked back at the painting, then put her hands over her eyes.

"You have a headache?"

"No, Mom, it's not a headache. Listen to me. Listen." She tried to control the tone of her voice, tried to sound calm and reasonable so her mother would really listen. "Something strange is going on here, and it has something to do with Dr. Lawrence's vitamins. And something in the air, some ringing."

"What? What ringing? What are you saying?" Her mother's smile widened. "Something in the air?"

"I don't know all the facts. But everyone's kind of weird. I didn't notice until Lois Wilson pointed it out, and she was able to do so because she stopped taking the vitamins. The kids are strange. Brad deliberately burned his own hand," she said quickly, "because he . . . he accidentally touched me here," she said, indicating her breast. "And at night, at a certain time, everyone's watching the same videotapes made by Dr. Lawrence, listening to his opinions about things and believing them, just the way you and Daddy are believing them."

Her mother stepped back as if she had been slapped.

"I don't understand this. Do you have a headache or don't you?"

"It's got nothing to do with a headache!" Justine screamed. Her mother closed her eyes and shook herself as if a chill had just passed through her body. "These kids aren't normal. They're worse than nerds, and you and Daddy . . . you've changed. You've got to listen to me. You're forgetting things and doing things you never did and—"

"Justine, I don't like this. You don't sound right; you sound sick."

"I am sick, sick of what's happening here."

"Happening here?" Her mother looked confused, surprised. "Don't you like it here?"

"Oh, God. I hate it here!" she said, clenching her fists and pounding the air around her head. "That's just it."

Elaine Freeman stepped back farther and brought her hands to her throat. "How could you say that?"

"I can. I couldn't before, when I was taking the vitamins, don't you see? Now something's happened to Lois. They found out what she was doing, and Dr. Lawrence came to her house and today she was like all the others again. She forgot everything she told me. It was horrible, frightening. I felt like I was talking to a zombie. And she was the one who told me to stop taking the vitamins."

"You're not taking the vitamins?" Her mother smiled. "But I saw you take your vitamin this morning."

"I just pretended," she said.

Her mother stared at her, her smile fading quickly as she understood what Justine was saying.

"You're a very ungrateful girl," she said. "I think you had better go up to your room until your father comes home," she added.

"Mom, don't you understand anything I'm telling you?"

"I understand that we've done all this for you, and you turn on us like this. Don't you realize how embarrassing this could be for us if these ridiculous ideas got out . . . and just when we've made so many good friends?" She nodded, confirming a thought. "Dr. Lawrence was right—there are substantially bad influences polluting you."

"Dr. Lawrence is . . . is a maniac," she said. Her mother stepped forward to slap her across the face. "Go to your room this instant," Elaine said through her teeth.

Her mother's look of intense hate and anger frightened Justine. She burst into tears and rushed away, charging through the house and up the stairs to her room where she shut the door.

Now she lay on the bed, waiting, confused, frustrated, frightened.

Perhaps her father would listen. Her father was brilliant and cunning. How else could he have become so successful so quickly? He would see things her mother couldn't see. And he wasn't here all day under the influence of these people and the development.

When she heard him enter the house, she sat up quickly, waiting in anticipation. Her mother had greeted him at the door and was filling him in on their confrontation. Very soon she heard his footsteps on the stairway. He didn't knock, but she didn't care.

"What's going on here, Justine?" he demanded, standing in the doorway. Her mother stood right behind him, her face knotted in a grimace of pain and sadness. "You haven't been taking your vitamin, and you hate it here?"

"Oh, Daddy," she said, starting to cry.

Kevin Freeman moved into the room and sat beside her on the bed. His face softened, and he put his hand on her shoulder. "Well, what is it, princess? Tell me."

Looking into her father's eyes, Justine thought she saw the old warmth and affection. He looked concerned, interested. She sat up, encouraged.

She went through her story concerning Lois, describing how things looked differently to her once she stopped taking the vitamin. She told him about Brad and about Lois's mother. He listened attentively as she described peeking in on the Wilsons and seeing them watching the videotape at the same time he and her mother were watching. Then she told him about the paintings Christy Duke and her mother were doing.

"Something's happening to everyone here, Daddy.

Something terrible. I know it has something to do with the vitamins and with this ringing in our ears. Lois was about to show me more before Dr. Lawrence got to her."

Her father listened, then nodded thoughtfully. Her mother moaned and sobbed in the hallway until he turned around and glared at her.

"Elaine," he said. "Why don't you just go downstairs now? I'll handle this, okay?"

Her mother nodded and left quietly.

"She won't listen to me," Justine said. "All she's worried about is being embarrassed."

"Well, you've got to be more understanding about your mother," he said. "This is a dramatic move for her, even more than it is for you. You see, I was brought up in a semi-rural environment. I'm used to small towns like Sandburg Creek, and small-town life where everyone knows everyone else's business. Your mother lived in a penthouse in the most exciting, bustling city in the world, and suddenly, she's here.

"Now you come to her with these stories, so it's understandable she would be fragile and emotional, isn't it?" her father asked softly.

Justine nodded and wiped her eyes.

"What are we going to do, Daddy?"

"Well, let me think about all this and look around a bit. The main thing is, you shouldn't let any of these ideas out. Don't talk to any of the other kids about it, not even Lois Wilson."

"I can't talk to her anymore, and it's useless to talk to the other kids."

"Right. Okay, why don't you rest up a bit and I'll see if Mommy can cook, or if we should all go out to eat, okay?"

She nodded and lay back as he got up.

"I knew you would listen. I knew you would understand," she said.

He smiled. "I'm not going to let anything happen to my princess," he said. "The idea was to bring us to a beautiful, safe environment where we would all be happy and secure. Anything that interrupts or damages that won't be tolerated," he added, his face tight with intensity. For a moment, he looked absolutely furious. "Be back in a little while," he said and left the room.

She closed her eyes to do just what her father had suggested—relax for a little while. She felt she could now. She had put her problems into her father's capable hands. She should have gone to him in the first place. He was always the strength in their family; he was always there whenever she needed him, no matter what the problem or the situation.

She felt her heartbeat slow down, and the pounding in her head receded. Feeling protected and safe, she drifted off for a short nap. Her father would take action. That was all that mattered now.

The ringing in her ears woke her. She opened her eyes abruptly and sat up quickly, listening. It was happening again, only it wasn't doing anything to her because she was off the vitamins. Still, if she could hear it, her father could hear it. She had to tell him and make him aware. This was the sound she had described, the ringing her mother claimed she had never heard.

She slid out of bed and left her room, but hesitated when she reached the top of the stairway. She could hear voices in the living room below. There was a stranger in the house. Her heart began to flutter again and her stomach felt so empty and light it was as though some-

one had sliced her in half and her torso was floating away
from the rest of her body.

It was Dr. Lawrence. Dr. Lawrence was downstairs
with her parents, and he was talking to them as if they
were little children.

"I don't care how loose it is," his second self began
the moment he opened his eyes, "you're not going to go
down there and just lift it off that other body. Your father
took great pains to place it securely where it is."

He sat up and looked around. His door had been left
open, but the nurse was not hovering about. He thought
he heard tiny voices and listened hard. Soon he realized
what it was—she was watching some soap opera in her
room. It was safe to move about. She was half in and
half out of the television set, walking beside her heroines
and heroes, kissing the men she admired, being the
woman of her fantasies.

"I know that," he whispered, wiping his eyes. They
felt like two blobs of jelly. He looked down at his arms.
The skin on them was so translucent now, he could see
the tiny wires and sockets. It occurred to him that his
father probably put the girl together the same way he had
put him together.

"So what are you going to do? Or has this all been just
talk?"

He glared at the shadows.

"It's not all talk. I know what to do. It's a matter of
cutting some wires and unplugging her head. That's all."

"How do you know that?"

"Look around you. It's how everything's been put
together."

"So? You'll still need some tools, won't you?"

"Yes." He thought about it for a moment. Then he slipped off his bed ever so softly, moving inches at a time. The tiny television voices continued in the other room. He went to the doorway, sliding his feet over the sheet of ice that covered his floor. He was barefoot and it was cold, but he had to tolerate it if he was going to be successful.

"Where are you going?"

"Shh."

"Be careful."

He peered out the doorway. All was quiet; all was still. The nurse was still half in and half out of her television set. It was his best opportunity. He tiptoed over the hall floor until he reached the kitchen. Then he went to the side door that opened to the garage and turned the knob a fraction of an inch at a time to subdue the sound of the click. When the door opened, he looked back and listened. She hadn't heard him; it was still okay.

Remembering where things were kept in the garage, he went directly to the bin that contained the tools. He lifted the lid as carefully as he had turned the knob on the kitchen door, and then searched within until he found the machete. When he was a young teenager, he used to enjoy clearing pathways in the forest, pretending he was on a safari in the jungle.

The edges showed some rust, but he thought it was still sufficiently sharp. He took it out slowly and lowered the lid softly. Then he made his way back to the kitchen and tiptoed through the house to his room. Once there, he shoved the machete between the mattress and bed springs.

"Good work," his second self said. He didn't respond,

but got back into his bed and lay there, waiting for her. He heard the tiny voices die, then heard her footsteps. He turned when she appeared in the doorway.

As usual, her face was flushed from the excitement she experienced living vicariously through television characters. Her thick neck was blotched red at the base of her throat, and her breathing was labored. He imagined how hard her heart struggled to lift that heavy bosom.

One of the buttons of her white uniform had come undone just at the center of her bosom. She was braless, and her nipples pressed vigorously against the garment. At this moment her breasts terrified him, but he couldn't turn away. He didn't want her to suspect anything.

She approached slowly, moving like a drugged gorilla, her heavy arms held low and away from her body. When she reached his bed, she undid the remaining top buttons of her uniform and leaned over to spill her breasts over him.

"Love me," she commanded, "love me like Cliff loves Tandy." She brought her hands to her bosom and pressed her breasts against his face, nearly smothering him. He tasted her salty skin and smelled her perspiration. It nauseated him, but he swallowed back the urge to dry heave and accepted her nipple between his lips, licking it like a hungry puppy dog.

She moaned. Her television lovemaking had brought her to the brink of orgasm, and now she quickly went over, revealing it in little cries of pleasure. His entire bed shook as she pumped her body against him. He was afraid the machete would fall out.

But it didn't, and soon her passion receded like the ocean tide. She backed away from him, her face red, her

eyes watery, her lips puffed. She ran her hands over her
hair, then rushed out to wash her face in cold water.

He knew what she was doing; she had done it before.

"That was disgusting," his second self said.

"What did you want me to do, drive her away and get
her upset? She might interfere with our plans."

"I can still feel disgusted, can't I?"

"It wasn't you."

"I feel what you feel."

"So then you know I'm not happy about it."

He sat up and checked the machete. Then he got off
the bed and went to the window.

"My father's down there," he said. "You don't think
he could be warning her, do you?"

"Of course not."

"I don't like it."

"You're not going to chicken out now, are you? Not
now, when you've gone so far."

"No."

"I'm coming with you."

He turned around quickly. "No. I don't want to have
to worry about you stepping into the light. I'll have
enough on my mind."

"You're going to need me. I can see that."

"I'll be all right."

"I'm coming with you."

"*No!*"

"No what?" the nurse said, appearing in the doorway,
her face cooled down, her hair brushed neatly, her
uniform buttoned. "What is it now?"

He looked at the shadows. His second self had
retreated sufficiently.

"I don't know," he said. "I . . . I had a bad thought."

"Only one?" She came into his room and went to his closet. "You're getting dressed up tonight. Your father wants you cleaned and dressed properly for dinner. You'll wear these slacks, this shirt and tie, and this jacket. What he expects you'll look like, I don't know," she said, turning to him. "Maybe he's testing some of those vitamins himself," she added and laughed.

Then she stopped thoughtfully.

"Maybe he's getting ready to demonstrate you. He's been mentioning that lately. Oh, well," she said, shrugging. "Ours is not to question why. Ours is but to do and—"

"Die," he said.

She tilted her head, and he saw just where the wires were connected in her neck. Surely they were located in the same place in the girl's neck.

"Very good. Okay," she said. "To the showers."

He started out, but just before he reached the doorway, he heard his second self whisper, "I'll keep my eye on the machete."

He checked to see if the nurse heard anything, but she was too occupied with his wardrobe.

"Thanks," he whispered, then left the room, confident all would go well.

"Her misbehavior," Dr. Lawrence said, "is not entirely her fault. Another girl, a problem child, has been a bad influence on her."

"Lois Wilson," Justine heard her mother say. She had gone far enough down the stairs to listen in on the conversation. "She said that Lois told her to stop taking her vitamins."

"That's right. The Wilsons have had a terrible time with their daughter. I've begun seeing her on a regular basis again."

"Maybe you should see Justine on a regular basis," Kevin Freeman said.

Justine couldn't believe what she was hearing. Hadn't her father believed anything she'd told him?

"That's why we called you right away."

"It's good that you did."

"But she won't take her vitamins," Elaine whined. Justine couldn't believe the sound of her mother's voice. It was more like the voice of a little girl, frustrated and tired. Justine thought she even heard her sniffling.

"That's all right," Dr. Lawrence said. "She doesn't have to take them herself."

"Oh?"

"For the next few days you can crush them up and put them in her food."

"Oh. What a good idea. Isn't that a good idea, Kevin?"

"Yes, it is. Should I keep her away from the Wilson girl, too?"

"No, that's not necessary anymore. The Wilson girl will be all right now. However, I have heard that Justine is paying too much attention to some problem kids at school, a girl named Bonny Joseph, and a boy named Tad Donald. Both are very bad influences. You must forbid her from seeing or talking to them. Ever," he added.

"I'll see to that," her father said gruffly.

"But you'll see her, won't you, Dr. Lawrence?" her mother asked, a frantic tone in her voice.

"Of course. Right after you start her on her vitamins again. You can bring her around to my office in two days," he said.

"Oh, good," her mother said. "I feel so much better now."

"Me, too," her father said.

"In fact," Dr. Lawrence said, "I'd like to have a few words with her now. Just to see how much damage has been done to her," he added. "It will give me a better idea of how to treat her later on."

"Of course," her father said. "She's up in her room. I'll get her."

Justine started back up the stairs quickly.

"No, that's all right," Dr. Lawrence said. "Let me go up myself. I do better with teenagers when their parents aren't present. Understandably, parents are a bit intimidating for them."

"Certainly," Justine's father said.

"Thank you," her mother added. "Thank you, Dr. Lawrence," she said as the doctor started out of the living room.

Justine had backed up to the top of the stairs when she debated rushing down and running out of the house. However, he was at the foot of the stairway already, and he would only block her exit. She retreated to her room quickly and stood there, frozen like a trapped animal. Moments later, he was at her door.

He tapped gently, and then opened it. "Hello, Justine."

She stepped back, obviously terrified, but he didn't acknowledge her reaction.

"I understand you're not feeling well today." He stepped farther into the room and looked around. "You have a very nice room, cozy and comfortable." He went to her window and looked out at the street. "And a beautiful view of the development, too."

"I don't want to talk to you," she said quickly.

He simply smiled. Dressed in a light gray sports jacket with a dark gray shirt and a navy tie, he looked tanned and relaxed, unruffled by the conflict around him. His calm, soft expression confused Justine. She expected rage and anger because of the accusations she had made against him and the development.

"I can understand that," he said. "You've been frightened and confused."

"I'm not confused. Something terrible is happening here, and not just to me and my parents."

"Terrible?" His smile widened. He had such soft, comforting eyes, eyes that lulled and soothed, eyes that mesmerized. She didn't want to look at him, but it was difficult to turn away. "What's terrible? Everyone is happy and healthy here. Everyone's prospering. I told you to call me if you had any problems. Why didn't you call me?" he asked, sitting at her desk so casually, it was as if he often came up to her room to talk to her.

"You did something to Lois," she said. "She's different."

"Uh-huh. She was in bad shape the other day, Justine. Her parents were very worried. Lois has been having hallucinations. I don't like talking about another patient, but in this case, since you have already been affected by her problems, I think it's all right," he added, crossing his legs and sitting back.

"Hallucinations?"

"That's right. Lois is a rather severe paranoid. Did you know that at one time she couldn't live at home because she thought her mother was poisoning her?"

"I don't believe you."

"It's true. I'll get her mother to tell you. She wouldn't eat anything. She was practically anoretic. Lost twenty pounds before I effected a cure. When she goes off her medication, as she apparently did recently, she suffers from paranoia again. Now I understand she was saying that my vitamin was another kind of poison." He laughed. "Funny, the forms the paranoia will take, isn't it? Something that can only be good for you suddenly becomes deadly." He shook his head.

Justine relaxed her posture and stepped away from the wall. "All the kids here are weird."

"Different, maybe, but not weird. They're more responsible. They have less street smarts, but they all come from good homes, so you think they're weird. It's just the way things are out here," he said. "After a while, you'll get to appreciate it. Believe me." He nodded knowingly.

But Justine's expression didn't soften. "Something's wrong with my parents," she said. "They're acting strange."

"How so?"

"They're saying and doing things they never did."

"Well, they're in a new place with new things to do, new people to meet. It's understandable they would change."

"Not like this. And my mother . . . she painted the exact same painting Christy Duke painted. Exactly the same," she emphasized.

He nodded. "I know."

"Well, that's not right."

"Maybe not right, but easily explainable. My fault, in a way. I showed them both a landscape someone did of the exact same location. It's hanging on the wall at the clubhouse. It influenced them. No harm. They'll realize it."

"I . . . don't believe you."

"Go down to the clubhouse and look on the wall in the meeting room if you don't believe me," he said.

"And what about the ringing in my ears. Lois said—"

"Oh, don't worry about that. There's a radio station just over the hill here, WBRO, FM, and occasionally they boost their frequency. Absolutely harmless. Oh, you might hear a dog howl once in a while, but other than that . . ."

She shook her head.

"No. Lois said—"

"I told you, Lois is a paranoid. She sees everything as potentially harmful. You can't let her influence you. Now why don't you try to calm down. You've got your parents very upset and worried.

"I'll tell you what," he said, standing. "If you still have these ideas after a day or two, I'll ask Lois's parents to talk to you."

"No, that won't matter," she said. "You own them."

"What?" He smiled widely again.

"I don't know how or why, but you own them. You own everyone here, even . . . even my parents."

His smile froze, and then faded. "You are suffering, Justine. I think it might be best for you to stay home from school for a few days. Get some rest. Eat well. I'll come around to see you from time to time."

"No. Don't come here anymore." She backed away again.

His eyes looked as if a thin layer of ice had formed over them. "Don't leave this house," he said slowly, in the tone of a command. "It's not safe for you to go out." He glared at her, and she felt the blood rush from her face. Then he turned and left the room.

She rushed to the door and waited until he went downstairs. Then she went out to the landing to listen to what he would tell her parents.

He told them to keep her at home. He told them she was a very sick girl.

But he told them he could cure her, and they were grateful, very grateful, sickly grateful.

More frightened than ever, she rushed back to her room and went to the front window to watch him get into his black Cadillac and head up the hill.

What would she do now?

She remembered what Lois and she had planned. Since Lois was out of commission, she would have to do it alone. She would sneak up to Dr. Lawrence's house and spy on his son. Then she would bring that information back to her parents.

It was her only hope.

11

WHEN JUSTINE DIDN'T respond to her parents' call to dinner, her mother came to her room. She told her she wasn't feeling well, and she had no appetite, but Elaine insisted she eat something and brought up some hot oatmeal. Even though there was no mention of Dr. Lawrence's visit, Justine knew why her mother wanted her to eat something.

She waited until her mother left, then emptied it all into the toilet. When her mother came up to collect the empty cereal bowl, she was satisfied.

"You'll feel a lot better now," she said. "I'm sure."

Justine didn't respond. She was disappointed that her father hadn't come up, but she was also relieved. With her dad out of sight, it would be easier for her to sneak out of the house. She waited until she felt sure they were having their coffee, and then she started down.

She hesitated at the bottom of the stairway, listening for the sounds of their voices coming from the kitchen. After she heard them, she slipped out the front door and started up the hill toward Dr. Lawrence's house.

As Justine drew closer to the house, she realized it was

much larger than it appeared. Viewing it from the streets
below, it was impossible to see the back of it. The front
facade made it appear deceptively narrower, even though
it was obviously bigger than the other ranch style
structures in the development. Its size made it more
intimidating, and she hesitated, her heart still beating
rapidly. She considered retreating, but she also found
herself drawn to the house the way someone might be
drawn to a dark cave. The mystery made it dangerous,
but thrilling at the same time.

Even though there was no one in sight, she couldn't
shrug off that sense of being watched, as if she were
trapped under some giant magnifying glass. She studied
the front of the house. To the right of the door was a large
bay window with a sheer blue curtain drawn across it.
The lamp that produced illumination within what Justine
assumed was the living room only revealed the silhou-
ettes of some furniture and a bookcase.

She moved very slowly, studying the house and
checking every few feet to be sure she hadn't been
discovered. Fortunately, the sun had just about disappeared beneath the horizon. Shadows were forming
quickly, cloaking her movements.

She stopped to listen. The silence from the house was
encouraging, yet also confusing. It seemed like no one
was home, but she knew the house wasn't empty. Dr.
Lawrence's car sat in the driveway. Yet all was so still.

Her legs wobbled. Her body, as if it had a consciousness of its own, rebelled. The movements were involun-
tary, instinctive, like fingers that shied away from a hot
stove. But her curiosity was stronger. Realizing she had
to discover something that would awaken her parents to

the terrible danger in their lives, she forced herself to move ahead.

The wooden part of the structure was comprised of the same type of cedar planks that had been used to build many of the houses below, but the facing was made from natural fieldstone. Dark blue curtains were drawn over the other front windows. She paused to study one of them, as the curtain seemed to be trembling. Someone might have been peering out at her, and then drew back. Maybe it was Dr. Lawrence. Maybe he was expecting her.

She waited for what seemed to be an eternity. When there was no movement in the curtain and no sign of anyone, she continued along the front of the house.

A black metal table and chairs were placed on the patio, but they looked cold and uncomfortable—nothing like the cushioned outdoor furniture her parents had behind their home.

Although there was a small garden in front of the house with rows of impatiens neatly planted along the walls, the grounds on the sides and rear were covered with silver and white stones. To Justine it looked as though Dr. Lawrence was trying to put up a false impression, a facade of a splendid home, when it was really something entirely different. It reminded her of the fake scenery she had seen when she and her parents vacationed in California and visited the movie studios in Burbank.

Triggered by the loss of sunlight, the solar sensitized switch turned on small spotlights placed along the front grounds of the house. Justine jumped back to the safety of the shadows. She thought someone might have heard her and turned the lights on, but still there was no sign of life in any of the front windows, nor did anyone come to the front door.

After a moment, she realized the lights came on automatically. The beams were focused on the front walkway, the garden, and the fountain. But the sides and the rear of the house were left in darkness.

Although she moved stealthily, her feet crunched loudly over the rough rocks. She paused, feeling that she was being watched intently again. Only this time, the strange presence seemed to be outside the house, in the darkness behind her. Was it some animal? She saw no movement. There were no eyes, and all was deadly silent.

In fact, the silence up here was so complete, it was as though she had climbed up out of the world. From her house she could sometimes hear the sounds of cars on the street in front of the development. Occasionally, noises of the outside world penetrated the walls of Elysian Fields. But up here, she heard none of that. The loudest sound was the thud of her own heartbeat, reverberating in the channels of her ears, vibrating through the bones in her face. She had to catch her breath.

For a moment, she considered turning and fleeing, but it was too late for that. She had to find out what Lois meant; and, anyway, her feet felt glued to the stones. It was as if a wall had formed in the air behind her, pressing her forward. She bit down on her lower lip and closed her eyes.

A slight movement in a side window caught her eye. Someone was inside; something was happening. There was something to see. She would have to take at least one peak before retreating.

Since there were no bushes or flowers planted near the

house on this side, she pressed herself against the building and slid along the walls until she reached the window. The curtain was partly open. Justine moved to the window frame and raised herself on her toes to peer in.

At first she saw nothing unusual—a large dark oak bed, a matching oak dresser, a plush-looking pecan-brown carpeted floor, and a standing lamp. She remained close to the window, but shifted to the other side of the frame to get a complete view.

Now she could see the entire room. It still looked like an ordinary bedroom. She saw another oak dresser and a desk, nightstands, and an armoire. She did note that the antique white walls were bare of pictures or ornaments, though a strange garment hung on a hook in the far left corner.

She heard some soft music, but still saw no one in the room. Justine's legs ached from standing on her toes, but she dared not move. Surely the music meant something was happening or something was about to happen. She waited, her eyes on the bedroom doorway. She held her nose so close to the window, the end of it grazed the glass.

Suddenly, without any warning, a young man's face appeared in the window. Rising up from below the window pane, he pressed his nose and mouth against the glass to peer out at her. For a split second she was unable to move. In that moment, she saw the face of a corpse. His eyes were bloodshot, his skin nearly milk white. His lips were as pale and as dry as day-old dead worms. She couldn't be sure, but when she thought about it and envisioned him again afterward, she thought his closely shaven head had tiny wires emerging from the sides of his scalp.

Justine screamed and fell back on the stones. The face disappeared from the window as quickly as it had appeared. She struggled to her feet, then ran back along the side of the house the way she had come, tripping once and tumbling to the stones. Frantic, she pushed herself up with the palms of her hands, and scampered on.

She whipped around the corner of the house and ran right into the arms of the waiting Dr. Lawrence.

She screamed again and tried to pull back, but he held her firmly at the shoulders. His fingers felt like vises that penetrated to the bone.

"What are you doing here?" he demanded, but she couldn't respond. His face was in the shadows. Just before she fainted, she realized that he had been watching her all along, that he had been tracking her in the darkness, and he knew exactly what she had seen.

He was ecstatic. There was no way to contain himself; he disregarded all warnings coming from the dark corner. He danced around his bedroom like a drunken fool, raising his arms over his head in a frenzied motion. He rushed to the window to look out, as though the image of her face was forever implanted on the glass. Then he turned back to his second self, who, although just as overwhelmingly happy, was far more reserved.

"She wants me. She wants me," he said. "She came up here to show me. It was her way of asking me, begging me to help her. Didn't you see? Didn't you see?"

"I saw, but you're only going to make it more difficult if you continue to act out like this. Control yourself."

"I can't. I can't remember being this happy. Was I ever this happy, ever?"

"Of course you were. When she was here," he added.

"Yes, yes. Oh, I looked right into her eyes, and she looked right into mine. And she called to me—screamed to me."

"You've got to stop and think. Calm down."

"Then she was gone. But that was only because he came along." He paused and looked toward the window again. Then he thought for a moment. "He doesn't want this. He's going to try to stop it."

"Of course he will. That's why I'm telling you to calm down. You'll give everything away before you have a chance to take action. Is that what you want?"

"No. I won't let him or the nurse stop me."

"She's going to be coming in here any moment. You've been pounding the floor. She must've heard that scream."

"Yes, yes." He looked around and listened. "Where is she?"

"Maybe she's helping your father. Get back into bed. Pretend you're asleep. If they suspect anything, anything at all, they'll strap you in. And then what?"

"I won't be strapped in. I won't!" he said defiantly. He looked at his bed with hate. Then he moved quickly to it, lifted the mattress a little, and pulled out his machete.

"Put that away. She's going to see it."

"Not yet." He hacked at the first strap. It took a number of blows to cut through the leather sufficiently enough for him to tear it from the bed. Then he started on the next one. All the while his second self was begging him to stop, but he couldn't listen to anything but his own excitement.

She was here! She had looked in on him! She had called to him!

How could he disregard that? How could he wait any longer? It was time to put caution aside. This was his chance, his chance to right the wrong.

He hacked off the second strap, then held them both up like freshly killed snakes to demonstrate his new power and control.

"Big deal, you killed two leather straps," his second self said.

"I've permanently emancipated myself," he responded.

"Not quite."

"What the hell are you doing?"

She was in the doorway, her large body a huge barrier.

"I told you. I warned you," his second self said, starting to retreat.

"Stay where you are," he screamed at the shadows. "You don't have to hide anymore."

"Who the hell are you talking to?" she demanded. She stepped into his bedroom and looked toward the corner. "Damn you, what have you done? And just when your father is having a major crisis in the development."

"She was here," he said. "She wants to come home." He gestured with one of the straps.

"Who was here? How did you rip those off the bed?" She looked past him. "Where did you get that?" she demanded as soon as she spotted the machete lying on the bed.

"He reminded me where it was," he said, pointing to the shadows.

She glanced at the empty corner again. "Christ, you're a mess," she said, turning back to him. "And to think your father had hope for you, some actual plans for you." She shook her head. "I got news for you. I think either you or I have to go. I've had it, fringe benefits or not."

She started across the bedroom toward the bed, and he stepped in her path.

"Get out of my way, you idiot. Go sit in that chair," she said, pointing and commanding as usual.

He looked at it and smiled. "I can't. I have work to do," he said.

"Work? You? What kind of work could you possibly do now? You couldn't even sweep a floor. You'd probably stay in one corner and sweep until the broom wore out," she said with a laugh. "Go on over there before I lose my temper."

"I told you this would happen," his second self said.

"Stop worrying."

"Huh?" she said. She looked into the corner again and in that instant, he reached back, took hold of the machete, and brought it around in one swift motion, striking her on the left side of the neck.

The machete sliced cleanly through an artery and came to rest against her neck bone. Her eyes exploded. Her mouth dropped. Her tongue quivered, then retreated toward her throat like a frightened mole. She raised her arms reflexively. Before her body folded and collapsed, he was able to strike her again, this time hearing and feeling the neck bone crack. As she dropped to the floor, her head tilted to the right.

Blood soaked the rug and ran down her starched white uniform, crawling quickly over her left breast. He rather liked the way it formed crimson shapes over her shoulders, down her arms, and across her bosom.

Her entire body shook spasmodically, then came to a quick halt. Her fingers curled like thick worms trying to protect their middles.

"What a mess," his second self said. He was standing just at the border of the shadows so he could get a good view.

"He didn't do such a good job with this one," he said. "Look at those wires. Inferior materials. I always thought she consisted of inferior materials."

"He did the best with what he had."

"With something as important as this, you'd think he'd try to find the best possible parts. There's so much riding on it, know what I mean?"

"Uh-huh. Well, you'll do a better job than that, I'm sure."

"Damn right." He turned to the window again, recalling her face vividly, relishing the image. "I'd better get started."

"Put the light out in here so I can follow."

"I told you . . ."

"Just do it," his second self demanded. "You can't do everything yourself. It's that kind of arrogance that gets your father in trouble sometimes."

"All right, but remember. You stay well in the background. I can't be worrying about you while I'm concentrating on the job that has to be done."

"Don't worry about me. Worry about yourself. The lights."

He went to the switch and dropped the room into total darkness.

"Ready?"

"Of course," his second self said. "You just go about your business. I'll make my way in the shadows behind you."

He went to the doorway and listened. All was quiet. Then he slipped out through the house, turning off lights as he went along so his second self could follow safely. Once outside, there was no problem.

"I see his car down there. I'd better stay off the road."

"No problem. You know how to get down there quickly. He showed you himself the other night, the night when you left me inside."

"All right, all right. Don't keep bringing that up. You're outside now, aren't you?"

"And I want to be outside whenever I choose."

"You will. Once she's back here and we're all together again, it'll be different."

"I know."

"Can't wait, can you?" He smiled. "I don't blame you. You've been in the darkness long enough."

He took a deep breath.

"Here we go," he said, scurrying down the hill toward the rear of house number one, pausing only to hear his second self scampering behind him. Now that they were both outside, he was rather glad he had agreed to bring him along. It gave him confidence.

It was good to know he was no longer alone, and that he would never be alone again.

She awoke in her bedroom. Only a small, low-burning night-light was on, but the immediate sight of these now familiar surroundings gave her the impression all had been a dream. She sat up slowly and looked down at her palms, turning them in the dim pool of illumination. They stung slightly, and they were still smudged from when she had fallen face down on the stones. It hadn't been a dream, but how did she get back here?

She recalled running into Dr. Lawrence, who'd shook her. Obviously, he had brought her back. Who knew what story he had told her parents. She had to get to them and tell them what she had seen. If they didn't believe her, she would take them up to the house and show them. Then they would know; then they would realize that something horrible was going on.

No wonder Lois had wanted to bring her up there, she thought. She had seen that . . . that creature. No wonder Dr. Lawrence never let him out of his house. What horrible things had he done to him? She shuddered when she recalled the image in the window.

What time was it? she wondered. She listened. All was deadly still. The television wasn't going; she heard no one speaking below. She started to get off her bed and stopped. Suddenly, she had the strong sense that she wasn't alone.

She called, softly at first, her voice trembling so much she couldn't muster much volume. "Daddy? Mommy?"

She listened again. There was a creak in the floor-boards, and a shadow moved in the far right corner. Whoever was standing there, stepped forward. She turned slowly toward him. The weak, yellow light pealed away the darkness slowly and revealed the corpselike face, its teeth as white as bone. She couldn't scream; she couldn't move. For a few moments, she felt as if she had already died. None of her limbs obeyed her brain's commands. A chill gripped her heart, making her wonder if it had already stopped beating.

Then something glimmered in the light, and she saw the machete.

"Daddy!" she screamed. She jumped off her bed and ran to the door, pulling the handle before turning it. She thought the unmoved door was somehow locked from the outside and panicked, pounding it and screaming.

"Daddy! Daddy!"

She turned and saw him step farther into the light. She hadn't imagined it—there were the stubs of tiny wires in his temples, and his eyes were milky white. It looked to her like the pupils were liquid, leaking like punctured egg yolks because thin lines of blood crisscrossed their way into the corners.

He smiled.

"Mother," he said.

She screamed again and turned the handle to success-fully pull the door open. Without hesitation, she shot out onto the second-floor landing and rushed to the top of the stairway.

"Daddy!" she cried as she bounded down the stairs without looking back. She tripped and caught herself on the banister, then rushed on to the bottom. Once there, she looked back and saw him standing at the top of the stairway. But he made no effort to follow her down. He just stood there, looking at her and smiling madly, the machete in his right hand.

She screamed, pressed her hands against her ears, and twirled in a circle, frantically wondering which way to go. She started down the hallway to the front door, but stopped when she saw her parents sitting calmly in the living room. Her mother was on the couch and her father

was in the soft, blue chair. They were facing one
another, but neither spoke.

Was it possible they hadn't heard her screams?

"Daddy! Mommy!"

She charged into the living room and rushed to her
father's side. He looked up at her slowly, his face
wrapped in anger.

"How could you do this? How could you embarrass us
so?" he asked calmly.

"Daddy." She caught her breath. "Daddy . . .
there's someone in the house . . . that creature. He
was upstairs in my room," she said quickly, "and now
he's at the top of the stairs."

"To go and invade someone else's privacy like that,"
her father said, as if she hadn't spoken a word.

"Justine, Justine," her mother said. "How could you
do such a thing? When did we ever teach you anything
but good things?"

She turned to her mother. Elaine Freeman was shaking
her head back and forth slowly. "Everyone's going to
know; everyone in the development is going to know,"
she said.

"We'll be like outcasts," her father said, turning back
to her mother. "Of all people to abuse that way—Dr.
Lawrence! What am I going to say to Michael tomorrow
morning?"

"Listen to me!" she screamed. "I *had* to go up there;
I *had* to see what Lois wanted me to see. And I saw *him*.
Now he's here in the house."

Neither parent stirred. They stared at each other for a
moment, then her father turned back to her, the same
look of anger on his face.

"I want you to go back upstairs, Justine. You're

confined to your room. I agree with Dr. Lawrence. You shouldn't even go to school for a few days, at least until we have all this straightened out. Go on," he repeated.

She stared down at him in disbelief. Then she turned to her mother.

"Your father's right, Justine. Go on."

"Don't you hear me? Don't either of you hear me?" she asked.

"I hear all the terrible things you've done," her father said. "Refusing to take your vitamins, hanging around with trouble-makers at school, insulting your mother's artwork, spying on Dr. Lawrence. That I hear. Go on, go upstairs," he commanded, thrusting his right forefinger at the door. *"Now!"*

"I *can't* go upstairs. *He's* upstairs!" She backed away from her father, her eyes wide, her fists clenched. "Go look for yourself," she said, pointing to the doorway.

"You're not the one giving orders here, young lady," her father said, rising. "That's been the problem. You don't know your place."

"No, you don't, Justine," her mother agreed. "Dr. Lawrence is right about that, too."

"You're crazy. You're both crazy," she said, and her father slapped her across the face so hard, she stumbled before catching her balance. Her cheek sang with the sting, and her head spun with confusion.

"Don't talk like that to us," her father said.

"Such insubordination," her mother said.

She glared at both of them.

"Upstairs," he demanded.

Justine couldn't believe her father. His shoulders were lifted threateningly; his face was red with rage. He was unrecognizable.

"He's turned you into a monster," she said. "Both of you," she added.

"Kevin, did you hear her?"

Her father didn't respond. He stepped forward again, this time to grab her behind the neck. She cried out with pain, but he forced her forward, pushing her out of the living room.

She screamed, struggling to break out of his hold, but his passion and rage had given him unusual strength. A moment later, he was lifting her and dragging her toward the stairway.

"In your room," he said. "Confined to your room."

She wouldn't let her legs support her weight in hopes of slowing him down, but he reached down and scooped her up into his arms. Then he started up the stairway, disregarding her screams and cries.

He marched into her room and dropped her on her bed. When he raised his hand to strike her, she cowered away from him, folding herself into the protective fetal position. She gagged on her own subdued cries, and her body shook with the effort.

"Don't you move from this room," he said, spitting the words between his teeth.

"But Daddy . . ." She looked about, hoping to see the creature and make her father realize, but there was no one in sight. Maybe he had snuck into the hallway, or into her parents' bedroom. She reached up, begging her father for mercy, begging him to listen to her pleas. But he slapped her hands, and then turned away from her.

"You're not to come out until I say so," he declared, then stepped out of her room and slammed the door shut behind him.

The finality of that door slamming was like a death

sentence. For a moment, all she could do was sit there and stare at the door. Then her body started to shake. She sat embracing herself, shivering. She couldn't even get the words out any longer. All she could do was stutter and gasp.

What had Dr. Lawrence done to them? She took deep breaths to keep herself from passing out again. They were no longer her parents; they were creatures, too.

The creature! She raised her head slowly to search the room. It looked as though she was alone. She went to the door and flipped the switch on the knob to lock it. At least she was safe in here, she thought, until she could figure some way to make them understand.

She went back to her bed and sat there thinking. It was deadly quiet again.

And then, after a few moments, she heard the whispered words. They came from her closet.

"Mother, I've come for you."

12

SHE TURNED TOWARD her closet, then backed slowly toward her bedroom door. He didn't come right out; he spoke from within, as if she were in there with him.

"We've both come for you," he said. "At first, I didn't want him to come along, but now I'm glad he did. He told me to watch where they took you, and he told me to stay back and wait in here until you returned. I'm always rushing about, and he's always thinking, so you can see why I need him.

"It's been hard because we're not always together. But now we will be; we'll all be together again."

She saw the closet door begin to open, and she reached back behind her and fumbled with the lock on her own door until she had it released. When the closet door opened farther, she stole another look at him.

He was wearing a light blue shirt, a navy tie, gray slacks, and a dark blue jacket, but everything was splattered with blood. There were thin streaks and spots of dried blood over his cheeks and forehead, as if he had just butchered an animal. The crimson contrasted sharply with his sickly white skin. He smiled, his lips undulating as if they were loosely attached to his mouth. He was so thin that his Adam's apple moved emphatically up and down against his skin like a rodent under a bed sheet, searching in panic for a way out.

"He has to stay in here to be safe," he said. "It's the light; he can't be in the light. After I get you off that body, I'll turn off the light, and then we'll all make our way back through the shadows and darkness, okay?" he asked, opening the closet door fully. He paused and looked back inside. "I'm taking my time," he said toward the closet. "Don't worry."

Was there really someone else in there with him? she wondered.

"I'm sorry all this has happened," he said, turning back to her. "I know it's all my fault, but I'm going to make things right now. The doctor has shown me the way," he added, and then the smile left his face. "Although he wouldn't like this, so we mustn't let him know until it's over. Okay?"

She did all that she could to prevent herself from screaming and fainting. By now she realized that her screams did no good. Her parents were useless. As difficult as it was for her to think, she did have one clever idea. After she opened her bedroom door, if she flipped the latch on the knob again and slammed it closed behind her, he wouldn't be able to pull it open immediately. Perhaps the lock would confuse him and give her some needed time.

He continued to smile at her as he started to come forward.

"This isn't going to hurt," he said. "It's only a matter of detaching some wires. You can ask the nurse. She'll tell you."

He was less than three feet away. She opened the door quickly, backed out of the room, and slammed the door. And yet, she didn't run down the stairs. The prospect of running into her father was almost as terrifying as this creature. Instead, she walked softly to the top of the stairway and listened. The house was silent.

She heard the creature trying the doorknob behind her, and realized that, as she had hoped, he was having some difficulty with the lock. Slowly, she began to descend the stairs once more. This time, when she made the turn at the bottom, she tiptoed toward the front entrance.

Her parents were where she had previously found them, and they were both sitting just as calmly. As she approached the doorway to the living room, she heard their conversation. It was an eerie replay of what they had said to her before.

"To go and invade someone else's privacy like that," her father said.

"Everyone's going to know; everyone in the development is going to know," her mother said.

It was all like a tape recording. They spoke slowly, without much emotion. She had to move quickly, and she had to get past the doorway without being seen. When she heard rustling sounds above, she realized the creature was struggling with the lock. He wasn't going to wait upstairs much longer.

With a deep breath, she walked quickly past the doorway. She didn't wait to see if she had been discovered.

She went right to the front door, opened it as fast as she could, and ran out, charging down the walkway to the brightly lit street.

Once there, she hesitated. She needed help, but she

wasn't sure whether she should try to get out of the development. Yet she realized it was some distance to the front gate and that . . . that thing would be out of her house at any moment. Could it catch up with her before she reached the Elysian Fields entrance? Surely, if anyone saw him, he would know to help her, she thought, heading directly for the Dukes' front door.

She pressed the buzzer and pounded the door. A moment later, Michael Duke opened the door. Christy stood beside him, and the two boys were right behind them.

"Oh, thank God, Mr. Duke," she said. "Dr. Lawrence's son is in my house. He's after me and my parents . . . my parents can't help me. Something's happened to them. You've got to help me."

Neither Michael nor Christy smiled. The boys glared at her, both wearing a similar expression of disgust.

"You go right home, young lady," Michael said. "No one here is going to help you."

"What?"

"You did a terrible thing, Justine," Christy said. "Everyone's going to know; everyone in the development is going to know."

For a moment, she couldn't talk. Nervously she glanced back at her house. When she turned back to them, Michael Duke was closing the door.

"*No!*" she screamed.

"Go home, young lady. And try to behave yourself," he snapped, pushing on the door. She had to step back to avoid being hit as he slammed it shut.

The loud, sharp sound and the subsequent reverberation throughout the empty street was like the report of a gunshot. Indeed, she felt as though she were being executed. She stepped back in disbelief, but the sensation that she was no longer alone out here overwhelmed her. She backed away from the Dukes' house and began to run down the street.

"Oh, God," she cried, holding back her sobs. Even so, the tears were streaming down her cheeks.

She turned in at the Wilson residence, pushed the buzzer, and pounded the door. When Lois opened it, she felt a glimmer of hope.

"Oh, thank God, Lois. Thank God it's you. I went up there; I saw him, only Dr. Lawrence discovered me there. He brought me home, and that creature was in my bedroom. We've got to tell everyone. You were right."

"Get away from here," Lois whispered. "You'll get me in trouble. You're no good. You're a bad influence. We shouldn't have anything to do with you until you've had a session with Dr. Lawrence."

"What?"

"Who is it, Lois?" Mrs. Wilson called from the living room.

"It's no one," Lois replied. Then she leaned forward, her eyes wide. "Everyone's going to know; everyone in the development's going to know," she said and pulled back to close the door.

"Lois!"

Justine started to pound the door, but stopped when she thought she heard a rustling sound to her left. Indeed, it was the creature, moving slowly in the shadows, coming toward her, the machete's blade glimmering in the streetlights' glow.

"Oh, God!"

She charged away from the house, running with all she had, her legs flying out from under her, her feet pounding the pavement, each step shaking and jarring her body. Her chest ached from the pain of breathing, but she couldn't stop. The momentum she achieved by running downhill with all her might carried her beyond herself. She felt as though she were flying. She didn't look back once, but she thought she heard a chorus of parents and children, all of them in the doorways of their homes, reciting the same line, practically singing it as she rushed by their houses.

"Everyone's going to know; everyone in the development is going to know."

She brought her hands to her ears.

"No!" she screamed, running until the entrance to the development came into view. She stumbled, caught herself, and ran on, hoping she'd be safe once she left the grounds of Elysian Fields. For now she felt as if she were being chased by more than one creature; she was being pursued by every resident.

She charged at the gate like a convict seeing an opportunity to escape a life sentence. But just as she was about to burst out, the security guard appeared, seemingly from out of nowhere, and she couldn't prevent herself from rushing right into his awaiting arms.

They closed around her like two thick python snakes, and she collapsed in their grip, exhausted and defeated. She fought hard to remain conscious.

Justine looked up into the security guard's face. It was a blur, but she thought it was a weatherworn face, the skin dry with deep wrinkles in the forehead, the teeth bone white, the eyes yellowish gray.

"You can't just run out of here," he said. And then she heard him add, "Everyone's going to know; everyone in the development is going to know."

She passed out, convinced she had fled directly into the arms of another awaiting creature.

"Why did she run from me like that?" he asked after he put the light out in her room so his second self could emerge from the closet safely.

"What did you expect? She's afraid. She doesn't understand all this. Look what she's been through. And don't forget, your father's been influencing her all this time. He brought her back down here after she returned to the house, didn't he?"

"Yeah, you're right. What am I going to do?"

"Go after her, but go slowly, and try not to overwhelm her. There's time to tell her things afterward. You tend to talk too much. Just do what has to be done. There will be time for talking later, lots of talking, endless talking."

"Right. You know, I am glad I brought you along now."

"Tell me something I don't know. Go ahead, carefully."

He fumbled with the doorknob until he got the door unlocked and opened.

"It's very bright out here."

"Hit the hall light switch."

He turned off the light, then he and his second self made their way down the corridor to the stairway.

"Go on, there are sufficient shadows. I'm right behind you."

He went down the stairs and out the way he had entered—through the rear door of the house. Then he hurried around to the front in time to see her turn away from the house next door.

He had to run to keep up with her, and he had to stay

away from the bright streetlights. His second self was doing well, too, keeping right behind her, until his father came down the hill in his black Cadillac and turned his headlights on them. He left the street, driving directly at them, crossing a lawn to do so. There was no way to avoid the bright, wide high beams. It took only seconds. He looked behind him and saw his second self instantly burn away. He barely had time to scream, and what emerged was quickly silenced by the hot illumination.

He was alone again.

His father got out of the car, keeping the lights on him. He was unable to move out of the rays; they held him like chains.

"Eugene," he said. "Come to the car."

He didn't move.

"Now, Eugene," he commanded.

He looked longingly in the direction the girl had run, then turned obediently toward his father's car. Without further hesitation, he marched to the vehicle, his head down.

"You've been bad again, Eugene," his father said. "Very bad. We're going to have to start all over now."

He turned to look back at the darkness, where the car lights held back the wall of black. His second self lay disintegrated on the grass.

"You killed him," he said.

"Get in the car, Eugene," his father replied, looking down the road toward the front gate. "Quickly. I have other things to do now."

"I'll be alone forever."

"You were always alone, Eugene. You just never knew it. Now get in," he repeated, the tone of command even sterner.

He couldn't resist it. He slid into the back seat, and his father returned to the driver's seat.

As his father backed the vehicle onto the road and turned around, he studied the darkness where the light had been, hoping for some miraculous resurrection of his second self as the light retreated and the darkness rushed back. But that did not occur. He had lost the most important part of himself, and there was nothing he could do about it. There weren't any wires to detach and reattach. It wasn't the same thing. He lowered his head in depression.

"You did a very bad thing, Eugene," his father said, looking at him through the rearview mirror. "For a very long time now, you haven't done anything unless I told you to do it. Why did you do that to Mildred?"

"I had to."

"Why?"

"I didn't want her to stop me."

"Stop you from doing what? What were you doing down here, running around with that machete in your hand?"

He looked down in his hand. The machete was still there. It had almost become a part of him.

"I . . . was going to bring her back."

"Bring her back? Bring *who* back?"

He smiled. He could almost hear his second self. "Whom."

"What?"

"It's bring whom back, not who."

"This is no time to worry about grammar, Eugene. Well," his father said, turning into the driveway of their home, "you're going to help me with Mildred, and then we're going to go into the lab. I'm going to check you out." The garage door went up. "Put that machete back in the tool chest, and go to your room—quickly!" his father ordered.

But when the garage door opened, the garage light went on and low and behold, whom did he see standing there, unaffected by the illumination—his second self. And he was smiling.

"He's back," he said. "He's back!"

"What? Who's back?"

His father brought the car to a halt, but he jumped out before his father did.

"What happened? How did you get back?"

"I don't know. We thought the light was deadly, but all it did was send me back here. Imagine."

"This is great."

"What's great, Eugene?" his father asked, getting out of the car.

"He's back. The light didn't destroy him," he said.

"Who's back?" His father looked toward the door to the house. "What the hell are you talking about now?"

He didn't respond. He directed his attention to his second self.

"He wants me to help him with Mildred."

"Of course he does. He always wants you to do something you don't want to do. It's been that way for as long as you can remember, hasn't it?"

"Yes, it has."

"Get that machete back in the tool chest and get into the house, Eugene," his father said.

"Don't do it. Turn around and go back down there. You can still get her."

"Eugene, didn't you hear me?" His father tapped him on the shoulder.

"I've got to do what he says. I always have."

"He's not your father."

"Huh?"

"It's not your father. Don't listen."

He turned and looked into his father's eyes and realized his second self was right. These eyes were like glass. He could see right through them to the other side. It was another one of his father's creations, not his father.

"Eugene, move. Now."

"Where's my father?" he said.

"What?"

"Where is he?" he demanded. "What have you done to him?"

"Get into that house and go right to the lab. I don't want to hear any more of this gibberish, understand? Move. Now!"

"Don't listen. He's only a projection; he's all light and no substance," his second self said. "You'll see."

"Yes," he said, and the illusion of his father relaxed, thinking he had said "yes" to him and was about to obey his order.

But he wasn't.

He was about to prove what his second self said.

He brought the machete up swiftly, grasping it with both hands as he raised it, and drove it hard into the illusion's stomach, cutting a quick incision up and into the heart. Blood rushed up and out of his father's mouth as he grasped the machete to keep it from moving any farther. Then, he suddenly stopped resisting. It was as though the current had been shut off. All the lights and all the little motors stopped immediately.

He collapsed, then slid off the machete and folded to the garage floor.

"I don't know," he said. "I don't know. He didn't disappear." He looked at his blood-soaked hands. "There's real blood. I don't know."

He turned quickly to confront his second self, only his second self was gone.

"Hey!" He looked around the garage. He was all alone. *"Hey, where are you? Hey!"*

There was no response. He's inside, he thought. He went inside. He looked down at his father's body, then rushed into the house. Much of it was dark.

"Where are you? Come on out."

There was no response. He went through the house, switching on lights everywhere, but he didn't find him. He checked closets, searched behind doors, even looked behind curtains. He saw the nurse still on the floor of his room, her blood caked around her neck, her eyes wide but dull. Finally, he returned to the garage, but still, he didn't find him.

"Where are you?" he shouted. He ran out and looked down at the development. *"Come back,"* he shouted. His voice reverberated down the hill toward the homes. *"Don't leave me alone, please!"*

He waited, but he heard nothing. He looked back at the house, then down at the development. The machete was still in his hand.

There was a word coming to him, a word coming back to him, rushing toward him like wind through a tunnel. He could feel it coming, and when it reached his conscious mind, his eyes bulged. His mouth widened, and the veins in his neck strained as he lifted his head toward the stars.

"Mommy!" he screamed. *"Mommy!"*

Then he charged down the hill, running as she had run from him, picking up a momentum that carried him beyond himself until he lost all control of his limbs, until he was just a thought attached to a body flying through the air, pounding the pavement, running right down the center of those well-lit streets, under the hum of the lights, past the perfect, beautiful houses with the toy families, running toward the crowd of people who were gathering below at the front gate, all standing around his mother, waiting for him to take her back.

He raised the machete and charged forward, screaming one incoherent syllable. The crowd began to part and back away so that the security guard, kneeling over her body, could raise his pistol.

But the bullets passed through his body painlessly, for he was all light and no substance. This was why he couldn't find his second self; he *was* his second self. They had merged after he had driven the machete into his father. He laughed at the realization, then watched his body peal away and fall to the pavement, rolling over and over until it came to a stop at the edge of the street, just beyond the pool of light, just inside the darkness. He continued on, floating through the air until he was out of the development, out of Elysian Fields, safe, away, beyond the reach of anything painful and evil.

Epilogue

THE ELYSIAN FIELDS clubhouse was crowded and noisy. Normally, it was a well-lit, comfortably air-conditioned light oakwood paneled room. But today, almost as if the development itself were in rebellion, the air conditioner did not work well, and two of the fluorescent bulbs had blown out. Also, a custodian was having trouble with the microphone. A connector plug appeared frayed and was shorting out. He was working frantically to splice on a new plug.

A lectern and a small, light maple-wood table had been placed at the front of the room which was filled with every available folding chair. Some people in the crowd were directing their families as close to the front as possible. But some people stood aimlessly near the doorway, looking lost and confused.

Dr. Michael Feinberg, a six-foot-two-inch rather gaunt fifty-one-year-old man with coal-black, curly hair that grew in thick patches, stood in the far right front corner, smirking and shaking his head. A few days ago, he had told Agent John Hersh of the FBI and Sandburg Police Chief Jack Daws that some of these people were not completely detoxified. It was almost a waste to bring them here, but the two law-enforcement agents were eager to get this underway, and the FBI was especially anxious to end the continuous media coverage, coverage that began the night Dr. Lawrence was killed, and continued on the front pages, right up until today.

Once the explanations were presented and people were permitted to return to their homes, it was expected that the media would move on to something else. Representatives of the electronic and print media were present. They had arrived early enough to hoard the front-row seats. Photographers and cameramen had set up their equipment in the corner, so as not to block anyone's view. This presentation was not for them as much as it was for the residents of Elysian Fields.

Or, as Dr. Feinberg referred to them now, the victims. The agency had assigned him and his staff to the case as soon as they'd heard the news. Embarrassment aside, they had an obligation to these people; he was here to "mop up." They'd sent him because he had worked with Felix Lawrence. He knew the man; he knew what the man knew, and he knew what he had been capable of doing.

He had always been suspicious about Dr. Lawrence's abrupt departure from the project. Even though he'd suffered a rather horrible family tragedy, Felix had never impressed him with his emotions. He'd never thought of Felix as a devoted husband and father. Now, Feinberg's worst fears had come true. Felix Lawrence had been one of those special kind of madmen—brilliantly schizophrenic: suave, impressive, caring, and loving on the outside, but insanely ruthless and unfeeling on the inside. It was no accident that his victims worshipped him, even as he carefully and skillfully worked to destroy them.

He was a high-tech Iago, a Shakespearean villain in the most traditional and dramatic sense, convincing his victims that he loved and respected them as he destroyed them. Few, if any, were a match for his wit, for his charm, and for his evil nature.

And so, in streamed his victims, dazed and confused. Actually more like children, Feinberg thought. He watched them take their seats, their faces still marked with fear and shock. They moved tentatively, their eyes darting around to be sure they weren't violating some rule. Some of them were like beaten-down puppy dogs, afraid to raise their heads or stare too long at anyone or anything.

Mop up, he thought. How could he do that when even he wasn't sure of the extent of the damage? The main thing was to assure these people that they could be helped. The ironic part was that they looked up to him much the way they had idolized Felix. His words were gospel. He'd learned that during these last ten days. Yet he didn't want such trust; he didn't want blind faith.

That was why he was sort of grateful for the girl—the one with the skeptical eyes, the one, who in a sense, had brought it all down—Justine Freeman. She didn't believe anything easily now, and he sensed that she was still suspicious of him. In a way, she was right, he thought. He had been working on the same project with Felix. Only, unlike Felix, he hadn't had such an unrestricted group of subjects on which to experiment.

And if he had?

He saw that question in the girl's eyes and thought . . . I don't know; I don't know what I would have done. The trouble with people like Felix and me is we get caught up in our work. Maybe science is the devil's way to get at us, after all. He shuddered and drove these depressing thoughts from his mind as Agent Hersh and Chief Daws made their way toward the front of the room to greet him.

Hersh was the quintessential FBI man—tall, handsome, physically fit, and firm-looking, the defender of America who represented all that was good and wholesome. He had dark brown, short hair, slightly gray at the temples, almost as if it had been deliberately tinted to add a look of maturity. In his dark blue suit and matching tie, he walked with confidence and authority. The crowd of residents in the aisle parted quickly before him, as though he carried more of a religious than a bureaucratic significance.

Jack Daws, the thirty-eight-year-old chief of police, looked tired and haggard by comparison. He followed a step or two behind. He was nearly a half a foot shorter than Hersh. Although he had a wrestler's physique— thick neck, wide shoulders, and narrow waist—he looked more like an overworked ball-park security guard in his light blue uniform than the head of a police department. It was apparent to Dr. Feinberg, right from the beginning, that all this—the particularly brutal murders, the national media attention, the heavy responsibilities—overwhelmed the small-town law enforcement officer.

The three men shook hands, looking like mourners who had met at a funeral parlor.

"Just about all the residents are here," Jack said.

"I'll give them some of the background, and then I'll introduce you," Hersh said. "I'd like you to give the technical end of this, making it as simple as possible. I stress, as simple as possible," he added. "Don't go any further with it than you have to."

"What about questions from the press?"

"I'll answer what I can and refer to you for explanations when I think it's appropriate."

"This is like a never-ending nightmare," Jack said.

The other two men looked at him.

"The press hoopla is going to end today," Hersh said with a tone of finality that made Daws nod in agreement, even though there was clear skepticism in his eyes. "Let's get started. Jack, you bring the group to order and introduce me. They all know you. I'll take it from there."

"Right."

The three moved to the small table, and Dr. Feinberg and Lt. Hersh took seats. Jack went to the lectern and looked at the custodian who nodded all was now well with the microphone.

"Ladies and gentlemen," he began. The mere sound of his voice over the PA system was enough to silence the crowd. People who had not taken seats rushed to take them. A heavy wave of expectation washed over the faces of the people who sat obediently, their attention now fixed on the three men in front of the room.

There was the whir from cameras and some flashbulbs went off, then reporters sat back, pen and pad in hand.

"Just about all of you are here, so we'll start. As was promised, the FBI has sent a representative to speak to all of you, and most of you know Dr. Feinberg, who also has a few things to say.

"From my end of it, I can tell you that the criminal aspects are settled. It is clear that Dr. Lawrence's son

Eugene murdered his nurse, Mildred Stoeffer, and his father. That part of the investigation is completed. None of you have to worry about any of that."

With that settled, Daws introduced Agent John Hersh of the FBI.

There was a slight brush of applause, and Feinberg smiled to himself. Those who clapped were applauding the FBI and all that it represented. It was almost an automatic reaction for them, like standing for the national anthem. Of course, there was nothing essentially wrong with that; it was just that he knew their reaction was part of the residue, part of what was left in them from Felix Lawrence's brainwashing. Felix had been an arch conservative who, despite his facade, could have been president of the John Birch Society.

"Thank you, Chief Daws," Hersh began. "I have had the pleasure of meeting with some of you already. First, let me assure you that the FBI has come into the investigation for a number of reasons, the primary one being the protection of you people. Certain governmental regulations were violated by Dr. Felix Lawrence. A number of security codes were breached. To the mind of some of my superiors, his actions were equivalent to traitorous betrayal, even though he didn't sell the secrets to a foreign power."

There was a deep gasp in the audience, like the sound of a giant vacuum cleaner. Dr. Feinberg's eyes twinkled. No matter what was said here, some of these people wouldn't believe it, wouldn't accept it. He was reminded of the end of the famous American novel, *The Scarlet Letter*, when the well-loved minister confessed his adultery to the whole town and ripped open his shirt to demonstrate the A he had branded into his own chest.

Although the townspeople saw it with their own eyes, they refused to believe it, some calling it the work of the devil, some saying the minister was pretending to be guilty only to teach them a moral lesson.

People don't want their heroes to have feet of clay, he thought.

"Dr. Lawrence," Hersh went on, "was part of a top secret project undertaken by our government. As you all know, brainwashing techniques, propaganda techniques; methods to influence and program people are as old as . . . as Adam and Eve.

"We in the free world are in a war with the oppressors of freedom to win the minds and hearts of the neutral nations, as well as maintain the influence we have over our own people.

"Well, a number of years ago, it was discovered that the behavior of animals could be manipulated by bombarding their brains with low-frequency radio waves. These airborne waves, which could travel over distances, changed behavior. By stimulating the brain's electromagnetic current, the waves produced a trancelike state, stimulated pleasure centers, and caused a tranquilizing forgetfulness and disorientation, which, in effect, caused dependency on authority.

"We discovered that the Russians had developed the technique far beyond what we had accomplished, and we began to work seriously on it ourselves. The project was known as RADA, Radio Control Authority, and Felix Lawrence, as well as Dr. Feinberg, were leaders in the research.

"To make a long story short, Dr. Lawrence left the project and came here to work as a psychologist and a nutritionist, but unbeknown to us, he brought with him a model of the radio device and the research he had accomplished while working on the project.

"Part of that research involved the use of a chemical that lodged itself in the brain, making the brain more receptive to the radio waves. That chemical was in the vitamins you all cherished and welcomed into your homes.

"In effect, you were all guinea pigs. Dr. Lawrence carried out his experiments on you without your knowledge. He tested theories and devices on his own son as well, which, as we now all know, resulted in this terrible violent ending.

"We regret what happened to you people, and we will spare no expense or effort to correct the damage. For that purpose, Dr. Feinberg and his staff have been assigned to you for as long as he feels it necessary.

"Before I introduce him to explain in more scientific detail what has occurred, I would like to make one final point. We don't like devoting our energies and time to weaponry, whether it be the RADA project or nuclear development. But for defense purposes, we will do all that is necessary to protect and insure our freedom. Thank you. And now, Dr. Feinberg."

There was loud applause. Then Feinberg spoke.

"Actually, Agent Hersh has presented it well. I'll add a few scientific facts. Electrical stimulation of the brain is not a new technique. Shock treatment has been used as a tranquilizer for many years. As every brain function is directly related to or caused by electromagnetic activity, the radio device is just another way to stimulate that activity.

"Dr. Lawrence was able to put you all in a highly suggestive state, and then feed you his own person philosophy. In short, he was turning you all into extensions of himself. You would vote for whom he wanted you to vote for, buy what he wanted you to buy, raise your children the way he wanted you to raise them. It is the ultimate in thought control because you were not only manipulated well, you never knew it was happening. And you, in effect, welcomed it.

"Now that you are off the vitamin, your body is slowly returning to its pure state as the chemical is leaving your brain. Of course, the radio device is gone, so the residual chemical is insignificant, anyway. Although it will take you a little time to reorient yourselves, you should all be feeling normal soon. There is no permanent physiological damage. It's as if you've been under hypnosis, and now you're snapping out of it. It's over," Feinberg concluded.

There was a heavy silence.

When one of the television reporters raised his hand, Feinberg looked at Hersh, who stepped forward.

"Yes?"

"Why didn't the radio device affect people outside of Elysian Fields?"

"The model Dr. Lawrence had didn't have the range. It barely reached the borders of the development."

"What about people who went in and out of the development?" another reporter asked.

Hersh looked to Dr. Feinberg and nodded, giving permission for him to reply.

"The RADA, as we called it, could stimulate their pleasure centers and cause them to like what they saw and maybe become a little forgetful while they were here. Once they left the grounds, they would leave with the impression Elysian Fields was a nice place, but nothing more."

"Could ordinary radio transmissions do any of this to these people, since they still have some of the chemical in their brains?" a television reporter asked.

The cameraman closed in on Feinberg and caught the way he glanced at Hersh.

"Absolutely not," Feinberg said. "Dr. Lawrence's transmitting device is special."

"How special?"

"That has to remain classified," Hersh interjected.

"Will these people really ever return to a so-called normal condition?" the first reporter asked.

Feinberg hesitated and Hersh glared intently at him. "Absolutely," Feinberg said and took a deep breath. *I hope*, he thought.

Of course, he noticed that no one from Elysian Fields asked a single question before the session ended. They sat obediently, and listened attentively, but no one voiced any anger, no one expressed any fear. If they were going to do it, they were going to do it with and among each other.

They were still a very private, very special community.

Justine and her parents left the hall with everyone else. Feinberg had spent more time with them than he had with any other Elysian Fields family. Once Kevin and Elaine learned what had gone on in their home and what kind of danger Justine had been in, they both suffered great guilt feelings. Kevin's guilt transformed itself into rage, a rage he directed toward all the residents of Elysian Fields and especially toward Michael Duke. Dr

Feinberg finally got him to understand that Michael, despite his role as solicitor convincing Kevin to move his family to the development, was a victim, too.

In the end, the two families met and shared their outrage and shock.

After the session in the clubhouse, the Dukes and Freemans gathered in the Freeman house. Elaine, Christy, and Justine prepared food, and their meeting seemed more like a wake. Everyone ate wholeheartedly, relying on their appetites to help ease the sense of mourning.

Afterward, everyone sat around and listened as Kevin and Michael reviewed the session in the clubhouse. They spoke of Dr. Lawrence as if he were someone to be pitied now. It made them feel superior and secure to do so.

Suddenly Christy and Elaine got up, both having the same thought. They looked at one another and went off to each other's art studio. They retrieved their paintings, and then everyone watched as each woman destroyed hers. The act had the effect of a catharsis. They hugged one another, then laughed.

"Now we'll get down to some serious work—paint some nude male models," Christy said.

"Right away," Elaine said.

"Now hold on a minute," Michael said.

Everyone laughed, but Justine looked at Brad's face and thought she saw some hesitation. Dr. Lawrence's puritanical ideas concerning sex were still impinged on his subconscious. It would take time; it would all take time.

Afterward, Justine went out alone and walked slowly down Blueberry Street. It was a beautiful afternoon.

People were on the tennis courts, and she could hear the dull, monotonous sound of lawn mowers.

Elysian Fields resembled any pleasant housing development wending its way through a lazy weekend. She stared out over the grounds and took deep breaths, pressing the ugly images of Dr. Lawrence's son back into the closets of her mind, stuffing them in there and closing the doors. Justine was so engrossed in thought, she didn't even hear her father and mother come up behind her.

"Nice day, huh, princess?" her father said.

"Yes," she replied, turning to them. They were holding hands.

"We're not sure what to do," Elaine said, "but we want to be sure you're in on the decision."

"What do you mean, Mom?"

"Well, we've been talking about selling the house and moving back to the city."

"Really?"

Her father nodded.

She turned away from them and looked out over the grounds again. "I don't know," she said.

"You don't know?" her father said incredulously. "We thought . . . I thought you would jump at the idea."

"I'm . . . not sure," she said. "It's beautiful here, and maybe now, I can make new friends."

Elaine smiled, but Kevin shook his head.

"Teenagers," he said.

Justine merely shrugged, and he put his arm around her.

The three of them strolled on silently. As they walked Justine wondered about her reaction.

She did like it here now.

But did she really like it, or . . .

There was no more ringing in her ears; there were no more chemically loaded vitamins to take.

There was only the development itself, tantalizing, hypnotizing, reaching out to her like some orphaned child.

How could she turn away?

The three of them walked on, each smiling, each feeling so content, it was hard to tell whether or not they were under a spell.

And in the end, what difference did it really make?

229

199